Beneath His Hands

A Psychological Thriller / Romance Duology

Patricia Elliott

ISBN 978-1-7380272-6-2

Published 2024
Published by Patricia Elliott
Copyright © 2023
Cover Design Copyright 2023 Jessica Greeley

All rights reserved.
No part of this book may be reproduced in any form or by any electronic or mechanical means, including information storage and retrieval systems, without written permission from the author, except for the use of brief quotations in a book review.

This ebook is licensed for your personal enjoyment only. This eBook may not be sold or given away to other people. If you would like to share this book with another person, please purchase an additional copy for each recipient. If you are reading this book and did not purchase it, or it was not purchased for your use only, then please return it to your favourite eBook retailer and purchase your own copy. Thank you for respecting the hard work of this author. All characters in this book are completely fictional. They exist only in the imagination of the author. Any similarity to any actual person or persons, living or dead, is completely coincidental.

Foreword

If you've bought this story after reading the first book, "Her Prison, His Game," I want to welcome you to Book Two of the psychological thriller / romance duology. This particular story is the romance side of the duo, but it is filled with suspense, adventure, and the necessary need to fight to stay alive.

However, if you haven't read book one, don't fret. This story can be enjoyed as a standalone. However, if you read it, be aware you may find yourself wanting to read book one anyway.

Chapter One

Ethan Barrett stood there with his arms crossed, staring at her, as she walked down the dock towards his boat. She wasn't the kind of person he wanted on board. Young and cute. She would be a distraction. But his long-time steward, Craig Peterson, was away on medical leave, and Ethan ended up having to call the staffing agency his family often dealt with.

The last thing he wanted was a woman to fill in for his friend. He needed a testosterone-filled boat, not an estrogen-filled one. As he watched her, he couldn't help but notice she walked with a slight limp. He was tempted to lift her long black skirt to find out the cause. His gaze traveled up the length of her body until their eyes locked. Flames swam in her hazel eyes, like a blazing inferno.

"Yes, I know. I walk with a limp," Jenna McCay said, placing her hands on her hips. "Do you want to see the ugly reason why, so you don't keep staring at me this whole trip?"

"Don't you think that should wait until we're in bed?"

Her hands rolled into tight fists, and before he could prepare himself, she shoved him off the dock and into the frigid waters below.

His entire body stiffened as the water closed over him, knocking the wind out of him.

Breaching the surface, he gasped for air and swam back to the dock as quickly as his frozen body would let him. Hauling himself out of the water, he stood up. She turned to run, but he grabbed her arm and pulled her into a cold, wet hug.

"Welcome aboard," he said, teeth chattering.

"Let me go, you big buffoon," she said, giving him another shove.

He flailed backwards, almost toppling into the water again, but this time, he regained his balance. She may be small, but she definitely had some power behind those puny little arms.

"You'll find I don't enjoy being groped or touched, Mr. Barrett. If you try that again, I'll knock you on your fine ass."

"You think my ass is fine?"

Jenna shook her head. "Oh, God. This is the strangest interview I've ever had."

"I can't say I've ever been pushed into the water during one before," he said, motioning for her to follow him. "Let's go inside. Once I get changed, I'll show you around."

"You deserved it," she quipped.

He left her in the saloon and headed to his stateroom. Somehow, he had a feeling she wouldn't be a distraction at all. He'd be able to get his work done in peace and not have to worry about her hanging all over him.

His screenplay had to be completed within the next two months to meet his deadline. If it wasn't ready, his agent, Jen, would smack him up the side of the head. She had already pitched his story to producers who were gung-ho to get it.

Peeling off the last layer of wet clothes, he shivered as the air hit his cool body. He hadn't planned on going for a polar bear swim. They didn't live in the tropics where the water was warm twelve months of the year. It was mid-May, and the weather wasn't quite swimmer friendly.

When he returned to where he'd left her, she was staring at the Oscar trophy in his display cabinet, all wide-eyed.

She hooked a thumb towards his award. "So, you aren't just some rich kid who mooched off his parents, huh?"

"Is that what you're after? A rich kid?"

"I'm not after anybody, Mr. Barrett. I just have more respect for someone who works for a living."

"Please call me Ethan. The recruitment agency said you have experience working on a boat?"

"Ask me anything."

Approaching her, he ran his finger down her cheek. "That's a dangerous request, Ms. McCay."

In lightning-fast movements, Jenna knocked him flat on his back, knocking the wind out of his sails again. His head slightly grazed the edge of the glass coffee table as he went down.

"Hell, woman!" he said, propping himself up on his elbows. "Maybe I should hire you as my bodyguard instead."

"Let me make one thing clear *again*, Mr. Barrett. I hate being touched."

"Then why would you choose to work on a boat that puts you in close corridors with others?"

He stood up and moved a safe distance away from the cute, crazy ninja lady. Having her around was going to make for an interesting few months. But, at least, she wouldn't invade his personal space, like others before her.

Turning away from him, she stared at a picture of his sailboat on the wall and wrapped her arms around herself. "I have my reasons."

There was a hint of pain in her tone, and it tugged at something inside him. He suspected that she was running from something. Why else would you hide out on the water? Heck, even he had to admit that it got him out of the clutches of his own family. There was always someone who wanted something, and he enjoyed being a loner.

Maybe that's what drew him to writing. It was a solitary job, which suited him just fine, and he liked that he could do it from almost anywhere. All he needed was a computer and Microsoft Word.

When he'd saved up enough, he bought his pride and joy, "The Em-Dash," a 114-foot catamaran. It cost a pretty penny but was worth every hard-earned cent. The peace and quiet allowed him to devote more time to his career.

"What do you think of my galley?" he asked.

Jenna ran her hand over the back of the couch, as she rolled her eyes. "Either you're stupid or you think I am." She'd worked on boats long enough to know it was the saloon, not the galley.

She did have to admit that this boat was more deluxe than others she'd been on before. Her apartment could probably fit into this one living space. There was a sectional teal couch that lined one side of the room, along with a glass coffee table that she had almost shattered with Ethan's head earlier, and a huge fifty-inch television that sat mounted on the opposite wall. On the far side of the room, there was a mahogany bar, fully stocked with liquor bottles which lined the wall behind it.

Every square inch of the room appeared to have some use. He even had a reading corner, which had a large built-in bookshelf and a comfortable teal lounger. A place she could imagine herself sitting during her breaks.

"On this level, we have the outer deck, the saloon and my office," he said, bringing her attention back to him. "Above, we have the upper deck and the cockpit. Below, we have four staterooms, all of which have their own heads. And I can't stress enough how I like things kept tidy."

Jenna nodded her head and followed him down a set of stairs.

"There are two aft staterooms and two at the bow. In-between, you will find the galley and mess hall. Oh yes!" He snapped his fingers. "If you mess up Roger's galley, he'll be none too happy. So, if you want anything, ask him. He's quite the stickler."

"Aye, I heard that, Boss," yelled a voice from the galley.

Ethan grinned before continuing to walk down the hallway, stopping at a closed door. "This is your room, and the most important room on the boat."

Pushing open the door, her eyes fell upon a washer and dryer. Next to the machines was a pantry where they stored the linens. Along the opposite wall were a few rows of shelves, housing various cleaning supplies.

"You're a pig," she said, sticking her tongue out at him.

"No. I'm a writer."

He started walking again, taking her down another set of winding stairs. They entered a narrow corridor, only wide enough for one person at a time. "On this floor, we have the engine room and the crew corridors. There is a comfortable place for the crew to relax down here, but I'm not too stringent in that regard. I like my crew happy, so they have freedom to roam, just as long as they stay out of my way when I'm working."

That was fine by Jenna. She didn't go on trips like this to mingle anyway. Getting away from the world and her past was all she wanted to do. She hated the questions and the looks she got from people when she walked by. Everyone seemed to know her face. It hadn't help that she'd been prominently in the news for weeks. Reporters and television shows kept calling her, even years later. All she wanted was to be left alone.

But no one cared that her horrific nightmare happened five years ago, and she didn't want to keep being reminded of it. Her limp was memory enough. Jenna leaned down and rubbed an ache in her calf. Thankfully, her injury hadn't stopped her from learning how to protect herself. No one would ever get the drop on her again.

And what better way to minimize the amount of people she came in contact with than to serve on a small vessel. She got a chance to see the world and get paid for it. Most of her trips were along the west coast of Canada and the States, but this time, they were going to travel to the Caribbean. She couldn't wait to see the turquoise-coloured water.

"Will anyone be traveling with you?" she asked.

His eyes hardened, and his lips pressed together, forming a thin, tight line. "No. It's just me and the crew." Turning, he went back up the stairwell they had just came down.

She hurried after him. "How many crew members?"

"More people equals more noise, and I hate noise, so there will only be five of you. Roger-the cook, Jerry-the Captain, Mark-the Deckhand, Chris-the Engineer, and you. And you should know I'm pretty ticked off at having to bring someone new on board who doesn't know my routines. Let alone a woman."

"Don't make me push you into the water again."

Spinning on his heels, he backed her up against the wall. "I don't put up with dangerous antics on my ship either."

Jenna kneed him in the crotch, making him double over. "And I don't allow myself to be bullied into submission. If you can't handle that, you can go without a stewardess."

"Let me guess, no boyfriend, right?" he asked hoarsely, breathing through the pain as he held his crotch.

She shook her head, tears filling her eyes. Unable to stay aboard for another minute, she took off towards the saloon. "I'll see you Monday."

Jenna made it off the boat and halfway down the dock before she broke down, her body shaking uncontrollably. Taking a seat on the nearby bench, she leaned over and covered her face with her hands.

Men! They were all men. The temp agency hadn't told her that. Would she be able to hold it together long enough to work with just guys on a daily basis? Most of her other jobs were a mixture of men and women, or all women, which was her work preference.

That way she never had to worry about a guy taking advantage of—

Damn it.

She couldn't even think about what happened without her mind freezing up. Yet, at the same time, it was all she thought about. *God.* She hated her head.

It was always there, like a dark storm assailing her mind. Therapists tried to help, but what good were they when they couldn't change what happened? Those days were long gone, but the memories were like a never-ending movie. She wanted to forget her nineteenth birthday, but the scars and nightmares were a constant reminder of the events that occurred.

Even learning self-defence didn't take away the pain, although it did help her gain a bit of confidence again. And if she was going to face this crew, she would need every ounce of it, providing she didn't go into hiding first.

Standing up, she walked over to the bus stop, shaking her head along the way. She was torn between feeling guilty for tossing him around and feeling elated that she managed to take him down three times in a row. Letting out a loud *whoop whoop*, she gained some attention from the people passing by.

Tucking her chin to her chest, she hid her heated face as she pulled out her phone, dialling her best friend's number.

"Cleo, you'll never guess what I just did. I'll be there in fifteen minutes."

Once Ethan regained his equilibrium after Jenna hit him in the crotch, he rushed to the upper deck and looked around for the woman, but she was gone. Smacking his hand on the railing, he cursed into the afternoon air.

"You okay?" Jerry asked, walking out of the cockpit.

"What do you think? I've been knocked in the water, flipped, and kicked in the crotch," he said, his groin giving him another twinge of displeasure.

"By that tiny wisp of a thing?"

Ethan glared at him. "Shut up."

The captain threw his head back and laughed, his belly shaking.

"It's about time a woman got the better of you," he said, patting Ethan on the back.

"Hey, you're supposed to be on my side!"

"If she's that feisty, she has my loyalty. I wouldn't want to get on her bad side."

Growling, he shoved by the captain and went back inside, only to hear the man burst out laughing again.

"I should fire you, Santa," Ethan yelled.

"Then who would put your presents under the tree?" his grey-bearded, red-cheeked friend shouted back.

Shaking his head, Ethan went over to the bar and made himself a double scotch on the rocks before wandering into his office. He couldn't help but wonder if she would leave him high and dry. She was definitely spooked. He could see it in her eyes, despite her attempt to put on a strong front. It was that little weakness which drew him in.

She could be the best thing that happened to his boat or the worst thing. And which one she would be, he had no idea. Worst of all, there was something inside him that was in an uproar, and he couldn't tell if it was because of her or the nightmare he had last night. They had all drowned in a freak boating accident. He could still feel the water in his lungs.

That was probably why he wasn't on top of his game in the interview with Jenna. He wasn't usually so unprofessional, and the last thing he needed was a sexual harassment lawsuit, especially when he was at the height of his career.

He couldn't afford to have anything derail his goals. One of his screenplays had been bought not that long ago, and it was being filmed. The same Hollywood producer was vying for the one he was writing now. No rest for the weary writer. They figured this new fantasy story would top the charts.

Turning on his laptop, he stared at the blank page before him. He was three quarters of the way through, and it wasn't going smoothly. The characters had him backed into a corner, and he wasn't sure which way to go. His initial plan wasn't working out the way he'd wanted it to, and now he had to re-think his strategy. It reminded him of why he liked the freedom of flying free, writing whatever came to his mind, as opposed to having a strict outline.

But since everyone was expecting a particular story, he had to stay as close to the original synopsis as possible. It was giving him a bloody headache. However, being out on the water had a way of opening up his mind, and he knew it would be the same this time if he could forget his drowning nightmare.

Taking another sip of scotch, he leaned back in his chair, attempting to visualize the screenplay scene in his mind. But it was her face swirling before him, her hazel eyes mesmerizing him. And he found himself making a character of her in his head. She'd be the perfect assassin in his next story.

Grinning, he wrote the thought down in his idea journal, hoping to return to it at a later date, and then placed it in the bottom drawer of his desk. The book had better be kept under lock and key if he was going to have her work on board. She'd likely toss him overboard again if she read it.

Ethan ran his hands through his dark chocolate-coloured hair. He was thankful to still have a full head of it, unlike his dad, who had started going bald by the time he was twenty-nine. In a month, Ethan would turn thirty, and his goal was to be floating through the waters of the Caribbean by then.

Roger poked his bald head in the door, looking rather sheepish. "Sorry, I know you don't like being bothered while you're working."

"What's up?"

"I'm about to head to Costco to stock up. Is there anything you want me to get?"

"Can you pop by the liquor store on the way back and get a bottle of Scotch? I have a feeling I'm gonna need more by Monday." When Ethan looked back down at his laptop, he still felt Roger's eyes on him and glanced up again. "Anything else?"

"Do you need me to cook dinner tonight, or will you be okay on your own?"

"I'm sure I can figure something out. Why?"

With a shy smile, he said, "Mark asked me out to dinner."

Ethan grinned. "That's so gay."

"Well, duh," Roger said with a wink.

"Have fun. I'll see you guys later."

His friends were going to have more fun than he would tonight. He hated deadlines. They took the fun out of everything. As soon as this script was finished, he was going to take a nice, long break, spend some time enjoying life.

The phone in his pocket vibrated, and the specialized tune he'd set for his mom filled the air. Groaning, he pulled it out of his pocket and answered the call.

"So, do you like her?" she asked.

"Ya, she was a barrel of laughs."

"Now you be nice to her!"

"Tell her to be nice to me. She's the one that knocked me on my ass."

The phone went silent on the other end, and he'd thought she'd hung up for a second until her laughter made him hold the phone away from his ear.

"She didn't?" his mother said, laughing.

"She certainly did. Three times in fact."

"Good. You need someone who can stand up to you."

"Stop playing matchmaker, please! Trust me when I say you won't get any grand babies from her."

"We'll see."

"I gotta go, Mom," he said, hanging up the phone before she could say goodbye.

Great.

She was at it again. He could bet one hundred percent she was the reason they sent a female stewardess and not a male one like he'd requested. If it was the last thing he ever did, he was going to prove to her once and for all that he was fine on his own. He didn't need or want a woman.

~

"You what?" Cleo cried, smacking Jenna with a pink heart-shaped pillow.

"I didn't know it was thee Ethan Barrett."

"Girl, he's like the hottest scriptwriter out there! Didn't you see him on the front of People magazine?" She took another whack at her.

"You can work for him if you want to," Jenna offered, snatching the pillow away.

"I'd die to be in your shoes, but alas, Josh would kill me if I jumped ship on him. No pun intended." Cleo grabbed her drink off the coffee table and then folded her legs underneath her butt, sitting back on the couch.

"How are things going between you two?"

With her eyes sparkling, Cleo held up her left hand. Jenna's hands trembled as her grip tightened on the pillow. On her friend's finger sat a big, fat diamond ring, sparkling like a rainbow. Part of her wanted to squeal and rejoice that Cleo had found her one true love—if there were such a thing—but the other half wanted to grab her naive girlfriend and run away, far away. Forever. Away from every single male specimen of their species. Away from all the cruel things life could throw at you.

But what could she do? Pull everyone into her own personal hell? Cleo deserved more than that, and her boyfriend, Josh, wasn't the one who had previously hurt Jenna. He knew what she had gone through and had been nothing but understanding and caring. But she had no control over the tremors that rocked her body whenever he stood close to her.

"Please don't be upset," her friend whispered, laying a hand on Jenna's arm.

"I'm not upset," she said, pinning a tight smile on her face. "Honest."

"Are you sure?"

"Don't worry about me," she said with a wave of her hand, as she fought back the tears that threatened to breach the surface. "Have you guys set a date?"

"Middle of September, in between our birthdays."

Jenna's jaw dropped. "This year?"

"If Josh had his way, we'd be married tomorrow."

Jenna swallowed hard, her stomach sinking into a deep gargling pit of quicksand. Once Cleo and Josh tied the knot, she knew that things would never be the same. It would be like how it was with every other friend who got married. They all turned their backs on her, distancing themselves from her life. Who could blame them, though? No one wanted a wet, soggy noodle among them. She was the party pooper that dulled happy hour.

"Are you sure you're ready to get married?" Jenna asked. "I mean, you had like a new flavour every week, even after you started dating Josh."

Cleo tucked her long black hair behind her ear and smiled. "And Josh made sure he was always right there in the thick of it. Heck, he hip-checked the guy I was dancing with."

Jenna couldn't help but laugh. "I remember that. He knocked Andy right into the punch bowl. The poor guy was red for a week."

"I don't think Andy will ever live down the *tomato face* comments that went viral."

Laughter filled the room as the girls wrapped their arms around each other, but it didn't take long for Jenna's eyes to burn with tears, and she buried her face against her girlfriend's shoulder.

"Damn it, girl. You're going to make my mascara run," Cleo said, sniffling.

Jenna pulled away, wiping her eyes with her sleeve. "Well, you could always go for the Goth look."

"Have you forgotten my Morticia days already?"

"The Adam's Family, ba-na-na-na," Jenna sang, tapping the tune on the coffee table before doubling over with laughter again.

Her friend, who could pass for an Egyptian goddess, grinned, hitting her with another pillow. "Oh, shut up."

Jenna tackled Cleo, wrapping her arms around her. "You know I love ya."

"What am I going to do without you for two months? Who's going to help me organize the wedding?"

And with that, Jenna slumped back against the couch, closing her eyes. Going to a wedding would be bad enough already but planning one would be pure torture. It was that realization alone that solidified her need to take the new job. She could handle sitting in a church pew for an hour or two, but the wedding buzz in the months leading up to the ceremony would drain her completely.

"You don't need me. I suck at planning stuff like that."

"At least promise me you'll be my Maid of Honour."

Jenna didn't want to be in the wedding or play any part in it but knowing how much it meant to her friend, she agreed. She'd lost her childhood wedding fantasies a long time ago, but that didn't mean other people felt the same way.

Cleo slid an arm around her shoulders, pulling her into a hug. "I know it won't be easy, but it would mean so much to me to have you up there with me."

"Just don't make me dance with the best man."

Her friend squealed, hugging her tightly. "Thank you. Thank you."

"I can't breathe," Jenna gasped.

Releasing her, Cleo said, "Sorry. Oh gosh, I can't believe I'm getting married."

"You and me both," Jenna muttered under her breath.

She liked that the two of them were still single. Well, unmarried at least, but she knew that wouldn't last forever, as much as she wanted it to. They were twenty-four years old and not getting any younger.

Standing up, Jenna grabbed her jacket off the back of the recliner. "I had better go, got a lot to do before I leave on Monday."

"Call me as often as you can, okay? Don't disappear on me!"

"Once I get our itinerary, I'll text it to you."

"If I don't hear from you whenever you make landfall, I'll send out the hounds," Cleo warned.

Her parents would probably say something similar after they found out she was going on a boat with all guys. They would be painfully reminded of what she'd gone through. She didn't need anyone to refresh her memory though. It was still as bright as day.

Thankfully, she had some extra money in the bank in case she had to cut her journey short. She could even travel a little with the money she had saved up from her last job. And the pay she would earn from this one alone would fund another back-packing adventure across Europe, but she'd have to find another travel buddy. Cleo wouldn't want to abandon her new husband.

"Don't forget to send me pictures," Cleo said as they walked to the door.

"As long as my new camera doesn't get waterlogged."

Her friend shook her head. "You're the only person I know that still lugs around a legit camera."

"Creature of habit." Jenna gave Cleo one last hug before stepping into the dimly lit hallway of the apartment building. "Bye."

Dark shadows illuminated the path before her as she rushed towards the staircase, eager to find the light of day again. Shivering, she slammed open the door leading into the stairwell. Light flooded in from the window, and she breathed a sigh of relief.

No matter how hard she trained to defend herself, she couldn't escape the feeling of monsters hiding in the dark. She never used to believe in monsters, not even as a kid, but now...

Shaking her head, she refused to think about it. Instead, she focused her thoughts on the present, making a mental list of everything she had to do before the trip. Buying pepper spray was on the top of her to-do list. Carrying a gun was out of the question, but maybe she could bring her collapsible bo along. She had no intention of letting her skills grow rusty out on the water.

She had a feeling her training would come in handy, and, if anything, it would keep the men at bay. Hopefully, things would go off without a hitch, and she wouldn't have to head out early. However, something deep inside her made her wonder whether the job was going to be more than she bargained for.

Chapter Two

"Everyone must wear a uniform while on duty," Ethan said, motioning towards the crisp white and black suit on the bed. "When you're off-duty, you can wear whatever you want."

Picking up the suit, she noticed that the skirt would barely cover her butt, let alone the jagged scar on her calf. Jenna pulled the skirt off the hanger and threw it at him. "Hell no."

Catching it, he asked, "Is there a problem?"

She folded her arms and glared at him. "I don't wear short skirts. Ever." All of her mini-skirts, and even her shorts, had been tossed in the garbage after what happened. She preferred to swelter than for anyone to see her humiliation.

"You gotta wear something."

"I'm sure you don't make the guys wear a skirt."

"Those are real, right?" he asked, pointing at her breasts.

"How dare you!" She lifted her hand to smack him, but his fingers wrapped around her wrist.

"Chill, darling. I'm just making a point." He planted a kiss on the back of her hand before releasing it. "By the way, please control your knee jerk reactions. I won't have you attacking my crew."

"Don't be a dick then," she said, wiping her hand on her pants.

"I'll do my best, so about the skirt?"

"I won't wear a skirt and that's final."

Nothing anyone said or did would make her change her mind. She couldn't stand people asking about her injury, so she kept it hidden beneath multiple layers of clothing.

He motioned to her hip-hugging black pants. "Does it have anything to do with your limp?"

"That, sir, is none of your god-damn business," she snapped, as warmth flooded her cheeks.

Holding his hands up in the air, he said, "Geez, you're like this high-strung filly. But suit yourself. Don't come crying to me when you have heat-stroke in the middle of the Caribbean."

"I can take care of myself."

Rolling his eyes, he said, "Okay, princess. Under your pillow is a welcome package. Follow every rule to the letter and the trip will go smoothly."

"When do we leave?"

"Soon," he said. "Be in the saloon in forty-five minutes for a briefing." With that, he turned and left the room, shaking his head.

Jenna shut the door and locked it, letting out a heavy sigh. He grated on her nerves intensely, and she had no idea why. Her stomach did a weird flip flop whenever she looked into his dark brown eyes. It irritated her and made her want to knock him on his ass, which she'd done more than once already.

Chuckling, Jenna walked over to the bed and pulled out the package from under the pillow. Inside was a list of rules, the itinerary, and her schedule. Scanning the rules, she burst out laughing. Why would he make a rule about not walking around naked?

Heck. She never even walked around her own place naked. Never had and never will. She hated her body and just looking at it made her shudder. If she could get herself a new one, without all the painful memories, she'd be in heaven.

It was a good thing she kept her uniform from her previous job.

She could use the pants in place of the skirt. But they weren't going to be her friend once they reached their destination. However, she'd deal with that when the time came. The boat had air conditioning, so it shouldn't be too bad.

She was grateful that Ethan gave her one of the main staterooms as opposed to shoving her in the crew quarters with the men. Opening the drawer, she went to put her shirts inside when she noticed something stuffed into the back corner. She picked it up, and when the light fell on it, she dropped it as a shiver rippled through her body.

"A condom," she gasped. "Gross."

Jenna slid on a pair of latex gloves and picked up the used condom. With a forest fire lit in her belly, she marched towards the saloon. Ready to rip the head off her new boss. The men were all gathered around the bar when she entered the room. A few of them backed away, but Ethan held his ground with a grin on his face.

"Found a present, did ya?"

As she approached him, she flung the condom at his head. He ducked, and it hit the tall bald guy in the back, square in the face. Deep, rich laughter filled the room. The man picked it up and threw it at Ethan, hitting him in the back of the head. Jenna bit her cheeks to hold back a grin as her boss glared at her comrade-in-arms.

"Serves you right," she said, giving her newfound buddy a thumbs up.

The man smirked and nodded in her direction. "I've been waiting for someone to do that for a long time," he said, holding out his hand. "Hi, I'm Roger."

She pulled off the latex gloves to shake his hand. "Jenna."

"Nice to meet you. And by the way, ignore what he said the other day. You're welcome in my kitchen anytime."

"Hey," Ethan complained. "You don't even let me in the kitchen."

"Do I need to remind you of the last time I let you use my microwave?" Roger wagged a finger at him.

"How was I supposed to know potatoes could explode?" he said, shrugging his shoulders.

There was an easy comaraderie between the men that Jenna envied. It was something she hadn't been able to develop with anyone but Cleo. Come to think of it, she hadn't made any new friends since the incident. She kept refusing to let anyone else into their inner circle, except for Josh. He wasn't Jenna's friend as such, more like an acquaintance.

She didn't consider herself snobbish or anything. She just didn't trust anyone as far as she could throw them. She had the wool pulled over her eyes once before, never again. It even took her awhile to trust Cleo again. Her friend had disappeared with a guy on the night her life changed forever.

And if Cleo hadn't been so persistent, they probably would have gone their separate ways, but she refused to give up and kept apologizing until Jenna gave in. She was glad she did. Life would have been lonely otherwise.

Ethan waved a hand in front of her face. "Hey space-girl, come back to earth."

"I'm here. I'm here," she said, shoving his hand away.

"While on board, you need to remain aware of your surroundings at all times."

"I'm aware of that."

"Did you read the rules?"

Holding her hand in the air, she recited the eighth rule. "Thou shalt not walk around naked."

Jerry, who had just taken a drink of whisky, snorted in laughter and immediately started gagging as the liquor spewed out his nose. "Holy bat in hell, that burns," he cried, his eyes filling with tears

"You're supposed to drink it, not snort it, man." Mark patted him on the back. "Roger, can you go get him a glass of milk? Ethan, he might need an hour or two to recover."

"Damn." Ethan looked over at Jenna, his eyes narrowing. "We

haven't even gotten out of port yet, and you're already causing trouble."

A look that was mixed with guilt and humour danced in her eyes, as she brushed a strand of strawberry blond hair out of her face. "Don't look at me. I didn't write the rules."

"She's got you there, Boss," Chris told him.

"Shut up."

She'd only been on the boat for an hour, and she had already gained the loyalty of his crew. Gripping the back of his neck, he tried to figure out how she managed to do that. If he sent her away now, there would probably be a mutiny. Grumbling, he left the group and disappeared into his office.

Walking behind his desk, he sat in his black leather chair, and a loud farting noise made him jump out of his seat. "Damn it, Chris!" he yelled. On any other day he may have been amused, but today was not one of them.

He picked up the whoopee cushion and shoved it in the bottom drawer of his desk, making a mental note to find a way to surprise his new guest with it. Ethan would have to make sure he locked himself in the bathroom so she wouldn't toss him overboard.

Sitting down again, he turned on his computer. Since they were going to be delayed, he may as well make the most of it. Working on his story would hopefully get the annoying, new crew member off his mind. Something that had proven to be difficult to do. He hoped that this wasn't a sign of what was to come.

Putting everything out of his mind, he re-read the last page of his script and this time easily picked up where he'd left off. Word after word flowed from his fingertips while a silly grin played on his face. If this didn't get him another Oscar, he didn't know what would.

He wasn't sure how long he'd been typing before he heard it. A sweet melodious laughter sweeping by his office door. Opening it a crack, he peeked through. Jenna and Roger were walking down the hall shoulder to shoulder. Ethan scratched his head in confusion.

How come she wasn't knocking him to the floor? She never struck him as the overly friendly type when they met. He scowled in their direction before shutting the door. Why should he care what she does? As long as she did her job, he wasn't going to let her bizarre behaviour bother him.

His shoulders lifted slightly when he heard her laugh again. Not only was she bloody cute, but she also had a laugh that made you wake up and take notice. One that could easily wrap a man around her sweet little finger. Running his hands down his face, he said, "Oh God." She was going to be the death of him, and their trip hadn't even started yet.

Rubbing his chin, he wondered how hard it would be to keep his boat clean and do his work at the same time if he let her go. Previously he had managed to do it alone on a smaller boat but not for a long time. "Damn it," he muttered.

He'd have to remember to speak to her about remaining professional with his crew. Looking down at his watch, he noticed a few hours had gone by and was about to go check on things when there was a knock at the door.

"Come in."

Mark stepped into the room. "Jerry appears to be doing okay. We should be on our way in about thirty minutes."

"Finally!"

"Did you really add that as a rule?"

A cocky grin spread across Ethan's face.

Mark burst out laughing. "Were you trying to get knocked on your ass again?"

Ethan picked up an elastic band and whipped it in the man's direction, his face heating. "Shut up." His crew had ribbed him all weekend over getting his butt kicked by a girl, and it didn't look like it was going to end anytime soon.

Mark ducked as the elastic flew over his head and out the door, hitting Chris on the shoulder who chose that exact moment to walk by.

Beneath His Hands

"Ouch," Chris complained light-heartedly, picking it up off the ground. "Didn't we use up all the elastics last week?"

Ethan held up a bag. "New stash."

"I'd like to see you flick one of those at her and see what happens," Chris said with a grin.

"Don't you guys have jobs to do?" he grumbled.

The men left his office laughing, and Ethan laid his forehead on the desk, groaning. They were never going to let him live it down. There was only one way to solve this problem. He would have to get the better of her at least once on this trip. But playtime would have to wait. He had work to do.

Jenna rolled over in bed and punched the alarm. Five-thirty in the morning came far too early, especially after he'd woken her up last night when he had spilled coffee while working in bed. Didn't the man know how to make his own bed?

They'd been on the water for five days, and already she was a walking zombie. She knew the men would all be awake now, preparing for the day. She was always the last one up, and no one really gave her any guff about it, which was nice. Her schedule started a little later than them, anyway.

Her first visit was to the kitchen to grab some breakfast and talk with Roger. Their early morning chats had quickly become one of her favourite parts of the day. As she sauntered her way into the kitchen, another large yawn had her stretching her arms towards the ceiling. "Hi, Rog…"

Jenna paused mid-sentence and looked around. The room was empty. Did she miss the memo? Reaching up, she grabbed a plastic cup out of the cupboard when suddenly a voice boomed behind her.

"Boo!"

Spinning around, she flung the cup in the voice's direction. Her eyes widened as she saw Ethan duck, the cup barely missing his head.

"Sheesh, woman! When are you going to chill out?"

Recovering quickly, a smirk spread across her face as she shrugged her shoulders. "Everyone was gone. For all I knew, the ship could have been taken over by pirates."

"Don't worry. You'd scare them all away," he replied, as he walked beside her, grabbing his own cup.

She bumped him out of the way with her hip and wandered over to the fridge. "Aren't you supposed to be writing or something?"

"Just came in for my morning joe."

"Where's Roger?"

"Gave him the morning off so he's probably sleeping."

"You mean Mr. Oscar winner is going to make himself some breakfast?" Jenna said, quirking an eyebrow. "I thought you weren't allowed in the kitchen."

"It's my boat. Besides, I can cook you know."

"I thought you didn't like to get your hands dirty with such menial things. Hell, you wake me up to change your sheets."

He came to a stop in front of her, placing the mug on the counter. Water droplets glistened on his neck from his early morning shower, and he smelled of mint aftershave.

Leaning over, he reached for the sugar jar behind her, his breath tickling her ear. "Maybe one day you'll see what my hands can do."

Her breath caught in her throat as damp heat pooled between her legs, making her nauseous. No! She didn't want this. Didn't need this. "Back up before you see what my hands can do. Again."

Staring down at her, Ethan knew he had better take a step back. Something in her eyes, akin to a frightened foal, made him move away. "Sorry," he muttered as he finished pouring his coffee. At least this time, she didn't lash out like before.

Once it was ready, he turned to head back out the door, stopping to look at her one last time. Her eyes were fixed in the same spot on the cupboard, her hands shaking. It was easy to tell that the poor girl had been through something traumatic. If writing taught him one thing, it was that body language was just as important as what someone said.

"Jenna, I don't know what you went through, but you're safe here. I promise you that."

He meant every word. As long as she was on his ship, he'd watch out for her. No one was going to hurt her on his watch. She didn't know it, but he'd been watching her over the last few days. There was a story to be told. He could sense it in his bones.

There were two sides to her, the fun-loving one and the warrior—the *I'm going to kick your butt girl*. Ethan often had to contend with the warrior. Only Roger seemed to draw out the fun-loving side of her. He'd have to corner him and find out if he knew anything about her.

"Really, I mean it. You're safe here," he said.

Jenna looked up and gave him half a smile, eyes wary. "Thank you."

"Also, when you finish making your rounds, can you change the sheets on my bed?"

"Don't tell me you spilled coffee again?"

Oh God. If he told her what had really happened, he'd never survive the humiliation. His body had gone into overdrive since she came aboard, and it was more than happy to make him wake up in a puddle from a wet dream.

Certain that his face was as red as a tomato, he made a quick exit, saying, "Something like that. Talk to you later."

He hadn't had an orgasm in his sleep since he was a teen. His mother had assumed he was playing with himself and gave him the birds and the bees lecture, right in front of his younger sister.

On the way back to his office, he ran into his cook coming out of the washroom.

"Hey, Boss, what's up?" Roger asked, zipping up his sweater.

"Come. Let's chat." Ethan walked into his office.

Roger flopped onto the couch, resting his feet on the coffee table, looking expectantly at him.

"You might not want to let Jenna use your kitchen."

"Why not?" his friend asked.

"She threw a cup at me."

Roger choked back a chuckle. "What on earth did you do this time?"

"Nothing. I just said hello."

The man snorted. "Ya, sure you did."

"Has she said anything to you about her past?" Ethan asked.

"Sorry. She swore me to secrecy. But I would tread carefully with her, okay? She's been through a lot."

"Was she hurt?"

"That's putting it mildly."

He knew that Roger was a man of his word, and that if he swore to keep a secret, he wouldn't tell anyone, not even him. It's one of the things Ethan liked about working with him. Yet, he couldn't help but ask again.

"Is there anything you can tell me?"

"I think she'll tell you when she's ready."

Picking up another elastic band, Ethan let it fly, hitting Roger in the leg.

"There really are other uses for those damn things," his friend mumbled.

"I know, but this is more fun."

Roger leaned over and picked up the elastic, intending on whipping it back in Ethan's direction when the boat suddenly careened to the left, knocking them off their seats.

Jerry's voice came over the loudspeaker. "Attention, please. We're about to enter a storm front, make sure everything is secure."

"Damn." Ethan closed his laptop and locked it in the desk. He grabbed four radios off the shelf behind him and handed one to his friend. "Roger, check the kitchen. I'll make sure everything is tied down outside."

He met Mark and Chris as he stepped out of his office, handing everyone a radio. A rush of adrenaline coursed through his veins.

Beneath His Hands

"Looks like it's a bad one." Chris said, falling into step beside him.

"Do we have everything we need to make repairs if necessary?" Ethan asked.

"Yes. I made sure of that before we left," his engineer replied, sounding a little offended.

He didn't doubt Chris's ability to take care of his boat, but the last thing he wanted was to be stranded in the middle of the ocean. The storm could drag them to God only knows where.

"Mark, come with me. I might need your help securing everything outside," Ethan ordered.

He had never heard Jerry's voice sound so stern when issuing a warning before. That told him it wasn't going to be an ordinary storm. Hopefully it wouldn't last long. If he had to keep taking breaks from his writing, he wasn't going to meet his deadline, and he was already falling behind.

Just as they were covering the hot tub, Roger's voice piped up on the radio, "Mark, get down to the kitchen A.S.A.P. Bring the first aid kit."

Ethan released his rope, which flung across the deck in the wind. He rushed down to the kitchen, with Mark hot on his heels. When they entered the room, he saw Jenna's feet sticking out from behind the counter.

Roger looked up at them. "She must have hit her head on the counter."

Coming around the kitchen island, he saw her head cradled in Roger's lap, a long gash across her forehead. Mark kneeled down and examined her just as the boat jarred to the right.

"Can't Jerry keep the boat straight?" Mark complained, as he reached to check her pulse.

"Is she going to be okay?" Ethan asked.

After a few minutes of looking her over and tending to her wound, Mark said, "She's going to have one nasty headache, but ya, she should be fine. Why don't you carry her to her bedroom, Ethan, and stay with her while we batten down the hatches."

Nodding his head, he leaned down and carefully picked her up, resting her head against his chest.

"Be noble now," Roger commented, winking at him.

"Shut up," he replied before disappearing out the door. As he was carrying her down the hall, her pant leg rode up slightly, and a pink jagged scar on her calf caught his attention. He ran his finger along the pink skin. "What happened to you?"

She moaned and tried to burrow deeper into his chest. The sound awakened his cock, which rose to attention. *Crap.* His jeans were cutting off his circulation, and he couldn't adjust himself.

The boat jarred violently again, causing his shoulder to slam into the edge of a door frame. Sharp, searing pain shot down his arm. He dropped to his knees and cried out in pain, trying desperately to keep a hold of Jenna.

With one sore arm, he hoisted her up over his good shoulder and made his way to her stateroom. After gently placing her on the bed, he tucked her in nice and tight so she couldn't roll off the side.

Hopefully, she would sleep through the rest of the storm and not have to tend to a massive headache while the boat was being tossed around. He didn't exactly want puke stains all over his new carpet. Ethan gave Jenna one last look before rushing out the door.

Lightning flashed through the windows, followed by a loud intense rumble that told him the storm was directly overhead. The boat careened to the side again. He grabbed the handrail to steady himself, his heart pounding in his chest.

"Jerry, talk to me," he yelled into the radio, trying to be heard above the thunder.

"A waterspout is directly ahead. I'm trying to turn, but the waves are pulling us closer," Jerry responded, his voice strained.

"Give the order to evacuate if we need to." They have never had to abandon a ship before, and he hoped they wouldn't have to this time. He'd spent a fortune on this baby and didn't want to lose it.

Jerry gave the ship wide call to put on the life jackets and prepare to evacuate if he gave the call. Ethan rushed into the saloon and pulled two life jackets out from the compartment underneath the couch and went back to Jenna's room. She was beginning to stir, her hand gingerly touching her forehead.

"Rise and shine, sleepyhead," he said.

"Leave me alone. Let me sleep," Jenna muttered, squeezing her eyes closed as white spots flashed behind them.

"No can do, darling. You have to get up."

"Go away."

"Unless you want to go down with the ship, you gotta get up."

That made her sit up and take notice, her heart skipping a beat. "Say what?"

Jerry's voice came over the ship-wide speaker system, saying, "Brace for starboard impact."

In that moment, a loud crash shook the ship, knocking it sideways. Ethan lost his balance, falling into Jenna. They tumbled off the bed. Her eyes widened as she lay beneath his body, blood rushing into her ears.

"Abandon ship!" Jerry yelled. "Abandon ship! Mayday…"

Ethan stood up, pulling her with him. "You're going to do everything I say. Got it?"

Too afraid to say anything, she nodded her head. Jenna knew that declaring a mayday on the VHF radio only happened if their lives were in major danger.

Ethan helped her into the lifejacket, and then he opened the door. The alarm blared as he pulled her into the hallway, stepping right into a puddle of water. "Shit!"

Chapter Three

They sloshed their way towards the stairs, her heart thumping erratically against her rib cage. The boat tilted to the side abruptly, knocking her towards the wall, making it hard to move quickly on the angled floor. "What's happening?" she gasped as the boat tilted in the other direction, throwing her into his arms.

"We're taking on water."

"No duh, Sherlock," she snapped. "Tell me something I don't know."

"The ship's going down."

"I know that, too."

"Then move your ass up those stairs," he ordered, shoving her away from him and towards the stairs. By the time she placed her foot on the staircase, the water was already covering the first step and rising fast. "We have to move it!"

"Stop telling me things I already know."

She went up a few steps before she froze, causing Ethan to run into her, knocking her down. Her knee smacked against the edge of the stairs, and she cried out in pain. "Watch where you're going!"

"Gee, I so enjoy smacking my face into someone's butt," he said sarcastically, rolling his eyes. "Hurry up." He tried to shove her up the stairs, but she pushed by him and retreated back down. He grabbed her arm. "Where are you going?"

"Let me go," she begged. "I have to go back."

"You can't go back. The water is rising too fast," he said, refusing to let go of her arm.

Looking down, she noticed that the water had already reached the second step. "I don't care. I gotta go back." She jumped off the step into the rising flood waters. She gasped when the cold water snatched her breath away, goose bumps quickly covering her skin. She had to get it. If she lost it, she'd never forgive herself, but Ethan's hand was still firmly attached to her arm. "Let me go. I need to go get something."

"Get what?"

"A wooden box. It's on the shelf in my closet," she said breathlessly, trying to peel his fingers off her arm as tears filled her eyes.

Ethan smacked the wall with his other hand, making her flinch. "Damn it, girl! You're going to kill us both." Letting her go, he waded through the water and disappeared into her room.

The stuff in the box was irreplaceable. If it ended up at the bottom of the ocean, she'd never forgive herself for not leaving it at home.

"Please. Please." she muttered, crossing her fingers as she watched the rising waters. "Please find it."

A loud grunt, followed by swear words, echoed down the hallway. Jenna clasped her hands together, holding them in front of her mouth. When the water reached her hips, and he still didn't come out of the room, she couldn't wait any longer. Grabbing the handrails, she pulled herself against the current and returned to her room. Only to see Ethan struggling to get the closet door open.

"Something's jammed the door. I can't get it open." He punched the door in frustration.

"Let me help."

"There's no way we'll get it open now, not with the weight of the water. We have to go."

"I'm not leaving without it."

"God, woman. You're driving me insane!"

A light bulb flashed over her head. "I saw an axe in the hallway, next to the fire extinguisher."

Without wasting another second, Ethan disappeared down the hall. She continued to pull on the closet door, only managing to open it about two inches. Bracing one foot against the wall and the other against the right closet door, she leaned back and pulled with all her might. "Give me my box, you stupid thingamajig!"

The handle popped off, making her fall backwards. "Oh crap!" she cried. The water closed over her head, her back scraping against the bedside table. She opened her mouth to cry out and accidentally inhaled some water.

Gasping, she tried to breach the surface, but couldn't get her feet back under her body. Suddenly a hand reached down and pulled her up. "I can't leave you alone for two minutes," he snapped.

She wanted to give him a sarcastic reply, but when she opened her mouth, all she could do was cough and point to the closet again. Lifting the axe, he chopped at the door. After six good hits, the door was open wide enough to get the box out.

"Boss, where are you?" Chris piped up on his radio.

"We're coming," was his quick reply before turning towards her. "Can we get the hell out of here now?"

"Lead the way, *Boss*," she mimicked.

Glaring at her, he rested the axe on his shoulder and moved towards the door. She followed him, holding the box over her head. The freezing cold water was up to her chest now, stealing her breath from her lungs. Her whole-body shook, and the adrenaline coursing through her veins made her heart thump faster than ever.

They entered the saloon just as a large wave crashed against the window, followed by a distant high-pitch scream.

"Man overboard," Mark shouted on the radio.

"No. No. No." Ethan ran outside and found a drenched Mark struggling to keep a hold of the raft as it blew around in the wind. Mark pointed into the water behind him.

"The wave, it hit us. I couldn't stop it, couldn't help him."

"Who?"

"Chris."

Another wave crashed into the side of the boat, knocking Ethan to his knees and sliding him dangerously close to the edge. He reached out and wrapped his hand around a nearby rope. "Help," he tried to cry, but the wind took his breath away before he could speak.

He couldn't die. Not this way. Not before he did everything he planned to do with his life. He wanted to go see his movie that would be premiering when they returned to Vancouver.

Hell.

He wanted to have sex again before dying. Sex with his hot new stewardess to be exact. "Someone help me, damn it!" The boat was sinking fast, and if they didn't get off it soon, they'd go down with it.

"I'm trying!" shouted Mark.

Jerry and Mark reached him at the same time, pulling him back onto the deck of the ship. They didn't even have time to breathe a sigh of relief when another larger wave knocked the boat further sideways. The sail was almost horizontal with the water now as lightning lit up the sky.

"Where's Roger?" Ethan shouted over the thunder, which had quickly followed the light show.

Jerry and Mark frowned, shrugging their shoulders.

"Roger, where are you?" Ethan called into the radio.

The only response was the squeal from the nearby radios, and Ethan's stomach rumbled with displeasure. They had been together for years, and now he was watching his crew being stripped away from him. One by one.

"Come on, guys, we have to hurry," Jerry said, interrupting his thoughts.

"We have to search the ship and see if we can find Roger." Ethan wasn't about to leave one of his dearest friends behind, especially if there was some miniscule chance he was still on board.

Jerry looked over the side of the half sunken ship. "The two bottom decks are submerged. We only have a few minutes to get off the ship."

"Search wherever you can. If we can't find him in five minutes, we'll jump." Ethan stood up, his body angling slightly. The boat was leaning on its side, making it hard to stand up straight.

He spotted Jenna holding onto the door frame at the entrance of the saloon and approached her. "Hold tight. We'll be right back."

"Where are you guys going?" she asked, tightening her grip on the door frame, her knuckles turning white.

"To find Roger."

She released a hand and gripped his wet green t-shirt. "Don't leave me," she begged.

"We have to find him. The more of us searching the better."

"Then I'll come with you."

"No," he said, refusing to let her be put in any more danger. "I don't want to have to keep an eye on you, too."

Her eyes narrowed. "You're a dick."

He looked down at the crotch of his pants and shrugged. "I'll apprise you of the dick situation later. Right now, I have a friend to find. If we aren't back in four minutes, get yourself in that raft."

She didn't look too pleased with him, but she gave him a salute. "Yes, sir."

Flicking her on the nose, he walked by her to go into the room, but before he got too far away, she kicked him in the butt. When he turned to look at her, she said, "Tit for tat."

If they weren't in such an intense situation, he would have had his own response for that. Instead, he found himself listening to Jerry bark orders at them before they made their way back into the bowels of the ship.

He hated leaving her on the main deck when it was so dangerous, but she would be near the life raft if she had to jump ship by herself. That was the safest place he could think of right now.

"Roger?" Jerry called into the radio.

Nothing but squealing static replied back to them.

"He may have lost his radio," Mark said hopefully.

Ethan decided to check the floor that was submerged. There was still half a foot of room near the ceiling to get air. They wouldn't be able to get to the engine room, but he didn't think Roger would go down there, anyway.

The storm still raged overhead, and the lightning and thunder made the air around them hum with life. The waves continued to toss the boat to and fro. Slipping under the water, Ethan swam down the corridor, looking for any signs of life.

His friend had to be okay. Swimming up to the ceiling, he poked his face up out of the water and yelled, "Roger, you down here?"

Upon hearing a shout further down the hallway, he dove under the water and swam farther down. "Hello," he yelled when coming up for air.

"In here," came the choked reply, followed by banging. "The door's jammed."

"Hang in there. I'll be right back." Quickly he hurried back to the saloon and ran into Jerry and Mark already there with Jenna. "He's okay. He's stuck in the laundry room."

The three men left Jenna alone again to return to the room to rescue him. Water began to pool around her feet. She turned and looked out the door. The back of the boat was disappearing into the ice-cold water. They didn't have long before it went down completely.

She carefully made her way over to the staircase. "Guys, we gotta go. Like now," she yelled.

When they didn't emerge from the watery tunnel, she zipped up her life jacket and went outside towards the life raft. A huge wave rose on the starboard side of the boat. She tried to rush back inside, but with the angle of the deck, she couldn't move quickly enough.

The wave kicked her feet out from under her, and she slid down the same slippery slope that her boss did before. "Ethan!" she cried.

Ethan heard her frantic cry for help, and his heart stopped at the sound. He shoved his buddies aside and high-tailed it to the outer deck, only to see her strawberry blond hair disappear over the side.

"Jenna!" He didn't waste a second. He grabbed the lifesaver and jumped into the water after her, keeping a close watch on her hair which stood out in the churning water. His men shouted after him, but he wasn't about to lose another crew member. Not if he could help it.

"Swim, Jenna!" he yelled, unsure if she heard him amidst the thunderous noise coming from the dark clouds above them. Her life jacket was keeping her afloat, but she was struggling against the monstrous waves.

He could barely feel his freezing fingers as he held onto the lifesaver and kicked his way towards her, his clothes weighing him down. They didn't have much time before hypothermia set in, that much he knew.

Keeping his eyes trained on Jenna, he pushed himself forward, forgetting about everything else behind him. He knew his men could take care of themselves. They still had the life raft. She had nothing, except her life jacket, and his eyes trained on her.

Whenever he thought he was making progress in her direction, the current pulled her even further away. His breath caught when a wave pulled her out of his line of sight.

"No. No. Damn it!" He put the rope over his shoulder, letting the lifesaver float behind him so he could use two arms to swim. He wasn't an Olympic champion by any means, but he was in good shape. Thankfully.

Another large wave came his way, making him duck under the water. It wasn't like swimming in a pool. The ocean fought back with vengeance. Every muscle in his body ached with exertion as he breached the surface, frantically searching for Jenna. His chin trembled and his teeth chattered unceasingly.

"Ethan!" she cried. He whipped around in the opposite direction and found her riding the wave high above him. How the bloody heck did she get behind him?

Whether it was fate, destiny, or some other whacko element of surprise, she coasted right into him. "Oh, thank God," he exclaimed as she wrapped her arms around his neck, clinging to him like plastic wrap. Nothing had ever felt so good to him than the feel of her fingers gripping him tightly. Pulling in the lifesaver, he placed it over her head and felt a slight loss when her hands gripped the ring instead. His skin tingled from the aftermath of her touch.

He had no idea what they were going to do now, but at least they were securely attached to each other. Not that it would help if they stayed in the water much longer. The icy ocean was having a numbing effect on his limbs.

She gave him a tiny shivering smile, her lips slightly blue, which was not a good sign. If luck didn't come their way soon, they'd become one with the depth of the sea. Their frozen bodies would drag them down.

While he enjoyed a good scuba dive every now and then, he didn't have a tank to breathe today, and he wasn't a merman. That meant he would become fish food instead. He glanced at Jenna. She would make a gorgeous mermaid though, and that was something he definitely liked the idea of. If he had his way, she'd have a fiery red tail that looked like she was being licked by the flames, and she'd be braless.

Despite their situation, he found the corners of his lips curling into a grin. He could be the fearless captain, and she could be his siren. Her call wouldn't lead him to his death, but into her arms instead, where they would make passionate love on the beach all night long.

Oh ya. He was definitely getting delirious.

"I'm s-s-so cold," she said, between chattering teeth.

"Keep your limbs moving, don't let them seize up," he said,

rubbing his hands up and down her arms. Not that it helped. His hands were like ice cubes.

"W-what are we g-going to do?" she asked, her chin vibrating.

"Let me thi—" His eyes widened, and he quickly pulled her close. A gigantic wave was bearing down on them, along with a chunk of debris. "Watch out!"

"Ethan!"

The piece of wood, which was the size of a raft, must have come from whatever hit his ship. "We have to try and get on that," he said, pointing to the incoming debris.

She shook her head wildly. "Are you crazy? That's g-going to be impossible."

"It's our only chance."

Jenna knew he was right, but one of them could get seriously hurt trying to snag it. They didn't need their blood attracting all the meat eaters of the ocean. She'd seen enough horror movies and documentaries to know exactly what would happen if they mixed their red life force with H_2o.

"Wait for my command," Ethan said.

"Yes, *B-Boss*!" Her words were supposed to sound sarcastic, but she could barely squeeze them past her trembling lips. She lifted her lead-like arms to get ready. They felt heavier than ever before. In fact, her entire body felt like a concrete block, making her wonder if she was suddenly on another planet.

As the wave crashed down, saltwater sprayed in her face, stinging her eyes. Her vision blurred so badly she could barely see what they were supposed to be concentrating on.

"On the count of three," he yelled above the roar of the waves.

Rubbing her eyes didn't help. It just made them worse. How was she supposed to grab what she couldn't see? Her throat started to close, her breathing ragged. "Oh, God. I can't breathe."

"Focus, Jenna." He shook her shoulders. "We only have one chance."

Squinting, she focused on the chunk of wood coming in their direction.

"One...two..." he yelled over the raging storm as he lunged towards their only hope. "Three!"

Following suit, she dove for the debris, but passed by it completely as she tried to find something, anything to grab onto. The rope from the lifesaver flew up and landed in the middle of the debris, joining them on either end of their new-found raft.

She tried to climb onto it, but as she lifted herself out of the water, another wave knocked her off.

"Hang on," he said, pulling himself onto the large wooden plank. After he was safely on board, he grabbed the rope and pulled her up with him.

The chill of the howling wind cut right to her bones as they clung to each other in the middle of nowhere. She wasn't sure what she was more terrified of, the storm or the man who had his arms wrapped around her. If it wasn't for her desperate need to stay on the new raft, she would push him away and tell him to shove his help where the sun don't shine.

"Hey look," he said, pointing behind her.

She gripped the front of his shirt and turned to see what he was looking at. On the distant horizon, there were breaks forming in the dark storm clouds, and a brilliant shade of blue was peeking through. And the spout that had threatened their boat was gone, and the boat along with it.

"I think we've survived the worst for now," he said, as he rubbed the back of his neck.

"Survived the worst? Are you crazy? We don't have food. We don't have a boat and—Oh, my God." She pointed to his calf. "You're bleeding."

"It's just a scratch," he said. "It's nothing."

"It's not nothing if it attracts a shark bigger than this piddly chunk of wood. Take off your shirt."

"Take off yours first."

"I'd punch you if I could get my arms to move fast enough," she snapped. Her Grand Teton goosebumps made her skin stretch beyond normal. And she could feel the panic creeping up inside her. They were in the middle of nowhere, with no way out.

Eyeing him warily, she released his shirt and grabbed onto the edge of the wood as it went sideways with a wave. Why the heck hadn't she listened to the alarm bells that were in her mind prior to taking this job? Now, she was trapped with a man she didn't really know, and lost in the middle of the ocean. And she couldn't do a damn thing.

But she wasn't going to be helpless this time, not like she was before. Her forehead creased as she glared at him. "Not this time."

"Holy geez, if looks could kill." Ethan held his hands up, but quickly returned his grip to the wet wood beneath him. Her eyes had turned as cold as the seawater around them. He wasn't sure what changed besides the predicament they were in, but he hoped to God she wasn't going to pull out her kung-fu moves.

"Breathe, Jenna. I don't know what you're thinking about, but you need to breathe."

Not only did her eyes hold no warmth, but they also took on a dark look. It was reminiscent of what you'd see in a demon takeover. Ethan didn't even know if he was dealing with the real Jenna anymore or some weird split personality. Over the last week, he'd seen her be at least three different people. However, with each one, he could still see a shadow hovering in her eyes.

Now, as they sat there in the middle of the ocean, alone, on a five-foot by four-foot raft, he found it intimidating to be facing the full blunt force of that shadow. Whatever happened to her, she hadn't made peace with it. It haunted her like a ghost in a graveyard.

"Don't tell me what to do," she growled at him.

If they didn't need to hold on to the raft due to the waves, he was certain that she'd make quick use of her limbs and knock him overboard. He kind of hoped that the waves kept rolling so she wouldn't get that chance. Maybe the current would push them towards a shoreline.

Knowing her temperament, he said nothing more, giving her a chance to work through whatever was going on in her mind. He had learned quickly that she would charge like a bull if anything he did resembled a matador waving a muleta. If prodded, her horns could do some serious damage.

So, there wasn't much he could do but sit and study her as they got tossed back and forth on the ocean's surface. Every muscle in her body was taut, and her mouth and jawline tense as she held on tight.

She was an enigma, a puzzle to be solved, and that intrigued his writer's brain. He found it incredibly difficult not to act like a reporter and grill her with all the questions running through his brain, but he remembered one famous quote.

Curiosity killed the cat.

So, he decided to keep his trap shut.

Chapter Four

Meanwhile, back on the mainland...

Iris McCay, Jenna's mother, grabbed her fleece Yellowstone blanket and curled into a ball on the couch, burying her face into the soft armrest. She smacked the cushion with her fist, crying.

"*Let her go,*" everyone told her. "*Let her live her life.*" Twice she made that choice, and twice now her daughter had disappeared. She kept trying to tell them her family was cursed, but no one would listen. *"You're being over-protective,"* they said.

No one cared about their past anymore. "*Get on with your life*" was echoed endlessly into her ear. She hated them. Hated the world. They had no idea what her family had been through after they got her back. Iris had to watch Jenna struggle through many sleepless nights, screaming out in terror.

Even Daniel, Jenna's father, grew impatient with their daughter's lack of affection towards him and spent more time away than ever before. The ugly 'D' word had been thrown around far too often. And even though they never acted on the thought, he still kept threatening her with it because of how she babied their daughter after the incident.

He'd expected Jenna to bounce back and be her old regular self and thought Iris' behaviour was prolonging her healing. And maybe it was. But what mother wouldn't do what she did? Every caring mother would hold their crying child in their arms and lay beside them at night, helping them fall back asleep.

What were they going to do now? She couldn't even contact Daniel to let him know their daughter was missing in action again. He had his phone off, per his usual routine. She had only gotten the call from the police a few hours ago, but it felt like an eternity.

They said that a distress call had been made, and the coastguard was going to check it out, but so far the crew hadn't been found. Iris' stomach sank at the news and still hadn't surfaced yet.

What if her baby girl was sitting at the bottom of the ocean? Iris would never see her again. Her throat clogged as a loud cry burst through her lips. "Oh, Jenna." She wrapped her arms around her belly, trying to calm the tumbling feeling inside.

After receiving the call, she had gone to the police station, asking to speak with Detective Charleston. He'd helped find her daughter the last time, Much to her horror, though, she learned that he retired a year ago. She'd begged them for his number, but they refused to give it.

"Sorry, ma'am. That's confidential."

"I don't care. He's the only one who can find my baby."

Her hand had itched to smack the woman who stood behind the counter as she acted so superior. It didn't seem to matter that her kid was missing. Iris had shoved her fists into her jacket pockets and left the building. The last thing her family needed was for her to be charged with assault, so she had returned home and crashed on the couch.

Growing impatient, Iris threw the blanket over the back of the couch, and grabbed her phone off the coffee table, searching for the number for the Ontario police. If her husband wasn't going to answer his phone, she would get them to track him down before it hit the news.

Daniel wasn't due back for another week as he was filling in at the head office. The big boss had gone on vacation. She would have gone with Daniel, but he refused to let her. When she clicked the on button on her phone, a picture of the three of them standing on a beach popped up. She glared at her husband.

If she had her way, they would be together all the time, and she wouldn't have two wayward travellers on her hands. Being alone had left her with way too much time on her hands. Her mind kept using that freedom to tie her down by thinking of all the worst-case scenarios.

And right now, she felt like she was on a rollercoaster with every twist and loop you could dream of. She tried to talk herself down, but then another image or thought would take its place. Tears burned in her eyes. Was she doomed to die alone with no loved ones by her side?

It was bad enough that she got her prognosis yesterday and hadn't had the chance to tell anyone yet. Now her baby girl was gone, possibly *dead* already. Acid rose in her throat as a snake-like shiver slithered down her spine.

Please, God, let them find my baby girl!

～

Something didn't feel right to Daniel McCay as he sat there watching the news. A distress call had been made from a boat called *The Em-Dash* just off the shores of California. A powerful storm had moved into the region, and the sailboat didn't stand a chance. Why did the name of the boat sound so familiar? Leaning towards the television, he listened to the reporter.

"There were six people on board, including our very own Oscar winning script writer, Ethan Barrett. The distress call came in at six thirty-five this morning amidst a very powerful storm that gripped the region. The coastguard has been unable to locate any survivors. They will continue the search throughout the day. Another storm is due to hit the area tonight, which may hamper the search efforts..."

The reporter stopped talking for a moment, pressing her finger to her ear before looking towards the camera again. "In surprising news, we have just learned that Jenna McCay, the only survivor of the heinous murder spree committed by Mathew Graham, is one of the missing crew members. We will share more updates as they become available."

Daniel leaned back on the tan couch in his hotel suite in shock, running a hand over his balding head and through what little blonde hair he had left, as he tried to digest what he had just heard. Memories of his baby girl sitting in the hospital bed assaulted him. She wouldn't let him touch her, wouldn't even let him get close. He hated what that asshole had done to her.

The girl he got back was not the same girl that left. She was identical to his daughter, but he didn't know her anymore. And she treated him like a distant stranger, freaking out anytime he got close. They both blamed him for what happened. All because he tried to encourage his daughter to spread her wings. *Hell.* It wasn't like he was telling her to go to the moon. He had only encouraged her to take the job at the library down the road.

He knew bad things could happen in life. It was just one of those things, so he tried his best not to blame himself. His family did that enough for him, but it wasn't easy. He didn't know what to expect from his wife this time. She'd probably toss her ring at him. And he probably deserved it, too.

Picking up his phone off the glass coffee table, he stared at the black screen. He should phone Iris and make sure she was okay, but he didn't relish the idea of talking to her. His mind was too messed up to handle one of her outbursts right now.

Jenna was gone. Again. It was like their own personal horror movie. The ones his daughter liked so much. He never liked them, especially the sequels. Why not just leave the survivors alone, and let them get on with their lives? One time through the wringer was enough for any family.

Taking a deep breath, he clicked on his daughter's name. Hoping and praying that the news broadcast was wrong, and she would pick up the phone. He crossed his fingers and tapped them on his knee as he waited for it to connect.

"Hi, this is Jenna. Please leave a message after the beep."

He yanked the phone away from his ear and chucked it across the room. The screen cracked as the device bounced off the wall. Standing up, Daniel paced the length of the living room, running his hands up and down his face.

"Damn. Damn. Damn," he muttered, then released a round of obscenities that echoed off the walls. An abrupt knock at the door interrupted his personal tirade. "What?"

Christy, his young blond assistant, walked into the room. "I heard shouting. Is everything okay?"

His eyes slid down her body of their own volition. She was wearing a tight white halter top and a hot pink miniskirt. Heat pooled in his belly. He let out a long breath and turned away from her, walking over to the only window in the room.

He placed his forearm on the glass and leaned his forehead on it. "My daughter is missing."

She walked over and stood beside him, placing her hand on his shoulder. "Again?"

"I just don't know what I'm going to do."

Turning him around, Christy ran her hands up his chest and linked her fingers behind his neck. "You could let me take your mind off it."

Unlinking her hands, he took a step away from her. "If my life were any different, I'd take you up on the offer."

"You don't have to do anything. Let me give you pleasure just this once."

His body severely wanted what she had to offer, but the ring on his left hand told him that if he opened that door, another would close. A chapter he'd been living for twenty-six years, and that wasn't something he wanted to throw away. No matter how hard it was, he was going to be a man of his word from now on. That was all he really had in this world.

"It's not that easy," he said.

The look in her grey eyes was that of a cougar stalking their prey as she approached him again. "It can be as easy as you want it to be," she said, reaching for his belt.

Stilling her hands, he groaned, "You're a temptress, you know that?"

"I know you want me. I can see it," she said, acknowledging the growing bulge in his pants.

"Yes. But wanting you doesn't change the fact that I'm a married man."

"Married schmarried. I don't care."

"Christy, you are a beautiful woman. There are plenty of available men your age that would die to have you."

"They're all boys," she said, undoing his belt.

The fire was getting a little too hot, so he put some distance between them and fixed his belt. "You sure don't make things easy on a man."

Instead of taking the hint, she pulled her shirt over her head, revealing a pink lacy bra that hugged her tanned California skin. She was someone that you would expect to see in a Los Angeles beach movie.

"Please, hun. You deserve a man who can give you the world. I can't give you what you want."

She unzipped her skirt and stepped out of it, her long, sexy legs snagging his attention. Shutting his eyes, he took a deep breath. His body was craving the idea something fierce, as sex was a rare commodity in his life lately.

Daniel leaned down and picked up her shirt, holding it out to her. "Christy, you need to get dressed. I can't do this. You know I can't."

"We did before."

"That's beside the point."

She grabbed her shirt and threw it on the couch. Turning back to him, she gave him a slight shove, making him land in the recliner. "Maybe that is the point. You came to me before."

"I had separated from my wife. I thought I was getting a divorce."

Kneeling in front of him, she looked around the room. "I don't see her here."

"She's still with me wherever I go," he said, pointing to the ring on his left hand. "I really need you to put your clothes on and arrange a flight back home right away."

"Pissy old fart."

Daniel choked back a laugh. "See, the grass isn't always greener on the other side."

Picking up her clothes, she strolled towards the door and gave him a cheeky grin over her shoulder as she smacked her pink thong-covered butt. "Kiss my ass."

As Christy walked out of the room, Daniel said, "Let me know when you have the flight booked."

Sticking her hand back in the door, she gave him the middle finger.

The room became eerily quiet after she left, like she had zapped all the energy out of it. Daniel stood up and went over to the dresser to pack his clothes, his heart heavy.

"Jenna's a fighter," he muttered as he pulled his suitcase out from under the bed. All he could hope for was that they got on a life raft before the ship went down. If he ever got his hands on the man who got his baby into this mess, he was going to kill him...if the ocean didn't finish the job.

Chapter Five

Evening had fallen, and the first star appeared in the sky. Lying on the wooden makeshift raft, Jenna stared at the star. The waters had finally calmed, and she no longer felt like she was going to be tossed to the gods of the sea. The sun had almost disappeared over the horizon, leaving the sky a gorgeous shade of pink and purple.

"Making a wish?" Ethan asked, breaking an hour-long silence.

"I don't believe in wishes anymore." Jenna cringed at the tiny wisp of hope that invaded her voice. Wishes were for people who were too young and naïve to know about all the horrible things in the world.

"Why not?"

"Because."

"Because isn't an answer."

"It's all you're getting."

"You don't like talking about yourself much, do you?" Ethan observed.

She shrugged her shoulders, fighting off a full body shiver as cold water splashed against her skin. "Oh, that's cold."

"Come here." He took her by the arm to pull her closer to him.

"Let me go," she cried, pushing him away. Her actions knocked them both precariously close to the edges of the small raft.

He flailed his arms in a desperate attempt to stay on board. "Damn, Jenna. I was just going to help you stay warm."

Sitting up, Jenna pulled her knees to her chest and wrapped her arms around them. She took a deep breath in through her nose and out through her mouth as she rocked back and forth.

"Breathe, Jenna, breathe. You aren't there anymore. You're alive," she told herself. "He's gone. He's in jail."

"Who's in jail?"

"No one...nothing." She waved a shaky hand at Ethan. "Never mind."

"I think I deserve to know why you almost knocked me into the ocean. *Again.*"

"I don't want to talk about it," she said, her eyes brimming with tears. "Please."

Turning away, she hid her face. Her story had been splattered all over the news for months. If he hadn't heard about it, that was his fault. She wasn't going to repeat the story to anyone anymore. No one else needed to know. Certainly not the man she was stuck with. It might give him ideas.

"I'm not going to hurt you, Jenna," Ethan said softly, staying on his own side of the raft.

"That remains to be seen," she mumbled.

"I'm honestly not a bad guy."

Why couldn't she have been trapped with Roger or something? She knew she could trust him. In the short time she'd been on the boat, he'd been so easy to open up to. He even made her laugh. Something she didn't do as often as she used to.

"Do you think they're okay?" she asked.

"My friends?"

"Ya."

Ethan didn't see any point in lying to her. "I'm almost certain we lost Chris."

"What about the others?"

His gut clenched as he looked over the darkening sea. He hated the idea that he may have lost his best friends. "I don't know."

In a surprising move, her hand came to rest on his arm. "I'm sure they're okay. They have to—" She suddenly stopped talking, her eyes widening. She appeared to be frozen in place, her fingers tightening on his forearm.

Resting his hand on top of hers, he asked, "Are you okay?"

Jenna jerked her hand away and fell backwards, tumbling head-first into the cold water. Ethan bolted forward, tilting the raft dangerously to one side, trying to grab her hand.

When she went under and disappeared out of his sight, a chill rippled through him. He couldn't lose her. Not yet. Not now. "Jenna!" He scanned the surface of the water for any signs of her. Bubbles. Anything.

"Damn it, girl! Where are you?" The moment he spoke the words something bumped into the bottom of the raft. *Hell.* She must be underneath. Using his arms as paddles, he tried to move the raft, hoping it would help.

His efforts paid off when a hand breached the surface. Grabbing it, he pulled her back onto the raft and into his arms. "Holy shit, you scared me."

Jenna pulled away from him and knelt on all fours, coughing up water. When he went to pat her on the back, she held out a hand, palm facing outwards. "Don't."

"Stubborn ass woman," he grumbled. Seriously. Not even his mother was as ferociously independent as Jenna appeared to be.

She half laughed and half choked as she cleared the water from her lungs, her lips curling into a grin. "You know it."

"You aren't like a lesbian, are you?"

Her gaze pierced him like a laser. "We're l-lost in the m-middle of the ocean," she said, her teeth chattering, "and y-you're asking me about my o-orientation?"

It sounded like a perfectly legit question to him, but with her lips pressed into a firm line and her fierce eyes ripping him a new one, he wished he could take it back. His conclusion was logical though, especially given the fact that she gravitated towards Roger.

"I should k-knock you in the ocean," she snapped.

Holding up his hands, he said, "Sorry. You just seem to hate men, that's all."

"I could say the same about you, woman wise. I'm the first woman you've had on board in like forever."

He frowned, his cheeks burning. "Exactly how much did my friends tell you about me?" In the past, his career was almost side railed by the last woman he was with, and he didn't need them telling Jenna about it.

"Don't like the tables being turned, do ya?" she asked, rubbing her hands up and down her arms.

"Touché," he replied. Ethan glanced around three hundred and sixty degrees and saw nothing, especially as night was quickly falling. Things weren't looking good for them. He had no idea how far offshore they were because he often left the route planning to Jerry and focused primarily on his writing while they were out on the water.

He and Jenna had no food, no drinkable water, and were stuck out on the open sea, where a storm could strike at any moment. Even in his writer's mind, he couldn't figure out how they were going to get out of this one alive, but he wasn't going to tell her that. They had nothing to catch fish with. Nothing to keep from getting cold. It caused a dark cloud of doom descended over him. He knew they were screwed. They would only survive a couple days at most.

After a while, the odd quiet cry came from her direction. Not wanting to encroach on her privacy, he kept quiet. She deserved a moment alone, even though he was right there with her.

"Ethan?"

"Hmm."

"I'm sorry that I've been difficult."

"Don—"

"Shut up," she interrupted. "I'm trying to talk."

He quirked an eyebrow and almost chuckled at how even her apologies were a game of dominance. She had to be in control of her circumstances. It was something she seemed to need, and he couldn't help but wonder why. He should have googled her, but he'd been too occupied to think of the idea before they left.

"I've been a bitch. I know I have. You're my boss, and I shouldn't have treated you that way," she said, wiping a tear away. "I guess this is karma biting me in the butt again."

"You didn't cause this."

"It's because of me you got separated from the others."

"You needed me more than they did."

"You shouldn't have risked your life to save me. I'm a nobody."

"Honey, nobody is a nobody and certainly not you." His heart went out to her. Her self-esteem levels were so low, and he couldn't wrap his head around it. She was beautiful and funny, but it was like she didn't know it.

She made a non-committal noise, and then returned to her silence. Laying his head back, he crossed his arms over his abdomen and focused on the gentle rocking of the raft beneath them. Above him, the stars twinkled in the darkness, playing their own silent music, shining brightly for him to see. It's one of the things he liked about being on the ocean, away from all the city lights. No pollution to get in the way. He could see the well-known band of the Milky Way spreading out like a spiral of white cloudy lights.

The moon cast a glow upon their humble little raft, creating a snow globe effect, blocking them out from the real world. A feeling of freedom washed over him, rather than fear. The last few years of his life were stressful, filled with cameras and lawyers. No rest for the famous script writer and the accused.

Movement on the raft stole his attention. Jenna rolled over and pressed up against his side, breathing softly and evenly in her sleep, shivering occasionally. He wrapped his arms around her and held her close, hoping whatever body heat he had would keep her warm. He kissed the top of her head, breathing in her scent. Underneath the smell of the ocean, he noticed a hint of lavender.

She was different from other girls he knew. Most would be freaking out, yet here she was sleeping. Just who was she? Men freaked her out, but being lost in the middle of the ocean didn't? He thought she'd become hysterical, but her biggest complaint seemed to be him.

She was the only woman he knew that could whip his butt, which was kind of a turn on. Maybe that's why he kept holding on to her instead of letting her go, even though he knew she would start a fight the minute she opened her eyes. If he had to, he'd come up with an excuse in the morning. It didn't take long before she started moaning in her sleep, so Ethan pulled her even closer to him.

~

Dark. It was so dark. Jenna was alone, but Mathew's stench of onions and garlic still filled the room. His fingers were like hundreds of tiny spiders walking on her skin long after he left. She rubbed her thighs together until they were raw, trying to get the remnants of her experience with him off her body.

She was trapped. Caged like some animal in a zoo, placed there for someone else's pleasure. She struggled to break free from the chains binding her wrists to the wall. Blood dripped down her arms as the metal dug into her skin.

How many times had it happened, six or seven? She'd lost count of all the times he came and took what wasn't his to take. Stealing her innocence, her spirit, causing the light that once existed inside her to dim. Her eyes burned, but no tears would form.

"Why won't you let me die?" she cried into the darkness. It wasn't like she was a bad person. She hadn't lived a bad life. Hell, her life had barely begun. Why was she here? With every ounce of energy she had left, she screamed, digging her heels into the dirt. "I'm going to kill you."

Pulling and yanking on the chains, she yelled every expletive she had ever heard in her life and then some. It didn't take long for the door to open again. His silhouette filled the doorway, his dark shadow falling over her body. Jenna cringed and pulled her legs closed, pressing her body against the wall.

"Go away," she cried.

The dirt crunched beneath his boots as he walked towards her. Her chest tightened, and bile rose in her throat, creating a bitter taste on her tongue. When he was only a couple feet away from her, she kicked her legs out at him. Her foot connected with his knee, making him buckle. Swearing, he grabbed her legs and tugged them, so she was partially lying down.

"No. Please don't."

He pulled back his hand, smacking her across the face with his knuckles, her jaw cracking. "Never do that again," he said, his voice rumbling.

"Don't touch me!" But her words were useless, just like her hands that were chained above her head. He took her by the forehead and slammed her head into the wall. Jenna grunted as pain sliced through her, stars forming in front of her eyes. He held her down as he undid his pants.

"I can't, please!" she begged, her voice hoarse and breathing ragged.

She squeezed her eyes closed, trying to will herself away. Anything to ignore what she knew was coming.

"Jenna, wake up," a new voice broke through her subconscious.

Opening her eyes, she was blinded by a bright light and quickly closed them again.

"That's it. Come back to the land of the living."

Jenna froze. An arm was wrapped around her, and someone was tapping her on the cheek. Who was he? Where was she? An intense heat bore down on her face, like a furnace. She attempted to open her eyes, but quickly closed them again as a heavy band of pressure wrapped itself around her head, her forehead throbbing.

Images from the previous day zipped through her mind, and one very specific image had her bolting upright, gasping, "My box. Where's my box?" She frantically looked around. There was water on every side, and their raft was empty of everything but themselves.

"I'm afraid you dropped it when you fell off the boat," Ethan said softly, compassion filling his voice.

"No. No. No," she said, shaking her head furiously. "We have to go back. We have to find it."

"Honey, it's gone."

She pulled her legs against her chest and laid her chin on her knee, glancing out over the ocean as far as her eyes would allow. Hoping and praying that she would catch a glimpse of the box that held the most precious thing in her life.

"It can't be gone," she cried, her eyes despondent. Was this her luck? Was this all she could expect from life? One crappy thing after another? Maybe she should just jump into the ocean and get it over with. At least then she wouldn't have to fight with the pain anymore. She wouldn't be stuck on the raft with a man that could hurt her.

"I'm sorry." He reached out to her, but she shied away. He dropped his hand on his nearly dry lap, which he hoped would stay that way.

The only good thing right now was that the sun was shining, and there wasn't a cloud in sight. Thankfully no other storm rocked their tiny little raft during the night. Weather remained calm.

"I need to find the box. We have to go back," she begged.

"Even if we wanted to, there's no way of knowing which direction to go."

"We have to try." She swallowed a sob as she tried to use her hand like a paddle in the water. When he sat there and didn't help, she glared at him, her eyes filling with tears.

"Unless you have food and a satellite phone in that stupid box, we better try to find land instead," Ethan said.

"It's not stu—you know what, never mind. You wouldn't understand." She turned her back on him, which wasn't an easy task on such a small raft, and looked out over the water again. The white caps glittered in the morning sun. At least, it still looked like morning. The sun wasn't at its highest peak yet.

"You are really peculiar, Jenna McCay."

"Gee, thanks," she replied sarcastically.

"You seem more concerned about that box than the fact that we are in the middle of nowhere."

She shrugged her shoulders. "I've been in worse situations."

All she needed was to see the fin of a shark, and then she could say that her life had become every single horror movie she'd ever seen. It was like the grim reaper was playing with her life and having a blast doing it, poking her with his scythe whenever he darn well pleased.

"Roger mentioned that you went through some hard times."

Her shoulders stiffened and pain shot up her spine into her head, making it pound again. "What did he tell you?"

"Nothing."

"Good. I don't plan on telling you either."

"I saw the scar on your leg."

Jenna spun around. Her fists clenched. Why couldn't the man leave well enough alone?

Ethan held up his hands. "Don't worry. I didn't do anything dishonourable. Your pant leg rode up as I was carrying you. Is that why you limp?"

"Yes." *That was all she was willing to say.*

He didn't need to hear how she was kidnapped by a deranged psycho and held against her will, nor the many months of painful surgeries and rehab afterwards as they tried to put her leg back together. If she told him, he'd pity her, and she didn't want anyone else to feel sorry for her. She faced enough of that when she was rescued.

Maybe that's why she liked working on the ocean. It got her away from the crowds, away from their sympathy or their disgust. People often asked her whether she felt trapped on a boat because there was nowhere to go, but there was something about the ocean itself that allowed her to breathe. It didn't make sense, but it had become her world. Maybe that's why she wasn't freaking out.

Ethan tilted his head and studied her. "Maybe I can guess what happened."

"I wouldn't tell you even if you did," she said through clenched teeth.

"You have PTSD and a pretty gnarly looking scar, and you can take down a guy with ease. My guess would be that you were in the military. Special Forces perhaps?"

Jenna shook her head. "Just leave it alone, please."

"I'm right, aren't I?"

She clenched her fists, struggling desperately not to push him overboard. Her past was her past alone, and she didn't want to talk about it. The only reason she shared it with Roger was because she had run into him in the kitchen. She had wandered in there after her nightmare with tear-stained cheeks, and he happened to be awake. There was something about him that made her feel comfortable.

Snorting with derision, she said, "If only it were something that cool."

But no, her reality was far less cool, and a lot more disturbing. Mathew, the murdering psycho, took everything from her. Things that she could never get back, and he gave her things that would stay with her forever. She'd give anything to forget the days when she was locked in his prison. The snakes. The spiders. His touch. Jenna shivered.

"You cold?" Ethan asked, his voice temporarily breaking her free of her memories.

She crossed her arms over her chest and ran her hands up and down her arms. "I'm fine." It was far from the truth, but no one ever wanted to hear the truth. It's not like they knew what to say in her case, anyway.

"You're shaking."

"So what!" she snapped, and then she felt a pang of guilt for responding so harshly. Her past wasn't his fault, and she shouldn't be taking it out on him. "Sorry."

"Don't apologize. Whatever it is you went through was traumatic, and I'm sorry."

"Thanks," she said quietly, afraid to talk any louder. If she did, she might start crying in front of him.

Jenna lay down on her side, facing away from him, hoping he'd take the hint. The sun was so bright she was seeing stars. Letting her head rest on her arm, she closed her eyes. If only she had an extra layer of clothing, she'd be able to hide herself from the dangerous ultraviolet rays shooting all around her. She didn't relish getting a sunburn, especially one that would make her look like a freshly picked tomato.

Rolling over to look at him, she said, "I'm glad you didn't force me to wear a skirt."

"I'm sorry. That was a terrible joke on my part," he said.

If Ethan had known she'd been through something traumatic, he wouldn't have even attempted to joke around like that. Now, he had put her in another situation that could only add to the intense emotional pain he could see in her eyes. He felt like a heel. He should have said no to hiring her and went without a stewardess. Roger would have gladly picked up the slack.

Jenna gave him half a smile, but it didn't reach her eyes. "You didn't know."

"It was petty of me."

"Are you trying to ease your conscience, Ethan?"

He opened his mouth to deny her claim, but then quickly closed it. He was the one who brought them into the path of the storm because he had a deadline to meet. And now, what did it matter? His story wasn't done, and he was going to miss his deadline.

Things weren't looking good on the rescue front. He hadn't heard a plane or even a helicopter since the storm, which meant either no one was looking for them, or no one knew where to look. The longer they spent out here, the greater the chances they would die of heat stroke, hypothermia or thirst. All because of his foolish choices, and a wicked storm.

He knew that storms were possible whenever they went out to sea, but this time it seemed like the sea had a beef to pick with him. First, his friend was swept overboard, and then he just about went over himself, then finally Jenna. It was like the ocean was trying to tell him something.

He wasn't superstitious or anything, but there was always a story waiting to be told. Maybe even their own survival story, which at this point was sitting at the to-be-continued part. Ethan breathed in deeply, the saltwater smell saturating his nostrils, making him wish for salt and vinegar chips. His stomach growled. He was really beginning to wish he hadn't skipped breakfast.

"Well?" she asked.

"Well what?"

"Are you trying to ease your conscience?"

"Maybe."

He said nothing more, and she didn't pry. Ethan knew he had a lot of things to confess and a lot of sins to be forgiven. Pride was right up there at the top of the list. Whoever was in charge of the world was making damn sure Ethan was pushed off his pedestal, and it looked like Jenna was sent to do it. No one had ever flipped him on his ass before.

The two of them never talked much over the last week. He'd been too busy locked in his study writing or at least trying to write. He wanted to see if he could finish his story before his birthday. There was a bottle of the finest wine waiting to be opened in celebration for another job well-done. But now that expensive bottle was sitting on the bottom of the ocean with his laptop.

The raft rocked as Jenna sat up abruptly. "Hey, did you hear that?"

"Hear what?"

"I thought I heard a foghorn."

Ethan shielded his eyes and looked around. In the far distance, he saw a smoke trail low in the sky and the silhouette of a large boat. That meant they were near a shipping route.

Jenna stood up, cupped her hands around her mouth, and hollered, "Help! We're over here." In a desperate attempt to be seen, she started jumping up and down, and the raft rocked dangerously. Her left foot missed the raft, and she flailed her arms, trying to regain her balance. "Ethan, help!" she cried, reaching out for him.

He tried to grab her hand, but she fell backwards out of his reach. She hit the water with a splash, disappearing under the deep blue sea. "Not again." His heart stopped when she didn't resurface. If he jumped into the water, they could lose the raft; but if he didn't, he could lose her. Neither option was pleasing.

"Jenna?" he yelled, carefully searching the surface for bubbles. Anything that could tell him where she was. "Damn it! Where are you?"

As if on cue, she surfaced about fifteen feet away, coughing and sputtering. The heavy stone of dread that had clamped onto his heart rolled away, and he started paddling in her direction.

"Over here," he shouted.

When she turned and looked at him, her eyes widening in terror. "Sh...sh-sh," she stuttered, pointing at something off to the left. "Shark!"

The fin was barely visible, but it was unmistakable. He tried paddling towards her, but the current kept pulling him away. "Swim, Jenna, swim!" She was frozen in her spot, ignoring his pleas. "Damn it, woman, swim!"

She finally started swimming towards him. As the animal neared them, he watched the fin dip below the surface, disappearing out of sight. His pulse raced in fear, unable to do anything but watch. "Faster, Jenna."

"I'm t-trying," she cried. When she reached him, she grabbed Ethan's hand just as something brushed up against her leg.

Jenna screamed.

Chapter Six

"Hell, if they didn't have bad luck, they'd have no luck at all," Johnathan Charleston said, running his hand along the back of his neck. He'd been listening to the news broadcast all morning. They had just finished interviewing a very distraught Iris, who could hardly hold it together.

His wife, Jodi, came and sat down beside him, pity in her eyes. "I couldn't imagine if that happened to us."

"Same here. I'm going to see if there is anything I can do." He'd been off the force for a little while now but did like to help out every now and again, especially on cases that hit close to home. Ones that he had a personal investment in.

"What do you think the odds are of finding them?" she asked

"I wish I could say it was good, but that storm was brutal." He'd heard there were six distress calls yesterday, and those didn't include Ethan's boat. Every news station appeared to be focusing on Ethan and Jenna's boat today. Not surprising, given who they were. But it would be the last thing Jenna would want. She hated being the centre of attention.

John pinched the end of his moustache and rolled it between his fingers, watching the screen. If it were his daughter out there, he'd stop at nothing to find her. He had worked hard to find Jenna the last time she disappeared, and lost a few good men along the way. He wasn't going to let it be for nothing. And that alone was the very reason he found himself dialling Iris' number. She would need a familiar face guiding her through all this.

"Hello," she answered, her voice cracking.

"Hi dear, it's Detec—Johnathan Charleston." He'd have to remember to stop using that title.

"Oh, thank heavens. The ladies at the office wouldn't patch me through to you."

"I'm sorry about that. The department has strict protocols unfortunately."

"They could have offered to call you, and let you know that I was looking for you," she huffed.

"Have you heard any news?" he asked, hoping to move the conversation forward.

"I haven't heard anything," she said, sniffling. "Excuse me one second."

The phone was muffled, but he could hear her blowing her nose, sounding much like a goose. *Poor woman.* He couldn't even begin to understand what it must feel like to be going through this again.

"Sorry about that," she said.

"Don't apologize," he said. "Is Daniel home?"

"No, but he's taking the next flight home."

"Okay. I'm going to see what I can find out. I don't work in the department anymore, but I still have contacts."

"Please call me as soon as you hear anything."

"Will do, hun. I'm also going to text you a number for the helpline. It will give you someone to talk with."

His wife squeezed his hand and gave him a loving kiss on the cheek as he ended the call. "I couldn't have married a better man."

"You mean you don't mind being married to an old fogey like me?" he said, lifting her hand to his lips. They had been married for twenty years now, but it felt like he'd just said 'I do' yesterday. Their relationship was one against the odds, an age gap of fifteen years sitting between them. Nothing unheard of back in the day, but he did have to fend off the cradle robber comments every now and again.

"I wouldn't have it any other way."

Behind them, he could hear a ruckus in the bathroom as their ten-year-old daughter got ready. "Where's our monster off to today?"

"A birthday party."

John groaned at the thought of an empty house and the kind of mischief they could get up to without their daughter around. He'd love to take advantage of it. "I know we don't get much time together by ourselves, but..."

"Hey, don't worry about it," she said, framing his cheeks with her hands. "I know you'll make up for it later."

"You know it!"

He couldn't have asked for a better woman in his life. She'd always been understanding of his career. Well, mostly. They'd had the odd falling out over the years because of the dangerous nature of his work, but in a way, it brought the two of them closer together. They had learned quickly not to take anything for granted and made every second worth remembering. And he planned to keep having moments with her until death took him to the other side.

"Go get 'em, tiger." She kissed him on the cheek before getting up to go check on Crystal, their daughter.

John slid his arm around her waist, pulling her onto his lap. "Do you call that a kiss?"

"You want more?" Jodi asked with a grin as she linked her hands behind his neck and lowered her lips to his.

"Always," he murmured. People sometimes asked him what the secret to his marriage was and honestly, he had no answer. Some people clicked, and others, not so much. No other woman had ever captured his heart like she did. Even when she frustrated him, he couldn't imagine his life without her.

Her warm moist lips against his aroused the animal inside him. She tasted of peanut butter and Nutella, her favourite breakfast in the morning. He wanted to carry her upstairs and disappear behind a locked door, but their fun would have to wait.

As much as he didn't want to, he released her, allowing them both to stand up, before the bulge in his pants became more noticeable and uncomfortable.

"Stay safe, John." She grabbed his hand and gave it a squeeze. "I love you."

"Love you too." He held onto her hand a little longer than necessary, getting lost in her sparkling blue eyes. "More than you know." Letting her go, he watched her small frame walk down the hall, her long blond hair bouncing against her back. He leaned forward just to watch her a little longer as her tight ass caught his eye. He'd certainly lucked out. His friends were getting divorced left, right, and centre, but she seemed content to stick it out with him. She could have had anyone, and she chose him. It still surprised him to this day.

He went to the door and grabbed the Stetson that he could never quite get rid of, despite its patches of worn colour and frayed edges. His dad had bought it for him a few months before he passed away, and John didn't have the heart to send it to the hat graveyard yet.

"Dad, I don't know if you can hear me, but I sure could use a higher power to point me in the right direction this time." He'd found her once before. Hopefully, luck would shine down on him again.

He opened the door and stepped outside. "Bye, babe. I'll call you soon," he yelled.

"Dad, wait." His daughter's heavy-footed steps as she ran down the hall had him turning back towards the door. His bright-eyed, brown-haired pre-teen was barrelling towards him.

"Hi, honey, have fun today," he said, pulling her into a hug.

She hugged him back. "We're still on for our father daughter dance tomorrow, right?"

"I wouldn't miss it."

"Love you."

"Love you too." A fierce need to protect her washed over him, and he tightened his hold on her. Her face buried against his chest.

"Dad, I can't breathe," she complained.

"You be careful today, okay? Promise me."

"I promise. I gotta go finish my hair." She rushed back into the house again, leaving him alone on the doorstep.

He would die if he lost his own family, which was why he needed to do something, anything to help bring Jenna home. He'd done it once before and by George, he'd do it again. Shutting the door, he walked to his vehicle. It was time to go meet with Brody Coleman, his long-time friend and coast guard.

John crossed his fingers as he backed the car out of his driveway. "Here we go...for a second time."

Maybe fate would be on his side again.

~

Jenna's scream ripped right through Ethan. With all the strength he could muster, he hauled her out of the water, his muscles shaking under the strain. They both fell back onto the raft, with her landing on top of him. Her entire body was vibrating, and her lips were pale blue.

He stayed perfectly still, afraid to spook her. "You okay?"

"I...uh...I think so," she stammered as she rolled off him, breathing heavily.

Out of the corner of his eye, he saw movement. When he turned, a dolphin jumped out of the water. Ethan smirked and pointed to the newly revealed visitor. "Well, will you look at that? It wasn't a shark after all."

Jenna poked her head up beside him and glared at the dolphin, who was happily clicking away. "Sneaky twerp," she muttered.

Ethan laid his head back against the raft and chuckled. "I don't think they are capable of being sneaky."

"Look, he's laughing at me," she said, crossing her arms.

"Are they even capable of laughing?" He tried to hold back another round of laughter as she turned her killer eyes towards him, warning him that he could very well become acquainted with the cold water again. That wasn't high on his to do list. His clothes were already wet and cool from her landing on him.

"Why won't he shut up?" Jenna splashed the dolphin.

The animal promptly and happily used his fin to splash her back. Ethan couldn't hold back anymore, and he laughed so hard his belly ached. It's not every day you see a war between a human and a dolphin. He had a front row seat to the biggest aquarium sideshow ever.

"If only I had my phone." The scene playing out before him would be a perfect viral video-Girl gets bested by a dolphin. "I don't think you're gonna win this war, babe."

Jenna plopped down on her butt, her hair dripping and a pout playing on her sexy, inviting lips. "Stupid animal."

Collapsing into their familiar silence, he watched the dolphin leap and play around them as it swam in circles. Don't they usually swim in pods? What was he doing all by himself? He'd never been this close to one before. He'd seen them from his yacht, but not up so close you could look into his pure eyes and see the animal's soul in the depths of them.

After a while, Ethan saw a pattern. The grey dolphin would swim a little distance away and then swim back to click at him. Always in the same direction. Sometimes he would swim up to the other side of the raft and bump it in that same direction.

"I think he's trying to tell us something." Ethan sat up and continued to observe the animal.

"I wish he could talk and not use his nose as a battering ram."

"Come on." Lying on his stomach, Ethan started paddling, using his arms.

Jenna quickly followed suit, squinting her eyes. "I don't see anything."

He couldn't either. And maybe this was a hope and a prayer on his part, but he couldn't ignore what his gut was telling him. It wouldn't be the first time an animal led people to safety, and it was their best shot at surviving, especially with the dark storm clouds brewing in the distance. They didn't want to be on the water when it hit.

They paddled until their arms were so heavy they could barely move. He was impressed at her resolve to keep pressing forward. She didn't complain. She didn't whine. In fact, she didn't speak at all. Probably couldn't out of sheer exhaustion as they struggled to keep up with the animal.

He caught her glancing his way. She quickly averted her eyes, her cheeks turning a sweet rose colour, which made her look even more amazing. "Why don't you wear make-up?" he asked.

"You want to talk about make-up?"

"No, I want to talk about you."

Jenna glanced over at Ethan, his muscles rippling as his arm cut through the water like his own personal paddle. She turned her focus back to the animal, her insides heating. "Why don't you talk about your script instead?"

"The one that is now at the bottom of the ocean you mean?"

"What? Oh no, I-I'm so sorry. I know how much that one meant to you."

He shrugged. Well, as much as one could while lying on their stomach. "Not much I can do about getting my laptop back."

"You worked so hard on it."

"There will be other stories."

He said it with such conviction in his voice, and a fire in his eyes, that even her bowels squirmed inside her, trying to find a safe place to hide. She wasn't sure exactly what his encrypted message meant. Suddenly the raft seemed even smaller than it was, causing her to dig deep inside her spirit for any reserve energy to launch them farther ahead.

She didn't like the look in his eyes, didn't like the way her body responded to him. One way or another, she was getting off this hunk of junk.

Even if she had to swim.

Chapter Seven

Jenna rolled over, breathing heavily; her arms refusing to move, feeling heavier than ever. "I can't do it anymore." Her strength was gone. They were going to die out here. If not from the heat, from the hunger or dehydration.

The dolphin, in all this time, never disappeared, it still swam ahead of them, coming back every so often to apparently see how they were doing. It also seemed to take pleasure in splashing her every single time he did.

"That animal hates me, I swear," she grumbled.

"It might help if you stopped glaring at the poor thing," Ethan answered with an exhausted chuckle, collapsing onto his back.

She reached out to smack him, but her arm didn't want to comply; it fell back against the raft of its own accord. Looking up, dark storm clouds covered the sky as far as her eyes could see. Feeling the tearful burn behind her eyes, Jenna squeezed them closed. Their situation was hopeless. "I don't want to die." Maybe she did once, but not anymore.

"We aren't going to, not if I can help it." With that, he slid off the raft into the cool water.

"What are you doing?" she cried, reaching for him.

"I'm gonna save us," he said, gasping for breath. "Wowsers, that's cold, but not as cold as back home."

Much to her surprise, the dolphin dipped under the water and appeared beside Ethan. Why the animal was taking such interest in them she didn't know. Was he a dolphin that one of the aquariums rehabilitated and released back into the wild?

"Hey, do you think the dolphin..." She stopped talking when she caught the look on Ethan's face. His raccoon eyes were half closed as he began kicking while holding onto the side. The dolphin appeared to sense how tired he was and pressed its nose up against the raft and joined in on the rescue attempt.

She wasn't sure what good it was going to do because there was no land in sight...scratch that. Jenna squinted. In the far distance, a dark, but welcomed, shape loomed over the gloomy horizon.

Scrambling to her knees, she yelled, "I see it. I see it." That gave her a renewed sense of purpose and strength. Leaning over, she helped her team move towards the island. She wasn't sure how long it was going to take to get there, or if they'd make it before the storm, but it gave her hope. And that was enough.

Readying her arm to slice into the water once again, she jumped when the dolphin made its loudest, most irritating whistle ever and began nudging Ethan's side. Ethan grunted with each jab. The animal disappeared under the water and tried to shove him back on the raft.

"What's going on?" Jenna asked, looking around.

Placing two hands on the raft, he hauled himself out of the water, dangling his legs over the side. "I'm not sure."

That's when she saw it. "There!" she cried, pointing to a triangular dorsal fin approaching them. All she could hear in her mind was the foreboding music from the movie *Jaws*. Jenna closed her fingers around his hand, holding it tight.

Her move shocked him, but what surprised him even more was

that she didn't jerk away, didn't move away. She stayed in the same spot, staring at the creature as it approached them.

When the shark was about fifteen feet away, she released Ethan's hand and slapped him on the thigh. "Get your damn legs out of the water."

Ethan yanked them out of the water, and the two of them moved to the centre of the raft, as much as there was a centre. He couldn't believe that he almost became shark bait, all because she touched him. She huddled against him, and he wrapped his arms protectively around her. Jenna seemed lost in the shark's world, not letting her gaze lose sight of the fin.

"We'll make it out of this," he said, his voice gentle as he rubbed her back. She stiffened slightly upon his touch, as though she just noticed they were touching, so he stilled his hand. He didn't want her falling into the water again.

She shushed him. "He might hear us."

The shark could probably hear their laboured breathing, still panting from the exertion of trying to reach land. Much to his frustration, the current was slowly pulling them away from dry ground, and at this point, there was nothing he could do.

The shark swam underneath the raft, nudging it lightly. Jenna buried her face in her arm, letting out a muffled cry. Ethan held her close, lending her his strength. It was all he could think of to do. They were at the mercy of the large animal, which appeared to be at least fourteen feet long.

Thunder rumbled overhead and a drop of cool rain landed on Ethan's nose. Man, they couldn't catch a break. They were in for one hell of a roller coaster ride. The shark nudged the raft again, pushing it slightly onto its side. Jenna screamed as they scrambled to steady it again.

"Oh, my god," she cried. "We're going to die."

There were no comforting words he could speak. The animal was circling them, knowing that food was only a bump away. As if wanting to join in their misery, the heavens opened and within minutes their clothes were soaked.

Jenna shivered, and Ethan wished more than anything that he had a jacket to give her. He was glad in a way that her hard exterior shell was cracking, but then again, funny things happen when you are faced with your own demise. She might not soften any further once they reached the island.

Waves tossed and rolled their little raft. All they could do was hang on for the ride. He held on to the right side of the raft and slid his other arm around Jenna, securing his other hand at the front. She gave him a small, wobbly smile as she held on tight.

"Where's the shark?" she yelled over the thunderous noise coming from above them.

He opened his mouth to speak when a wall of water crashed over them, pulling them under.

As Jenna tumbled underwater and her lungs starved for air, her mind flashed back over her life. As clear as day, she could see the positive line on the pregnancy test. It wasn't possible. It couldn't be. Letting out a cry of anguish, she had thrown the test across the room and slid down the bathroom door. Her butt had hit the floor along with her fists; her crutches clanging against the bathtub.

"No. No. No." She shook her head, tears flowing down her cheeks. Her nightmare wasn't over. It wasn't God-damn over. Jenna gripped her stomach, wishing she could somehow rip out the horrible nightmare growing inside her.

Darkness descended upon her spirit, wrapping itself around her like a boa constrictor, squeezing any remaining life out of her. She had no strength left to face another day. The burning pain in her leg from the bullet that pierced her skin and the knee-high cast were enough of a reminder of what she went through when she was kidnapped.

There was no fight left inside her. Jenna was done talking to psychologists, psychiatrists, counsellors, repeating the same story over and over. She didn't want to see the hurt look on her dad's face when she rejected his touch, or the worry marks etched into the brow of her mother that appeared to grow overnight.

It would be better if she was gone. Her parents could finish mourning in peace, without having to look at her sorry face every morning. Her mom's eyes had taken on a constant red, puffy appearance and always seemed to be on the verge of tears whenever Jenna hobbled into the room.

The burden of knowing she was behind her mother's haggard appearance was too much to bear. Reaching up, she grabbed the painkillers off the counter and stared at the bottle. She rubbed at the ache in her chest, her mind lost in a dark void with no way out. All she just wanted was peace, wanted the pain to stop, and the horror of her life to end. She couldn't even remember what things were like before *it* happened.

Standing up, she filled the cup with water before placing it on the counter. Her hand shook as she opened the pill bottle, dumping all the contents into her palm, then Jenna looked into the mirror. Staring back at her was a woman with oily, matted strawberry blond hair and blood-shot eyes. Her cheekbones and jaw line were growing ever prominent, showing how little she'd been able to eat since she came home. Any food that went in quickly came back out.

She didn't want to go back to the hospital either. And didn't want to be stuck between four white walls and another patient who wouldn't shut up, or be locked away for being deemed crazy or unstable. Jenna stuffed a bunch of pills in her mouth and took a gulp of water, then repeated the process until nothing remained in her hand.

There was no fear of death. All there was, was a desire for the quiet rest it would bring. Jenna placed the bottle on the counter and took a deep breath. *It was done.* Grabbing her crutches, she made her way to her bed. She had no idea what waited for her on the other side, but it had to be better than this.

Lying back against the warm inviting mattress, she folded her hands on her chest and waited. She waited for the slow fade into black. And then black into nothing. Picking up her phone, she texted her best friend. 'Bye, Cleo.'

It didn't take long for her phone to notify her of her friend's response. 'Where are you going?'

'Away. I love you.'

'What do you mean?'

'Tell my parents that I love them. That this isn't their fault.'

'You're scaring me, girl.'

Jenna let her hand fall to the bed, cradling the phone in her palm. Her phone quickly vibrated again. She turned it off. No point in prolonging the goodbye. Never again would anyone take advantage of her or her body. And she wouldn't have to live with the regret of having an abortion. That was something she refused to live with.

After a while, her chest grew heavy, and her eyes refused to focus. The room filled with a whitish cloud, making it feel like she was watching a movie on one of those old school black and white reels rather than real life. Black spots danced in her vision, giving her one last show to watch before she left the world behind.

The room grew dark until there was nothing left to see or feel, darker than a starless night. Even her limbs seemed to join in the final farewell as a wet cool sensation swirled around her arms and legs, making her shiver. She gasped for air and inhaled a salty cool liquid in the process, as thousands of tiny, rough grains of sand pressed into her cheek. She propped herself up on her elbows, hacking. Her vision hazy, and her limbs like jelly.

Where was she? Was she dead? Was this hell? She tried to sit up, but her head throbbed, and her stomach revolted against the movement. Groaning, she held her forehead, which sported a large goose egg, and waited for the pain to subside—the past and the present colliding together inside her mind.

The second time she almost lost her life after her rescue, it was by her own doing; this time, it was the elements that were in cahoots with each other. Yet again, somehow, she was still alive, as though some God wasn't done with her yet. She rubbed her eyes and cringed when they burned. Had they made it to the island?

In the dim light, she could make out a long beach and ahead of her was a thick forest. The moon shone brightly overhead, which meant she must have been out for hours. How on earth did she survive long enough to make it to the island? The last thing she could remember was doing somersaults in the water after the raft flipped.

Oh, my God, Ethan!

"Ethan," she yelled, and then sucked in a quick breath when sharp pains accosted her again, blurring her vision. From what she could tell, she was the only one on the beach. She stood up, her body swaying back and forth as she tried to find her land legs.

"Ethan!" she yelled, but only the waves answered back as they lapped against the sandy shore.

She was alone in the dark...in a strange place. Where? She had no idea.

~

Ethan leaned back against a tree and pressed his torn shirt against the cut on his leg, sucking in a breath when the injury stung. He must have hit some coral or something along the way. The important thing was that he'd made it to shore, and he hoped that Jenna did, too. When he woke up, lying face down in the sand, he'd thought he was dreaming. They were so far away from landfall that it just didn't seem possible to be here, but he wasn't going to look a gift horse in the mouth.

Across the sky shot a shooting star. He watched it until it disappeared beyond the curve of the earth, and in a concussed daze he wondered what it would be like to live among the stars, to travel to planets beyond theirs? If he had the chance to go on the first spaceship to Mars, he would be the first in line. The chance to live out some of the stories in his mind would be a dream come true, instead of just writing about what could be. He loved mysteries and space was a giant one.

That's probably why he liked the ocean, too. The mystery of what creatures lay beneath its depths was always on his mind. And he wouldn't have it any other way. You had to dream—to look beyond yourself—otherwise life was too monotonous...boring. Well, it certainly wasn't boring right now.

Ethan shook his head and was greeted with a sharp pain. Pressing his palm just above his ear, he felt something damp. As he pulled his hand away, he was greeted by the sight of blood. Man, he was a walking buffet table. Hopefully, no animals would come seeking his scent.

He examined his body while keeping his ears open for any animals that might think he'd make a good dinner. Frogs croaked from somewhere behind him and the odd owl hooted in the distance, but nothing more ominous caught his attention yet. He wanted to call out for Jenna, but it would be a death wish if large predators were stalking around.

Satisfied with his examination and the noises around him, Ethan sighed in relief. Nothing was broken. The worst of it was a gash on his leg that was bleeding. He had no idea if the injury was from their raft, their shark or even some coral.

He wasn't even sure how he missed getting eaten by the shark that had been circling their raft. Did it go after Jenna? His stomach churned at the idea, and he quickly tossed it from his mind, refusing to even entertain the thought. She had to have survived. Roger. Mark. Chris. Jerry. *Oh, God.* He may have just led all his crew to their deaths. His own death he could deal with, but not theirs, too. He pounded the sand with his fist, growling inwardly.

Tears pricked the corners of his eyes. He squeezed them closed, as the knot in his chest grew. Why had he let Jerry take them so far offshore? It was all his fault. He should have just continued their usual route, instead of trying to do something special. When tears started to fall down his cheeks, Ethan opened his eyes and shook his head again. Crying wouldn't change anything. What's done is done. He needed to focus on the here and now. It's the only way he'd survive.

And what he needed was water. Frogs meant fresh water had to be somewhere on the island, unless Indonesian crab-eating frogs migrated to the United States and Mexico border. Boy, the things he researched for his stories.

A number of years ago, he did some research on outdoor living and medicinal plants, but do you think he could remember any of it now? He was hoping it would come back to him as he sat there, but his mind was drawing a blank. How could he remember the stupid frog, but not how to treat the wound on his leg or head for that matter?

"Stupid brain," he muttered.

Maybe he'd recognize certain plants if he saw them, but he didn't dare leave the beach until daylight, otherwise he might get lost walking around in the dark. Ethan grunted, partially chuckling. He was already lost, so it's not like it would matter. But, at least, on the beach, it was more open, and nothing would be able to surprise him.

Eventually, light peeked over the horizon as the sun started to rise. The owls went silent, but the frogs kept up their banter, like a croaking musical, from the soprano to the bass. He could almost tell the different ones apart after listening to them all night, despite the waves almost drowning them out. Joining in the chorus were birds, tweedle-deeing and tweedle-dumming away, grating on his ever-growing headache. Thankfully, their chirping meant no danger was lurking about.

Reaching over, he grabbed a broken tree branch that could act as a cane and used it to stand up. He turned to face the forest and scanned the tree line. The brush was heavy, but there had to be an opening. A path somewhere that took him more inland. He didn't exactly want to go trail blazing and not be able to see what he was about to step on.

Limping his way along the brush, feelings of helplessness festered

Beneath His Hands

inside him. His leg was throbbing, and there appeared to be no end to the thick forest. Up ahead, the beach curved around a corner, but with the blood dripping down his leg, he wasn't likely to make it that far.

"Hello?" he yelled, his voice echoing back at him as it bounced between the walls of an unseen ravine. "Jenna?"

The only response was a fluttering in the trees as birds sought safe haven from the new and disturbing lunatic on the island—namely him. Even the frogs grew silent as he dragged his sorry ass down the beach.

Carefully and slowly, he reached the corner, and much to his delightful pleasure, there was a creek flowing into the ocean, coming from the forest. Along one side there was a pathway wide enough for him to walk.

"Here goes nothing."

Using the tree branch cane, he hobbled his way along the creek's edge, barely able to keep his balance on the uneven, rocky terrain. After he followed the creek for a short distance, the beach eventually disappeared from his sight as the forest swallowed him into its waiting clutches.

∼

Jenna shoved branches aside as she forged her through the forest, following the sound of rushing water, not giving a darn as to what hid in the bushes surrounding her. She wanted a drink, and nothing was going to stop her from reaching her destination.

What she liked most about this experience was that she didn't have to fear being attacked by a crazed lunatic. She hadn't come across another soul so far. The animals would be easy enough to handle, but people were another matter. Jenna shivered. If she didn't see another man for as long as she lived, she'd be perfectly content.

Traipsing about the island made her feel like she was on an episode of the Swiss Family Robinson or Gilligan's Island.

Sheesh.

Did her mind ever think of anything but television shows? The culprit might be her night-time routine of watching DVDs on her laptop which led to the movie scenes jumping in her head.

"Damn." It, too, was nestled comfortably on the ocean floor, along with her irreplaceable treasure box. She'd have to buy another stupid laptop, which was going to cut into her travel funds.

Up ahead, she could see a clearing. Placing her hands on a fallen log covered in moss, she hoisted herself up and over, but just as quickly as her feet hit the ground, they flew out from under her. Jenna shrieked as she landed in a conveniently placed mud puddle, her butt growing acquainted with the cool, squishy mess.

She held her arms out to her side and shook them, globs of mud flying everywhere. One landed directly on her nose. "Gross!" Using her sleeve, she tried to wipe it off, but her wet and dirty shirt just spread the mess around even more.

Scrambling to her feet, she prayed, "Please let me find fresh water." There had to be some on the island somewhere. Animals could only drink fresh water, and there seemed to be plenty of them—birds, squirrels, owls, etcetera. She even saw a snake, and if it kept its tongue to itself, she was more than okay with sharing its space.

By time she pushed her way into a clearing, her pants were blood-stained and covered in holes. She turned back to look at the path she'd just exited and acquainted herself with the heart shaped rock and the twisted tree next to the path so she could remember where the path was. There was no way she wanted to get lost out here. She wanted to be on the beach to keep watch for any boats sailing by. Finally, Jenna took a moment to look around the clearing.

"Wow!" Ahead of her stood a large waterfall, cascading down a large rocky cliff and falling thunderously into the turquoise-coloured pond below, mist rising from the base. Surrounding the pond were multicoloured flowers, giving off a sweet honey scent. She had no idea where the water was coming from, but she was more than happy to take what she was given. A frog, sitting on a lily pad, paused to look at her before disappearing into the welcoming water.

The sun was beginning to peek over the trees. Its rays made the water sparkle and the air around her warm under its glow, feeling much like a summer morning. Jenna slid off her shoes and socks and walked to the edge, dipping her toes into the serene waters. It was slightly cool but felt rather heavenly.

Backing up, she removed the remainder of her clothes and then kneeled beside the pond to rinse them off. Without her Maytag, they weren't going to be squeaky clean, but she should still be able to wear them. Once they were all done, she placed them over a low tree branch and then dove into the deeper end of the pool, the water closing over her body.

Under the water, near the waterfall, she noticed a dark cave. That must be where the water goes to keep the pond from flooding. Swimming up to the surface, Jenna spread out her limbs like a starfish, staring up into the sky.

"I think I just discovered paradise." Maybe this was the fountain of youth, and she'd look years younger, and her leg would be healed if she stayed in it long enough. Either way, it felt divine, like her very own outdoor bathtub with no peeping toms. She knew the wildlife didn't care about taking advantage of her, except maybe having her for dinner.

Floating on the water made her feel light and fluffy, like the cotton clouds flying overhead. Jenna wished she could stay there all day, but she knew that no one would find her so far away from the beach. Also, there were a few more pressing matters to attend to, like shelter and food before it got dark.

She didn't want to leave yet though and chose to stick around for a bit longer, but only until the sun passed its midway point in the sky. The good thing was she now knew where to get a drink. The water looked and tasted okay. The only thing that sucked was she had nothing to store the water in, so it was going to be quite the trek back and forth.

Pushing the thought away, Jenna cleared her mind and allowed herself to feel the water caress the crevasses of her soul. For once, peace filled every corner of her heart. And that didn't happen very often. With the darkness momentarily gone, it allowed her to breathe. There was nothing else to focus on but how good it felt.

No creeps. No reporters. No story to tell. There was just freedom in that moment to just be. Nothing more. Nothing less. No worrisome glances from her mom. No friends begging her to get out and socialize. No weddings to be a part of. Only the island and she existed.

A hoarse scream made Jenna turn upright as she looked around, trying to pinpoint the sound. When it sounded again, she looked up and saw a red-tailed hawk circling above, as if to say it wasn't just her on the island.

"Oh, shush already," she said, sticking her tongue out at it.

That's when she heard it, a loud twig snapping. Jenna spun around, her own scream joining that of the hawks.

Chapter Eight

"We've lost her for sure this time?" Iris cried, throwing her arms around her husband.

Daniel held her close, resting his chin on the top of her head. They'd just heard the news. The coastguard found three of the crew alive on a life raft, floating miles from where the boat went down. Jenna and Ethan were not among them.

Hope faded as they listened to the crew tell their tale of how Ethan jumped off the boat trying to save their daughter. They knew the waters in that area were infested with sharks, and their chances of survival dropped immensely with each day that went by. He didn't want to accept it, but he knew the odds. Even the coastguards were thinking of calling off the search, but he managed to talk them into searching the islands that were in the vicinity.

It was a long shot. None of the islands were close enough for them to swim to, but he wasn't about to give up yet. He'd call in a few favours from his friends if he had to. He'd bailed them out of enough jams that they swore they'd always be there for him.

Brent was the only one who had a boat though. He practically lived on the thing. Pulling out his phone, he clicked on his buddy's name.

"Hello?" Brent answered.

His friend listened intently to all that Daniel shared and remained silent for a moment. The wheels in his friend's mind were always turning, and that was one thing Daniel liked about him.

"I'm sorry, Dan. She seems to get hit with the worst luck," Brent said. "Let me check my maps. I'll see if I can find any type of a pattern with the currents."

The coastguard probably thought of all that too, but so far, they'd had no luck. No one believed they could have made it to an island, not after their freefall into the water. But his daughter had to be alive. She had the soul of a survivor. He didn't raise his baby to be a sissy.

Okay, technically, he wasn't there most of the time, but that was going to change. No more traipsing about the world. He was going to find a job close to home and be the husband and father he should have been from the start. That is...if he got another chance.

"Thanks, Brent. Call me back as soon as you can."

His wife's sobs quietened a bit, turning into the odd sniffle. She looked up at him with pleading eyes. "Please, don't go away again."

"I'm going to help them look for her, but when I come back, things are going to be different around here. I promise," he said, framing her face with his hands. "I'm going to change."

"You mean it?"

"More than I've ever meant anything in my life. We have a lot to talk about after this is over."

"Kiss me, please," Iris whispered as she looked up at him with her deep brown eyes, hesitant but full of love for him. A love which he knew he didn't deserve. He'd have to tell her about Christy, and Daniel wasn't sure how she was going to take it. Her values were strongly linked to right versus wrong. There were very few grey areas in his wife's mind.

When they first met, she was happy and always smiling, and then he started doing boneheaded things and that smile slowly faded away. Now, she was a nervous little thing, and he was to blame. His new personal mission was to make her laugh and smile again. He was never going to take what they had for granted again. He did that far too much already.

Leaning down, he tentatively brushed his lips against hers. It was their first kiss since he'd gotten back, and he didn't want to scare her off, but pleasure rocked him when she deepened the kiss, exploring his lips with her tongue.

Groaning, he pulled her up against himself, showing her just how badly he needed her. "Please?" Now it was his turn to beg, he wanted her more than he'd wanted her for a long time.

"Yes," she murmured. "I need you. I need a distraction."

"Happy to oblige."

He would have kicked his heels for joy, but he wasn't about to let her go, especially not now. He finally had her in his arms again. Tonight, he would be in his own bed with his wife. And he was never going to be apart from her ever again.

Placing one arm under her armpits and another behind her knees, he picked her up and carried her to their room. "I love you, Iris."

Fresh tears filled her eyes, but not from sadness this time. He spoke the words he knew she'd been waiting to hear for so long. Words that had been locked away for longer than they should have been. They never came easy for him. His parents never said it, so most of the time he didn't think about it, even more so when they were having difficulties.

Walking into the bedroom, Daniel closed the door behind him. Tonight, was going to be all about her. Only her.

～

"Don't just stand there staring," Jenna screeched, trying to cover herself in the crystal-clear water without sinking, knowing Ethan could see pretty much everything. "I thought you died."

"As you can see, I'm very much alive," he said, smirking. "And you don't seem any worse for wear."

"You are such a pig!" she said, attempting to splash him with water, glad to have the ripples in the pond hiding her body temporarily.

He laughed and attempted to duck out of the way, but his grip on the tree branch cane loosened, and he fell over, landing on his injured leg, with a loud painful grunt. It was only then that she noticed his leg, and his blond hair caked with blood.

When he didn't move, Jenna's insides shifted. "Ethan?"

He didn't answer, and she couldn't tell if he was breathing.

"Damn it, Ethan! Answer me." she yelled, smacking the water with her hand. If he made her get out of the water naked, with him right there, she was going to smack him silly. Picking up one of the lily pads beside her, she threw it, smacking him on the back. "Hey you, bonehead, wake up!"

He didn't jump. Nothing. Biting on her bottom lip, she cautiously swam closer and then waded to the edge of the pond to get a better look at him. His back was facing her, so she couldn't even tell if his eyes were open or closed. Jenna crawled towards him, attempting to keep her body out of his line of sight.

"You better not be faking or so help me God, I'll kill you myself." She placed two fingers on his neck to check for a pulse, breathing a sigh of relief when she found one. It was faint, but it was there.

Why didn't the meathead stay with his crew? He shouldn't have come after her. *Damn it.* She wasn't worth his trouble or his time, and now the man was making her responsible for his life, and she hated him for it.

He needed to wake up and then disappear to the opposite end of the island, leaving her in peace. What she hated most was the feeling of being indebted to him. A life for a life. But here they were. Rolling him over, she checked for injuries. He had a deep, long gash on his leg. She'd have to deal with that somehow. His head injury appeared to be fairly minor, but if she didn't get his leg to stop bleeding, he would die.

She wasn't a doctor, and she didn't have a first aid kit or butterfly stitches, but Jenna knew how to take care of herself. It's the only way she found the will to survive by learning everything she could about the great outdoors.

Mathew had taken her into the boonies, and she vowed to never let anyone get the drop on her again. Man nor wilderness. She'd learned every single medicinal healing recipe you could find in the wild. It was just a matter of finding what she needed. However, she didn't want to leave him in the middle of the forest while she looked for everything. That was a death sentence.

Putting on her wet clothes, she glanced around and tried to find something she could use as a stretcher—sticks, vines, anything—that would help her move him back to the beach. Jenna laid two large branches parallel to each other, and placed some smaller branches across them, tying them to the larger ones with vines that she found. After she tied the last vine, she stood up and examined her handy work, wiping her hands off.

"Not bad, if I do say so myself."

It was a little crooked, but it should do the trick. She put it down beside Ethan, pressing it as close to his back as possible and then rolled him onto it. Took a bit of pulling and tugging, but she managed to get him squared away on the make-shift stretcher. She tied a few vines around his body so he wouldn't roll off and then picked up the branches near his head.

"Holy jeez, you weigh as much as an ox," she groaned as she tried to pull him forward. The edges of the branches dragged along the ground, adding extra friction. He was going to kill her before they even made it back to the beach.

Along the way, she saw some small white flowers and slowly lowered him to the ground. "Hot damn. Yarrow." Grabbing some of the leaves, she rolled them around in her palms and shoved them into the wound on Ethan's leg. If this plant didn't stop his bleeding, nothing would. Her mom often used the plant herself, and swore by it. Grabbing a few more of the flowers, she slid them under the vines across Ethan's chest to use for later.

"Alright, lummox. Let's get the show on the road," she said, picking up the head of the stretcher. "I still can't believe you're making me save your stinking butt."

But she knew she couldn't leave him to die. The world wouldn't forgive her if she let their beloved screenwriter die, and she wouldn't be able to forgive herself. She didn't have to be happy about the idea though. The man was a pig with a capital P.

When she reached the beach, she carefully lowered him to the ground and checked on him. His leg had finally stopped bleeding. She removed the leaves and did what she could to pull the deep wound closed, adding more yarrow leaves on top to help with the healing. It was tricky trying to keep the wound closed when she had no official bandages, but she made do with some vines. The job wasn't perfect, but it worked well enough to keep him alive. Jenna hoped anyway.

She was shocked by how low the sun was in the sky. Did it take them that long to get back to the beach? She still had to make a shelter and find food, but her whole body ached from dragging his ragdoll ass back from the pond.

Jenna was thankful that his fainting episode had allowed her to get out of the pond with a bit of dignity, instead of him standing there staring at her, which he surely would have done, with that stupid, crooked grin on his face. And she knew her body would have reacted to it and tingled in places she didn't want it to. The warm glow inside her had already begun when he stood there all sexy and annoyingly cocky. Just like it did when they were in close proximity on the boat.

Walking away from him, she sat down and leaned against a fallen tree. "What the heck am I going to do with you?" Jenna groaned.

She survived. He survived. And, apparently, they were alone together. A cool breeze blew through her body, making her shiver, reminding her of a ghost walking over her grave. A grave that had nearly been hers the last time she was trapped with a man. Jenna dug her fingernails into the palms of her hands.

"He's not Mathew. He's not the same guy," she chanted. "He's not going to hurt me."

But the reassuring words did little to settle her fears, and she found herself praying, "Please, don't let him be like Mathew."

Jenna repeated that mantra until she fell asleep, forgetting all about shelter and food. She was way too exhausted from their trek out of the forest and the ghost she was battling in her mind to care. Sleep wasn't about to let her recover, though. It was about to awaken the frightened animal inside her.

And worse yet, it was about to unleash another monster upon them, one that had not shown its face in two years. One she fought to keep contained, but this time, no chains were going to be strong enough.

Because it wanted out—needed out—and it wanted blood.

Chapter Nine

"Come on, stop playing hard to get," Ryan, Joshua's friend, said, grabbing Jenna roughly by the shoulders.

"Let me go. I mean it," she said, her fists clenching. If the man didn't remove his hands soon, she wasn't going to be responsible for the rage building inside her. The monster was never too far from the surface and was ready to take over her body the minute a slimy man tried to touch her.

"I just want a good night kiss." He hauled her up against him, his hard crotch pressing against her belly, making her dinner rise in her throat.

"I'm not going to warn you again. If you don't let go of me, you'll never use that dick again."

Ryan twisted her around, wrapping his arm around her neck, forcing his way into her house. "How about if I use it right now?"

Jenna gasped for air as his grip tightened, blood roaring in her ears. She pulled at his arm and tried to scream as she fought to get loose. All the while fighting the monster inside her from breaking free. If she let go, there was no saying what it would do. She couldn't let go. She had no restraint if she did.

The quick hiss from the zipper on his pants knocked the rest of her control away. No one was ever going to do that to her again. Sliding her leg back, she grabbed his arm and by shifting her weight, she flipped him over her shoulder. Ryan landed flat on his back, wide-eyed with his mouth hanging open.

"You men think you can do whatever you want, don't you?" Jenna circled him, her eyes narrowing. "No more," she growled in a voice that was no longer her own. Lifting her foot, she dropped the edge of her stiletto right through his open zipper, twisting it mercilessly against his dick.

He screamed and reached for her foot. She pulled it away before he could grab it.

"You're a bitch," he snarled.

With her fingers closing into a solid fist and digging into her palm, she drew it back and let it fly, hitting the pointed tip of his nose. The cartilage crunched against her knuckles, his head snapping back.

"You don't know who you messed with tonight," Jenna said, her fist connecting with his face again and again, blooding pouring out of his nose.

He shoved her away and attempted to crawl towards the open door. She stepped on his back, dropping him to his stomach.

"Let me go."

"Not so fun being on the other side is it," she said, taunting him as she kneeled on his back, grabbing a clump of his thick brown hair. "Never again." Jenna slammed his face into the hardwood floor.

"Jenna, what the hell!" Her dad's voice boomed from behind her. His arm went around her waist, hauling her off the guy.

That's when it happened. Her dad was the next over her shoulder before she even had a chance to stop herself, smashing him right through their glass coffee table. Iris raced into the room, her hands flying to her mouth as she cried out in terror.

"Iris, call 911," her husband groaned.

Jenna reached for Ryan who almost made it to the door. "I'm done playing nice. You don't deserve the air you breathe." She raised her hand, poised to strike his throat.

"Honey, please!" her mom begged. "Stop."

But there was no stopping. There was no end to her nightmare. She struck out at him, her hand passing right through him as though he were a ghost. The world spun around her, swirling like a white hazy mist.

Shocked, Jenna jerked backwards, her head connecting with something hard and jagged. She closed her eyes as a sharp pain reverberated through her skull. When the pain settled, she opened her eyes and looked around, her gaze following the sandy beach until they fell upon Ethan's unconscious body. Men. She'd hurt them all for what they did to her. As the sun shone down on his dirty, unshaven face, Jenna crawled over and straddled him.

"You. You're like all the rest!"

~

"I really wish you wouldn't go out on the boat," John told Daniel while standing on the docks. "The crews are going to comb every island. The best thing you can do is stay close to the phone. We don't need you guys getting lost out there."

Daniel took a breath before responding. "You can't expect me to sit back and do nothing."

"I know I wouldn't if it was my daughter, but it really is the safest thing you can do for your family," John replied, staring at the tall mast of Brent's sailboat, shielding his eyes from the glare of the sun.

Taking a step up the gangplank, Daniel turned and looked back at the retired detective. "I'm going, John. It's not that I don't trust you guys to find her, but I need to do something. I need to help."

"If I can't dissuade you, make sure you have your radio set to our channel and notify us if there are any problems or a break-through. By the way, is Iris okay with you going?"

"No, but she agreed to it. The more people out there the better."

His wife fought him over it, too, but in the end, she understood it was something he needed to do. Although, he doubted she would have let him go if it was anyone other than Brent taking him.

"Not if they have to rescue your crew, too." The retired detective folded his arms across his chest.

"With all due respect, Brent has been sailing the seven seas about as long as any coastguard. We went on a trip with him when Jenna was little. I trust him."

"It's not him that you need to worry about. It's the storms, they can hit without warning. Jenna was on a huge yacht."

The man had a point, but nothing was going to stop him from going out there and bringing his baby home. "I'm aware. Is there anything else you want to say, or can we get this show on the road?"

"Call command every hour on the hour, got it?"

"Yes, sir," Daniel saluted him, and then disappeared into the cabin.

He found Brent pouring over the maps spread out on the table in the Saloon. A cigarette was tucked neatly behind his ear, and another dangled from his mouth.

"So?" Daniel asked.

"I've circled some of the most likely islands, but it is going to take us time to get there. I'm not sure how helpful we're going to be, Dan."

"How long is it going to take to get there?"

"A week or more, depending on the weather."

Daniel thumped his fist on the table, his voice deepening. "My girl might not have a week."

"Maybe you should go with the coastguard then. Their boats can move faster, and they can search in the helicopter."

"They won't let me go."

The 'professionals' thought he would just get in the way. He volunteered to help, but he didn't have the proper certification. But John was going to be on one boat, so Daniel, at least, had some eyes and ears there.

"There are a total of ten islands in that area, most of them unoccupied, except for two." Brent pointed to the island closest to the vicinity of where the boat went down. "This is the best place to start."

"Okay, let's get going."

"I'm just waiting for three of my friends to get here. They will help us cover more ground when we reach the islands."

"How long until they get here?"

Brent looked down at his watch. "Another hour or so."

Dan clenched his fists and took another deep breath, his face heating with frustration. He wanted to be on his way already, not losing more time waiting. For each hour they were docked, daylight wasted away. It didn't care about them or their mission. The world kept going around. Never stopping. Never waiting. Why he hadn't noticed it before was beyond him.

Brent came around the table and patted Daniel on the back before starting his pre-embarkation check. "We're going to do our best to help you find her."

"How could I have been so stupid?"

"Dude, not even you can predict the weather."

"It's not that. If I was around and forced her to interact with the world, she would not have been on the run."

"Or she would have done it anyway. Kids are their own people, Dan. They are going to go where they want and do what they want with their lives. Hell, I should know. My three are all over the globe."

"That's different. They never..." Daniel walked over to the window, unable to finish his sentence due to a large lump taking residence in his throat. Between the kidnapping, and the last rape attempt, his daughter had quickly faded away from him, wouldn't even look at him. He couldn't tell if it was hatred in her eyes or guilt after everything that had happened. Jenna had become impossible to read, disappearing whenever he was home.

He was angry, yet grateful at the same time because he wouldn't have to worry about offending her or making her more upset, but if he found her again, he wasn't going to let her hide so easily. They were going to get help and work through this god-forsaken mess.

"Why don't you take your stuff down below to your usual room? I'm just gonna finish my pre-check, make sure everything is ready to go for when they get here."

Daniel nodded, happy to be doing something different than standing there, like a bumbling idiot. If they talked much longer, he was going to cry or punch something. His wife had cried enough for the both of them with plenty of tears to fill the Nile River.

Taking his bag, he wandered down to the lower deck and into one of the empty rooms. Last time Daniel was here he shared it with his wife, and Jenna had the room across the hall. Jenna was ten years old on their first outing. He could still hear her giggles filling the ship with Brent's daughter, Meghan.

Oh, how he missed Jenna's carefree days. The days of picking her up and tossing her over his shoulder, tickling her, were over. Gone like the wind. She wouldn't even sit at a table with him now and part of that may have been his fault as he avoided it whenever possible himself. He hated the awkwardness. The cautious glances and the snappy responses were anything but pleasant.

Daniel dropped his bag and sat down on the bed, resting his hands on the mattress. He *should* have..."Coulda, shoulda, woulda," he muttered. The *should haves* didn't matter anymore. It's not like they could change anything. "Where are you, chick-a-bee?"

Flopping back on the bed, he threw an arm over his eyes and mumbled, "God, if you know where she is, please show us."

When nothing happened, he smacked the bed. He wasn't exactly sure what he had been expecting. Maybe a rainbow to show them the way? If God wanted to, he could send them a cloud like he did the Israelites, but maybe his small, screwed up family wasn't worth the big man's time.

"Sorry, I know I've made a mess of our lives, and I don't deserve to get her back, but please, for my wife's sake, help us," he pleaded, staring at the pure white ceiling. It reminded him of exactly how dark his own soul had become over the years as regret, anger, humiliation, and more built up inside him.

You could call this search a cleansing of sorts for him. A renewal of his lost soul. And maybe, just maybe, Jenna wouldn't just see him as an evil guy anymore but as her father.

That was his wish.

～

Jenna was shocked to find herself straddling Ethan when she regained control of her mind. Standing up, she took off running, pushing her aching calves as fast and as far as they could go, trying to burn off her anger, guilt, and frustration. When she reached the pond, she fell to her knees. Her lungs burned, and sweat beaded on her forehead. She never wanted to hurt Ethan.

Resting her hands on her thighs, she screamed as loud as she could. Leaves on the trees rustled as birds took haven in the air, and squirrels clamoured to escape. They were lucky. They could run away from her, but she couldn't get away from the images that thrust themselves into the forefront of her mind.

"Get out of my head." She jammed her hands in her hair, grabbing a fistful. Why couldn't the demons leave her alone? They were forever there, reminding her and haunting her, saying that she will never be who she was again. And after what just happened, she was beginning to believe them.

During her episodes, it was like someone else took over completely, and she was only an observer along for the ride. She'd gotten better over the last while, more in control, but the dreams did it almost every time. All Jenna wanted was to be normal, but normal went out the door the moment the cloth went over her mouth in that alley way, and she woke up in a house in the middle of nowhere. Some guinea pig in a psycho's murderous game.

She thought the dreams were over. That they were gone. Her training had helped her regain a little control over her life, over her circumstances. That was the only reason she had the courage to take the job on Ethan's boat.

With her heart racing, Jenna took a deep breath and tried to gather herself. She pushed away the evil monster that dug its talons into her psyche and cleared her mind. There was no way she was going to let the damn thing win.

"Breathe, Jenna. Don't think about anything else."

Slowly she breathed in the clean crisp air, gathering it deep in her lungs. As she released it, she counted to ten, repeating it as many times as was necessary to refocus. It took a few rounds, but her heart slowed, and the brain fog cleared away.

There was no doubt about it. She had to stay as far away from Ethan's side of the island as possible, which meant it was time to find a spot to hunker down and build her shelter, gather food, and try to survive until help arrived.

Jenna returned to the side of the island that she first arrived at, staring out over the water with her hands on her hips. In the distance, dolphins playfully jumped in the surf.

"You guys are so lucky." What would it be like to have so much freedom? To be able to go wherever the tide flowed. To swim, jump, and play without a care in the world. She knew that growing a tail would never happen, as that idea belonged in books and movies, but that didn't have to stop her from swimming though. The weightlessness while floating in water made her feel like she was transported to a whole different world. Fear and anger disappeared, replaced by a restful peace.

Looking around, she tried to find the best spot to build a shelter. And as if things were perfectly planned, there was a three-foot tree stump near the tree line. All she needed to start making her little hide away was a long sturdy branch. There were ferns and other types of brush around that would easily stay on top of a wooden frame.

While working away on her temporary home, her mind wandered. Who would have thought that she'd actually need to put her training to use like this? Learning self defence and survive were all things she did to find herself again, to feel confident in her own skin. The sad part was that it did little to settle the horrifying experiences that lived in her mind—the ones she could never forget.

Was it strange that being out in the wild felt more natural to her? Away from the hustle and bustle of life. Away from the crowds. No need to worry if that wandering hand was anything more than an accidental brush as men walked by, or whether their smile held something more sinister underneath.

She could breathe here. Something that hadn't come easy to her over the years. Reaching up, Jenna took hold of a decent sized branch. After a few hard tugs, it cracked, and she landed on her butt. The branch hit the ground beside her.

"Oh, that smarts." Her butt was going to be black and blue before this was over. Dragging it over to the stump, she placed one side on top and tied the other end to the tree. Satisfied with the results, she started looking around for decent sized branches to use for the wall. It was going to be nice to fall asleep to the waves crashing against the shore. If she had her way, she'd purchase this island and make it her home.

After she finished building her temporary home, Jenna plopped down on the sand in front of it, her legs stretched out in front of her. This would be the perfect place to live if she had an endless supply of food.

Leaning back on her hands, she watched the surf roll and tumble against the shore, white caps bobbing. The dolphins had disappeared, but that didn't take away from the beauty of the ocean.

Her stomach rumbled, crying out for food. Folding her legs underneath her, she stood up. She could remember seeing a patch of blackberries somewhere. Saliva pooled in her mouth at the thought of a plump juicy berry. Plodding her way back through the forest, she stayed on her ready-made path as to not get lost.

She found them on the same path leading to the waterfall, full and ripe. The berries fell into her hand with a simple touch, red juice streaking her palm. Licking her lips, Jenna popped a handful in her mouth and revelled in the burst of flavour.

Beneath His Hands

As she grabbed another mouthful, a large, black fur-covered back appeared on the other side of the bush. Jenna gasped and slapped a hand over her mouth, smearing blackberry juice across her face.

A bear.

He couldn't push his way through the thick bush, could he? When his ears popped up over the top, Jenna ducked and held her breath, wishing for bear spray. Not wanting to make a sound, she froze in place. She'd never been this close to a bear. A wolf. Yes. A bear. No. They were not known to be aggressive, but a solid wall between the two of them would make her feel a lot better right about now.

The cracking of twigs alerted her to the fact that the bear was on the move. As the sound faded and the bear moved on, the tension in her shoulders released as did the air screaming in her lungs.

"Too close for comfort," she mumbled, grabbing another handful of berries in her juice-stained hand.

Wandering back to camp, she picked up a few pieces of broken glass near the water's edge and then plopped down on the sand next to her shelter.

∼

Ethan groaned, throwing his arm over his eyes to block out the sun beating down on his face. Now he knew what it felt like to be a piece of hot coal in fire, being roasted to their core. Rolling onto his side, he hissed in pain as something sharp dug into his hip. As he propped himself up on his elbows, his butt slid between two branches of his 'bed.'

If you could call it a bed. It kind of looked like a survival stretcher that was thrown together. Looking around, he saw the beach and the waves crashing against the shore, but no Jenna.

How'd he get from the waterfall to here? And why the heck couldn't he remember making the journey? Reaching down, he gingerly touched the cut on his leg, peeling the dried plant leaves off.

His wound wasn't bleeding anymore. He was sure he had her to thank for that, but where the hell was she?

Careful not to get any sand in the cut, he cautiously stood up, testing his weight on the injured limb. It hurt like hell, but nothing he couldn't manage. He ran his sandpaper tongue over his cracked, dry lips.

He didn't want to go back through the forest and risk irritating his leg, but he needed something to drink. Salt water wasn't going to do the trick. Thankfully, the stick he had been using was on the ground next to the bed, along with a large leaf full of fruit. Even though his stomach grumbled at the sight, he didn't want to eat anything until he eased his parched throat.

Ethan had a sneaky suspicion that since the food was there, Jenna had no intention of coming back. After their encounter, she was likely running scared. She didn't like him. That much was obvious. But why? What had he done wrong?

"Jenna?" he called, his voice gruff as a tickle rose in his throat, causing him to break down coughing. Leaning over, he gasped for air, his throat stinging as cough after cough made breathing impossible.

He was going to call out for her again but decided against it. He needed water. The only thing he could do was go to the waterfall and hope that this time he was strong enough to make the journey.

Part of him hoped he'd find her naked in the water again, but he doubted he'd be that lucky. He wanted to kick himself for fainting at such an inopportune time. His body hardly had enough time to register seeing a naked woman before his leg injury knocked him out cold.

Stupid. Stupid.

Leaning down, he picked up his walking stick and hobbled his way to the edge of the riverbank. He was right back to where he started, except Ethan knew he wasn't alone this time. She was somewhere on the island.

Come hell or high water…he was going to find her.

Chapter Ten

Empty. The turquoise-coloured water was void of the one life form Ethan wanted to see. Glancing down at the pool, he was left with a conundrum. If he knelt beside the water to get a drink, he'd get sand in his wound. If he got it wet, it would likely re-open and start bleeding again.

Not having any other option, he took off his shirt and wrapped it around his leg. He was determined to get a drink before he died of dehydration. They always warned you to never drink water in the wild without boiling it first, but that wasn't an option.

Kneeling, he leaned down and scooped the cool water with his hand, hungrily drinking as much as his body would allow. His first swallow stung like hell, but, man, did it feel good going down, cooling his insides like a cold shower.

Leaning back on his heels, he looked around. The area was completely untouched by man. He couldn't help but wonder if this was what the Garden of Eden would have been like. He wasn't religious by any means, but he'd heard the stories of a garden so beautiful that it would put most of the world to shame. Mankind apparently destroyed the opportunity to stay in it by never being happy with what they had. A trait we apparently never got rid of if the modern world was anything to go by.

What would happen to this beautiful island when their rescue team arrived? If it wasn't on the map yet, it would be then, and greedy developers would have their wicked way with it. As soon as his leg would let him, he was going to explore the island and see if anyone else was there with them.

Ethan sat on a rock, his leg stinging. Unwrapping his shirt, he tore it down the middle to create a better bandage. The last thing he needed was for the cut to get infected. He'd be in a bloody pickle if that happened. No meds or antibiotics meant death would be inevitable, or at the very least, losing his limb would be. And gangrene would not be aesthetically pleasing to the eye.

When he stood up, he froze as the hair on his nape stood on end. A low guttural growl came from somewhere behind him. The sound was distinct. Clear. Whatever it was, he had no hope in hell of outrunning it. Ethan tightened his grip on his walking stick. His knuckles turned white as he slowly turned around. There on the other side of the pool stood a large, hairy Mexican wolf, baring his teeth at Ethan.

"Well, shit!" he muttered. His leg smelled of day-old blood, which was a smorgasbord in the wolf's eyes. Injured prey always appeared more appealing. No matter the size. He could just see the headlines now,

"*Screenwriter Ethan Barrett Bested by the Big Bad Wolf. No Little Red Riding Hood to save him.*"

He liked Jenna's headline with the dolphin much better. A raw, untamed spirit glinted in the animal's eyes as it snarled at him, running on pure instinct. He has probably never seen a human before. Ethan's heart raced at the prospect of becoming someone's dinner.

They stood facing each other, only the water separating them. He tried to wrack his brain for what he was supposed to do in this situation, but he drew a blank. The synapses in his brain didn't want to fire and save his ass.

Keeping his eyes on the animal, he bent over and picked up a stone, testing the weight of the palm-sized rock. He wasn't a pitcher. Hell, he had never even played softball, but he did shoot darts back in the day. He could only hope the rock did the trick and his aim was pure so that it scared the creature off. Wiping his sweaty palm on his pants, he transferred the rock to his right hand.

"Get the hell out of here!" he yelled, waving the rock in the air.

The wolf snarled at him, slowly moving around the pond. Raising his arm, Ethan chucked the rock, hitting it on the back. The animal jumped and yelped, but it didn't back off.

"Go eat something else," he yelled, backing up slightly, keeping his eyes on the ever-nearing wolf. Behind him, another noise caught his attention. *Oh, God, don't let there be another one.* It wasn't growling, so he hoped that was a good sign.

Leaning down, he picked up another rock and tossed it at the hungry animal, smacking him on the snout. It yelped and dropped to its belly, rubbing its nose with its paw. Ethan held his breath, hoping that was enough to detour it.

But the damn thing was persistent. Before long, it was back on its feet, racing towards him. Holding the stick, he swung it like a baseball bat. The animal ducked and jumped at him. Ethan held his stick sideways in front of him, hoping to knock the animal away. But the wolf's weight knocked the stick out of the way easily, hitting Ethan square in the chest with its paws.

Falling backwards, he hit his back on a rock and knocked the air out of his lungs. Gripping the stick tightly with both hands, Ethan held it against the wolf's throat, trying to keep the nipping teeth and bad breath away from his jugular vein.

"Eat a breath mint," he grunted, his biceps shaking from exertion. His strength was dwindling. The trek to the waterfall had drained him. He didn't have the energy to fend off the attack. Jagged lines appeared in front of his eyes, and his mind grew foggy.

Soon, those jagged lines formed that of a child, one that had long strawberry blond hair. She wore a white sundress covered in pink-flowers and was running towards a faded woman in the distance. Behind the woman was a man. His hands were on her shoulders.

As he watched this play by play, the woman's face came into focus. It was Jenna. His eyes widened as the man's face swirled into his vision. He blinked rapidly. He was the man. And Jenna wasn't shying away from his touch. Instead, her hand was resting on his as they smiled at the child running towards them.

It was like watching a movie projection from the old days with a screen full of black scratchy lines. The young child, smiling and giggling, jumped into Ethan's arms, and he spun her around and around until all that could be seen was a tornado like mist, growing larger until everything disappeared into it.

"Come back," he yelled, swiping his way through the impending darkness as the daylight was sucked into the mist, taking his breath away with it.

～

Jenna heard Ethan yell, and she groaned. She wanted to ignore him for the rest of the trip for his sake, but it didn't look like she was going to be that lucky. At first, she thought about not responding to it, thinking it might be a ploy, but the urgency in his voice made her heart skip a beat.

"So much for peace."

Grabbing the pointed stick that she'd carved last night with the sharp glass, she crawled out of the shelter which had been protecting her from the morning heat. She heard him yell again, and then he was silent.

Heading off in the direction of his voice, she held the stick above her shoulder, ready to strike if she had to. The island was not quite human friendly as she found out earlier that day when she tried to go for a swim and the fin of a shark appeared.

She had managed to make it to shore in time, but it took forever for her speeding heart to return back to normal, every beat feeling like an impending heart attack. In the distance, an animal was growling, but Ethan could no longer be heard.

"Please be okay," she begged.

As she neared the watering hole, she stopped and listened. A deep snarling growl came from the other side of the bushes.

That can't be good.

Moving into the clearing, she gasped. A large wolf was on top of a barely conscious Ethan, its paws on his chest. It turned and looked at her, its eyes wild, saliva dripping from its mouth.

Bending down, she grabbed a rock and threw it at the animal, as she charged towards it. "Get away from him!"

The wolf snapped at her, attempting to ward her off.

"Don't snap at me, damn it," she yelled, throwing another rock its way. When she was finally about ten feet away, the animal turned its large body and faced her, challenging her.

Jenna gripped her stick with both hands, ready to stab it if need be. "Don't make me kill you," she said. "Because I will."

Not that she wanted to. The animal was just following the instincts it was born with. No different than what she was doing right now. Sweat gathered on the back of her neck and near her armpits, the only visible sign of uncertainty. She ignored the corner of her mind that wanted to run.

She learned to push past all the anxiety and fear and stand on her own two feet, and this animal was not going to take that from her. "That man is mine. Go find your own," she snapped, shoving the pointed end of her stick at the wolf, hitting it on the thigh.

Yelping, it took off, disappearing into the forest. It wouldn't have gone too far though. The animal was slightly on the skinny side, so it was obviously starving, and Ethan looked like a deluxe buffet that would keep him fed for weeks.

As much as she didn't want to be around him, she'd have to hang around until he was properly back on his feet and not a travelling lunchbox for the animals on the island.

"Upsie daisy, big man," she said, grabbing his hands and pulling him to a sitting position, ignoring her queasy stomach due to their close proximity.

"W-we have a daughterrr youuu know," he slurred, his head wobbling as he tried to look at her.

She put her arm around him and helped him stand up. "If I didn't know any better, I'd say you were drunk."

"She looks like you, cute as a but-button."

"Keep dreaming!" she replied.

She could already tell that taking care of him while he recovers was going to be a barrel of laughs. A painful barrel of memories. Maybe she could find a way to knock him out until he was well enough to fend for himself.

Jenna chuckled. That wasn't going to happen, but she could dream, right? She didn't know why Mother Nature was pulling this crap on her, but it was definitely having a laugh. It pulled the old switch-a-roo. Wasn't the woman supposed to be the damsel in distress, not the guy?

She didn't have the strength to carry a half-conscious man back through the forest and his stretcher was in the opposite direction. "Come on, Ethan, move those legs," she said, slightly tapping the back of his knee with her foot.

Instead of helping, his body pitched forward, making them fall face first into the mud.

Lifting her head, mud dripping from her chin, she said, "I swear you're doing this on purpose."

He turned to look at her, his eyes cross-eyed. "Are we mud-wrestling?"

"Just shut up and get up," she said, putting her arm around him again, helping him up.

"Did you become a twin? I see two of you."

"Man, what did you eat? You're higher than a kite."

Beneath His Hands

By the time she managed to get them back to the shoreline, he grew too heavy to support anymore. Using her last bit of strength, she helped him get into the shelter. It wasn't long before he was out like a light.

"Sleep tight, sleeping beauty," she said, patting him on the head before turning to the fire pit she made last night. Only glowing embers in the bottom showed any signs of life.

"I wish starting my life again was as easy as blowing on an ember."

Just when she thought she was getting back on track again, nature always had something else planned for her. "What are you trying to do here?" she asked Mother Nature. "I'm not going to fall for him, you know."

Suddenly a breeze blew by her and into the forest behind her, making a cackling witch sound. Jenna shivered. She didn't like that noise. Not a single bit. Leaning down, she blew on the embers, trying to bring them back to life to get rid of the cold chill passing through her body.

Somehow, she didn't think her life would ever be in her control again.

∽

Ethan lay there watching Jenna. She wasn't stirring yet, which gave him time to study her. When he first woke up, memories of the night before flashed in his mind, and he thought for certain he'd be alone again. But it was a pleasant surprise to see her sprawled on the ground on the other side of the dying fire, her head resting in the crook of her arm.

Streaks of mud still lined her cheek, but it didn't detract from her simple beauty. Her slightly parted lips gently blew air at a strand of hair that had fallen across her face. When it landed on her cheek, her nose twitched like a bunny, making Ethan grin.

He liked seeing her at peace. Free from whatever memories assailed her. His stomach often ached seeing the pain spinning like a

Patricia Elliott

tornado in her eyes. But she never spoke of it. That could only mean the depth of agony and horror inside her went so deep words couldn't even describe it.

No one deserved to be trapped beneath such a heavy burden. Her real personality still existed, but the glimpses into her true character were few and far between. When she came out to play, he quite enjoyed her company, even if the moments were fleeting.

Like when she flung the condom at his head and joked about the naked rule, making his men choke over their drink. That was the woman he wanted to get to know. The one who knew how to have fun and relax. Not the guarded one that held a death grip on her protective shield.

She stirred and stretched her body like a cat, sighing softly. The sound tugged at his heart. There was something about Jenna that filled him with a desire to learn everything he could about her.

"Hey sleepy he..." he said.

Her eyes shot open as soon as he spoke, and she jumped into a crouched position, scanning her surroundings, hand ready to pick up her stick.

"Man, you're quick on your feet."

She swivelled around with her stick in hand, pointing it directly at him. Her eyes were as though a stranger was looking back at him. No recognition.

"Jenna, it's just me," he said, grabbing onto the end of her weapon. "Easy there."

He could see the internal war going on inside her. Her eyes narrowed, and then widened as a flash of recognition passed through them. Her hands shook as she held the stick against his chest.

"Jenna, it's Ethan. I'm not going to hurt you," he said softly, fighting the instinct to yell at her to come back to earth.

The battle continued to rage, almost like she was fighting another soul within her. Her eyes would grow hard and then soften as she looked at him, bouncing between the two faster than he could blink.

"Please, sweetheart, put the stick down."

Shaking her head, Jenna squeezed her eyes closed and sat back on her heels. He watched as she took a deep breath in and then out, tapping her fingers alternately on her knees. When she reopened her eyes, her composure was back. She was back.

"Where were you just now?"

"It's a long story," she sighed.

He did a wide sweep with his arm. "I think we have all the time in the world."

"I suppose with all the times I've tried to hurt you, you deserve to hear the truth. You might not want me around once I tell you though."

Ethan sat across from her, watching as she stared into the dying campfire. He couldn't believe that he was finally privileged enough to hear her story. "Let me be the judge of that."

Jenna picked up some dried seaweed and picked away at it. Much of the horror she went through had been locked away, and she'd refused to talk about the worst of it, even to counsellors. Not even her friend Cleo knew of the extent of the torture she had endured by Mathew's hand.

"It was my nineteenth birthday, and my friend, Cleo, insisted on celebrating. I thought it was going to be just the two of us, but she roped me into allowing two guys to come. If I knew what was going to happen, I would have stayed home," she said, rubbing her arms. "Cleo and her new boyfriend disappeared, leaving me alone with Derek, a fellow co-worker. Anyway, he was always hitting on me. I felt so awkward that I took off out the back door of the bar and into the alley.

"You know what's funny, people always talk about how characters in horror movies make dumb decisions, and I've seen enough of them to know better, so why I did that is beyond me, but I did. I went into a dark alley to get away from him. Next thing I know, I'm waking up in a cabin in the middle of nowhere."

"You were kidnapped?"

Swallowing hard, she nodded, tears forming in her eyes.

"You don't have to tell me if you don't want to."

Jenna shook her head. "No, I want to. I need to. I've let it have a hold on me for long enough."

"Okay," he said, reaching for a handful of berries on the leaf beside him.

Her stomach rolled as she watched him pop the food in his mouth. She doubted she'd eat anything for a while. "I didn't know what was going on. Whoever it was locked me in the cabin and just left me there."

"That doesn't sound so bad. More like a free vacation."

She let out a hard chuckle and rolled up her pant leg, giving him an unabashed view of the jagged scar that ran up the length of her calf. "Does this look like it was fun?"

"What happened?"

"My captor tortured me with snakes, locked me in a coffin with spiders, and trapped me in a dungeon where he raped me over and over again for his own fucking pleasure, and then he shot me when I tried to escape." The words tumbled out of her mouth quickly and all in one breath before anxiety had a chance to take over, preventing her from speaking like it always does. Jenna placed a hand on her cramping stomach, trying desperately not to puke as acid rose in her throat.

"My God, Jenna."

She spat bile on the ground, pretending it was Mathew as the fear turned to anger. They'd taken so much from her, but she was going to take her life back. She no longer wanted to be ruled by fear or anxiety. That's why she chose to tell Ethan more of her story. "Apparently Derek organized it with his crazy ass foster brother, just so he could play the hero, hoping I'd fall for him."

"That is some messed up shit."

"You think that was bad. I got pregnant by that bastard and his foster brother, not sure which one."

Ethan's eyes widened and his jaw dropped. "I'm so sorry."

"That's all I ever heard after I got home. I'm sorry, Jenna. I'm so

Beneath His Hands

sorry that happened to you. I hate it," she said vehemently, as she crumbled the seaweed in her hand. "I hate the look of pity in people's eyes. The look of being damaged goods."

"Is that why you started working on boats?"

"Sort of. After it all happened, I was in rough shape. I thought hearing him get sentenced to life in prison would help, but it didn't. I spiralled into a deep depression. To cope, I guess you could say my mind split in two. The first time I experienced the split personality was when I tried to go out with my friend again. She thought it would help if I got right back into the saddle, and she introduced me to another friend of someone she knew, Ryan."

"Don't tell me—"

"Yep," she interrupted. "It just seems to be my luck. Anyway, Ryan dropped Cleo and her boyfriend off at Cleo's boyfriend's place and then drove me home. He hated that I was so cold towards him. He assumed I was playing hard to get and tried to force himself on me. When he did, something inside me snapped."

"Can't say I blame you. You've been through hell."

"You don't understand. I broke his larynx, nearly killed him. I—" She choked back a sob. "I hurt my dad when he tried to pull me off the guy. I couldn't stop myself. It was like I was locked inside watching it all happen. The police arrived and took me away, locking me in a mental hospital for the second time."

"And now I got you into this mess."

"More like I got you in this one. You did jump into the water to rescue me, remember?"

"And I'd do it again. Curious though, if you've struggled with this kind of stuff before, how come I didn't see anything to this extent on the boat?"

"I'm on medication or at least I was."

"Is that what was in the box?"

Pulling her knees up to her chest, she wrapped her arms around them and rested her wobbling chin on her knees. "It was one thing in the box, yes," she replied. She didn't have the heart to share the other.

He'd already heard enough of her story and didn't need to hear the rest.

"Why do I think that wasn't the only thing in there? You wouldn't risk your neck just for medication. That's easy enough to buy back on land."

"I don't see a store nearby, do you?"

Curiosity flashed in his eyes, but he didn't push her and for that she was grateful. Her heart felt a little lighter for sharing some of her story with him, and she was glad that he didn't get up and move away from her, but she couldn't help wondering whether she should leave to keep him safe from her crazy mind.

"Do you want me to go?" she asked.

"If I wanted you to go, I'd tell you."

"You're stupid then."

Ethan chuckled. "Hardly. You've already had a few chances to hurt me, and you didn't. You might have more control than you think."

Standing up, she said, "Then you have more faith in me than I do."

"You're a strong woman, Jenna. You can do more than you realize."

"Just because I can hurt people doesn't mean I'm strong."

"The fact that you're still alive tells me you're strong inside and out."

"No, it just means people found me before I could kill myself," she said, as she started to walk away. "I'm going to get some water."

"I'll come," he said, struggling to stand.

"Just rest that leg today. I'll be back."

"Promise?" he asked, holding out his pinkie finger.

"Seriously, you're going to make me pinkie swear?"

How old was this guy, twelve?

Nevertheless, she held out her finger and wrapped it around his, ready to declare that she'd be back. But her words fell short when their link sent an electric shock up her arm, spreading throughout her body.

"I...uh...I'm going to go now," she said, attempting to pull her hand away.

He squeezed her finger, refusing to let go. "You haven't promised me yet."

"Shut up."

Appearing to sense her need for space, he released her hand. "If you aren't back by the time the sun starts to set, I'm coming to look for you."

"Deal."

Chapter Eleven

Ethan glanced towards the sun, which was just above the horizon. His prickly princess hadn't returned from her water trip yet. He wasn't sure if she was just scared to come back or if something had happened to her.

He knew she could take care of herself, but would she leave him high and literally dry? He never had a chance to drink anything all day, and he needed to get some water before it got too dark to travel.

Grabbing his walking stick again, he stood up, gingerly testing his stiff leg. His scar was going to match Jenna's. Ethan shook his head. He still couldn't believe the story she had told him. How could one person have such bad luck? In his writing research, he'd read about generational curses, but he thought they were all utter hogwash. Now, he wondered if there was any truth to it.

First, she went through the kidnapping, and then after that another attempted rape, and now she was trapped on an island with him. He had to do everything he could to make this easy for her and not make it a horrible experience. Now that he knew her story, he'd do his best not to get inside her personal space. How do you recover from something like that?

He limped his way back to the watering hole, half expecting Jenna to be there relaxing, but it was empty. A large pit opened up in his stomach. Did the wolf come back? Ethan looked around, checking for blood. Nothing out of the ordinary caught his attention.

"Jenna," he yelled, "can you hear me?"

Her faint cry could be heard in the distance. He turned towards the noise, following another path already blazed through the forest, by Jenna no doubt. As he limped his way along, another path branched off to his left.

"Keep yelling," he yelled out again, straining his ear to listen.

"Help me!" she cried.

Her voice vibrated in his left ear. Hobbling his way down the path as quickly as he could, he followed her cries of anguish. "Where are you, Jenna?"

"Over here," came her muffled voice.

"I can't see you."

"Be careful. I'm down a hole."

Treading his way carefully, one foot in front of the other, he followed the sound of her voice. He didn't want to become the second victim. How on earth had she fallen down a hole? After taking a few more steps, he found a cave-like hole in the ground.

"Hello?"

"Took you long enough," she grumbled.

The hole curved like a slide, so he couldn't see her. "Are you hurt?"

"No, but I can't climb back out. I'm in some sort of cavern. Just wait till you see what I found. You aren't going to believe it," she said, excitement lacing her voice, the anger dissipating.

"I'm going to look around to see what I can use to pull you out."

"There should be some vines around, like I used to make your stretcher."

"Right."

He had to backtrack a bit, but sure enough, he found a tangle of vines hanging down. Giving them a good hard tug, he expected them to fall, but they stayed firmly in place. That was good and not good at the same time. Good in the fact that they could support his weight and not break. But how the heck was he supposed to use them if he couldn't get them down?

Ethan picked up a stick and tore it down the middle, hoping it was jagged enough to do the trick. Yanking hard on the vine, he pulled it down as much as he could so that it gathered on the ground and used the stick to cut through it. It was an inch in diameter, like a good-sized rope.

Unsure of how far down she was, he tied a couple of them together, threw them over his shoulder and wandered back to the hole.

"I'm tossing the vine down. Let me know if it reaches you."

"Okay."

He tied one end around a tree and then dropped the other down the hole until there was no slack left.

"Well?" He asked.

"I see it, but I can't reach."

"How many more feet do you need?"

"At least ten."

Ethan pulled up the rope, saying, "Okay, hang on."

"It's not like I'm going anywhere," she quipped back.

"Smart ass," he replied, chuckling.

At least she didn't appear to be in any distress down there. He could only hope that he wouldn't run into any wild animals again while he played hero. Getting her out of the hole was going to require all his left-over strength.

Cutting another vine, he dragged it back to the others and tied it to the end, and lowered it once again, hoping it would reach her this time. The rope tugged in Ethan's hand.

"I've got it," she yelled.

He braced himself against the tree and helped support her climb back up, pulling the rope as much as he could, hand over hand.

When her fingers grappled the edge of the hole, he crouched beside her and helped her the rest of the way.

Resting on all fours, breathing hard, she said, "I owe...you one."

"You saved me, it's the least I could do. Now I need to go get some water before I keel over."

"I'm really sorry. I got chased by a wolf."

"Same one?"

"How am I supposed to know? They all look alike to me."

"Easy, spitfire. I'm the hero, remember?"

"Have you forgotten that I've saved your life twice since we got here?"

"Well, if we're keeping count, I saved yours twice, too."

Jenna muttered a curse word under her breath. The man was right. She didn't have a leg up on him in the rescue department. But she did have something he didn't, so if he didn't play nice, she wouldn't share.

Picking up a few rocks, she made an X next to the hole. "If you can play nice until we get back to camp, I'll show you what I found."

"Nice-nice or spicy-nice?" he asked, as he offered his hand to help her up.

"You're a p—"

His eyes darkened and a slight smirk played on his face as he backed her up against a tree. "If you say that word again, I'm going to kiss it right out of your mouth."

She snapped her mouth closed, pressing her lips firmly together, but she couldn't look away from his eyes. They...They should have scared her, but the only thing she felt in her stomach was a case of nervous butterflies.

She was losing it. It must have been all the time she spent in the cavern, waiting for her saviour to come. That's it. Yes. Her mind was going crazy. She didn't really want him to kiss her. She couldn't.

"I...uhh...we should get back to camp," Jenna said, ducking under his arm, making a beeline for the self-made path back to the waterfall.

"Chicken," he said, half chuckling.

He didn't know how right he was. She didn't pride herself on being scared of something that came so easily for most people. But it was something she'd never done, by choice, beyond kissing her parents on the cheek.

She hadn't even kissed her dad since it happened. Now, here she was, thinking about kissing a man she barely knew. What the hell was wrong with her?

She stood there waiting while Ethan drank some water for what felt like an eternity. "Come on. Let's go before it gets dark," she said, tapping her foot. The sun was already behind the trees, making their branches cast dark shadows across the ground.

Finally, he stood up, and they were on their way again.

∽

The sky wasn't quite pitch black by time they made it back, but it was getting close. The first stars of the night were beginning to appear, twinkling to their own musical song. Despite being stranded, it really was a beautiful spot. Maybe when she got back to land, she'd inquire about whether the island belonged to anyone yet. It would be the perfect getaway from civilization, away from the crowds. She could likely afford it now.

"You look deep in thought? What's on your mind," Ethan asked.

"Have you ever watched Island life?"

He leaned down and grabbed a handful of waiting berries, mushy from the heat of the sun. "You mean the show where people buy their own islands?"

"Yeah."

"Once or twice."

"That's what I want," she said, grabbing a mango and taking a bite.

"To be on the show?"

"No. I don't want to be on camera again." She'd had enough of that before when she faced questions people should never have asked on camera. Private things no one else had the right to know.

"If we get rescued, you do realize that they'll want to interview you right?"

"Ain't gonna happen. My plan is to disappear, and I finally have the means to do it."

He tilted his head and studied her. "How so?"

Jenna reached into her pocket, and her fingers closed around her earlier discovery. Gently, she removed her hand from the zipped pocket, not wanting to scratch her find. She held out her hand and slowly opened her fingers, watching with pleasure as Ethan's eyes widened.

"Hot damn!" he said, his jaw dropping.

In her hand sat the largest blue diamond the world had ever seen, still partially encased in rock.

"Do you realize how much money you're holding right there?" Ethan asked.

"Enough to buy this island. If it is for sale, that is."

"Darling, you are going to be one of the richest women in the world. That thing should sell for at least seventy million."

Jenna gasped as she held it up in front of her, examining it in the dark. She hadn't realized it would sell for that much. She figured fifteen to twenty million maybe. Her and her parents would never want again. Her dad would never have to travel and leave her mom behind. They could finally have the retirement they deserved.

Ethan held his hand out, and she passed him the diamond. "Were there any more down there?"

"I couldn't tell. It was too dark. This one happened to be on the ground beside me when I landed."

Two inches the other way and she would have landed right on top of it, crunching the first good thing in her life. Mind you, her find would only matter if they were rescued. And now, more than ever, she wanted that to happen. She wanted to sell it and get oodles of money.

Ethan held it up in the air to examine it. "There must have been an earthquake or something that loosened it from the rock face. We could be sitting on top of a diamond mine."

"Or Blackbeard's treasure," she said jokingly.

"That would be the find of the century."

Excitement filled her. "We have to go back."

If there was a possibility of more treasure existing down there, she had to find out. There could be whole cavern full of money just waiting for them to discover it.

"Without a torch or a flashlight, it's going to be pretty impossible to see what's down there," Ethan said.

"We could find a stick and wrap moss around it or something."

"Women!" He threw his hands in the air. "You always want more bling."

"Hey, even you said we could be sitting on top of a diamond mine."

"That doesn't mean I want you to risk your neck going back down there. We should wait until we have the right equipment."

Jenna groaned. He was right. There was no way she could climb down the vine and hold a flaming torch at the same time, and Ethan was in no condition to do any climbing. But she hated the feeling of not knowing. She had never been one much for jewellery or sprucing up her appearance, but the idea of having her own private cavern full of treasure, like the little mermaid, was not easy to resist.

He handed the gem back to her. "I know a guy who works with high-end diamonds like this. He can help us appraise it and get it ready to sell."

The thought of handing the diamond over to some stranger didn't sit well with her, but Ethan was well-known, and she knew he had connections she didn't have. "It's not going to be easy giving it to someone else, especially when I can't prove that it's mine to begin with."

"I send business his way all the time. I trust him."

The pressure of a yawn built up inside her, and her mouth

widened in response. "I'll thi...abou... it," she said, her words garbled by the yawn as she covered her mouth. Lying down, she cradled the diamond in the crook of her arm, her cheek resting on her forearm.

"Tired?" he asked.

"Very. How's the leg?"

"Sore, but I think I'll live."

Lifting her head off her arm, she said, "Maybe I should look at it."

He smiled. "Just lay your pretty little head back down and get some sleep."

Pretty? Did he go blind or something? Choosing not to respond, she rolled over and tried to ignore the butterflies in her stomach. It had been a long time since anyone called her pretty or dared to try for that matter. She didn't like the giddiness it created inside her. It made her feel shallow and needy, and yet oddly fulfilled. Warmth spread throughout her body. A feeling unknown to her.

"Stop it," she grumbled under her breath.

"Did you say something?" Ethan asked.

"No."

If he knew the reaction her body had towards him, she'd never hear the end of it. And she wasn't going to go there. No way. No how. Jenna shoved her hands between her legs and pressed them against her crotch, willing the annoying ache to dissipate. She could feel his eyes on her and that heated her core all the more.

"Stop looking at me," she snapped.

"You look so cute over there. It's hard not to."

Jenna let out a hard laugh. That was the biggest lie she'd ever heard. "Kids are cute. I'm..." She let her voice trail off. She didn't even know what she was anymore. Cute was the last word she'd use to describe herself.

"And the cutest thing is, you don't even realize how cute you are."

"There's nothing to realize."

"Why do you do that?"

"Do what?"

"Put yourself down so much. I get that you went through something horrible, but you don't have to let it define who you are."

"Isn't that what you're doing, too, *Mister I don't want a girl on my boat?*" she commented, rolling over to face him.

"I suppose you're right in a way. But I have a very good reason for my choice."

"I told you my sordid details. Let's hear yours."

Picking up a stick, Ethan pulled it through the sand, creating a line in front of him. What he went through was nowhere near as horrific as her experience, but it was still a defining moment for him. He had learned when it came to women, they always had their own agenda. Sex wasn't all they wanted from him. They wanted his money and would do anything to get it. Twice burnt taught him a lesson he would never forget.

Jenna didn't appear to be like them, though. She wasn't interested in him, and that made him very interested in her. He wanted to break down her defences. And sharing his story seemed to be one method of drawing closer to her.

"I didn't always have an all-male crew."

Sitting up, Jenna crossed her legs, placed the diamond in the centre—a spot he would love to be occupying right about now—and watched him intently. "What happened?" she asked.

"The first one wasn't too bad. She sold a few semi-naked photos of me to a magazine."

"And how did she get those photos, sir?"

Ethan smirked, his steamy eyes locking with hers. He opened his mouth to speak, but she raised her hand, shivering. "Forget I asked. What else happened?"

"Her name was Naomi. She was an old family friend that I thought I could trust. Turns out, she was a witch in sheep's clothing. I knew I shouldn't mix business with pleasure, but I was a rising star and let it go to my head. It didn't take long before she wanted more than I did, and when I said no, the shit hit the fan," he said, grimacing at the memory. "She carefully planned a setup and claimed she wanted to role-play. And me, like the idiot I was, went along with it. I had no idea what she had planned until the police hauled me off the boat the next day, arresting me for assault and rape."

"Dang."

"She didn't get away with it, but it took forever to clear my name. After that, I swore to never let another woman on my boat or in my arms."

"Can't say I blame you. I haven't let myself get close to anyone ever since..."

"Do you ever want to?"

Her gaze fell upon the fire, the flames dancing in her eyes as confusion swirled inside them. "Sometimes I think I want to, but..." she started to say. A visible shiver rocked her body, eating her last few words, her cheeks turning a slight pink colour in the dim light.

"Afraid that it will hurt?" he asked.

"And that I'll hurt somebody because of my, you know," she said, with a wave of her hand.

Having been on the receiving hand of her episodes a few times, he could understand her fear, but he had a feeling that the right person could make it through that barrier. They could show her that there was more to making love than being afraid.

"It can be amazing," he said softly.

Jenna smiled wryly, obviously choosing to ignore his response. "Why do we always have the weirdest conversations?"

"Your guess is as good as mine," he replied, shrugging his shoulders. He didn't know why these topics came easily for the both of them, considering their history. But nevertheless, here they were yet again. And since they were just getting to the good stuff now, he wasn't about to drop the conversation. "Have you ever had sex, aside from what happened?"

She buried her face in her hands, but not before he saw her cheeks turn a bright red colour. "I'm not going to answer that question."

"You don't have to. I already have the answer."

"How? I could have slept with 50 guys, and you wouldn't even know it."

"I'd know it all right. I'd see it in your eyes."

"How?"

"Experienced women have this air about them. They don't get flustered. And you can't even say the word *sex* without turning red."

"Yes, I can." As if to prove her point, she moved closer to him. "Sex. Sex. Se..." When their eyes locked, her mouth stopped moving. Awareness moved through her gorgeous hazel eyes as she bit her bottom lip. "I...uh...."

Ethan reached out and rested his palm on her cheek, running his thumb across her bottom lip. Satisfaction filled him when she leaned into his touch. And all the blood in his body pooled between his legs. He prayed that she couldn't see it in the dark. "Do you realize how sexy you are?"

As soon as he spoke, she broke their connection, diving for the other side of the fire again. He hung his head, shaking it softly as he swore to himself. He should have just stayed quiet, but he couldn't help it. Her quiet sensuality sang to him. Even though she was timid like a deer, she was beginning to trust him and that made him feel good. He knew he couldn't move too quickly, or she'd retreat into herself again.

He had to balance a fine line and keep his animalistic passions at bay until she caught up to them. And he hoped to God that it wouldn't take long, or he might find himself going off into the bushes to take care of his arousal. A permanent hard-on was not fun.

"Good night, Ethan," she said, her voice husky.

He could hear the need in her voice, but also the fear and hesitancy that laced every word. She was entering a new territory, and the way was unknown to her and quite frankly, he was beginning to feel outside of his own waters as well.

"Good night, Jenna." He let her name roll off his lips.

She shivered again, and he relished her response, his own body trembling with anticipation. There was no doubt about it. He was getting in over his head, but he didn't want to stop. This was the first time since it all went down that he wanted to be with a woman again. Even if it was the woman who pushed him into the ocean.

Ethan laid himself back on the sand, propping his arm behind his head, grinning like a fool. Could life get any more interesting than this? He closed his eyes, dreaming of the day that Jenna would let him in. His whole body tingled at the thought.

He couldn't help but laugh. This was exactly what his mother had hoped for. She was always telling him it was time to get back on the horse again. She wasn't getting any younger and desperately wanted grandkids before she was too old to enjoy them.

Mother, you old coot!

Chapter Twelve

Jenna wasn't sure whether she should feel horrified or fascinated as she stared at the sight before her. She went to bed aching, wanting to try something she had never done of her own accord, and now the feeling was a thousand times stronger. The crotch of Ethan's pants stretched out like a tent pole, and she itched to reach out and touch his erection.

Smacking her forehead, she whispered, "What is wrong with you?"

Rolling over, she tried to erase the image from her mind and stop the warmth from pooling between her legs. Her body was acting like an alien from outer space, invading every part of her sensibilities. She didn't want to want him. She didn't want to feel this way. It scared her. And she hated it.

She was surprised that Ethan never said anything after they said good night, leaving her alone with her thoughts. He loved being outspoken. Never seemed to be afraid to share what was on his mind. If he held back because he knew she needed space, damn him for caring. She wanted him to say something to turn her off, like he did at the beginning. But he didn't.

Instead, he risked his life to retrieve her box and then jumped off the boat to save her, not even knowing if he would survive. And he even came looking for her after she fell down a hole. Just knowing someone cared enough to do that was incredibly humbling. He didn't even seem to want anything in return. Wasn't forcing her to do anything that made her feel uncomfortable.

It's like they finally reached an understanding. Upon hearing him stir, she turned to face him again. Her eyes immediately honed-in on his erection, still blatantly evident against his torn sweats. When she managed to pull her eyes away, she glanced up at him, his eyes dancing with amusement.

"Like what you see?"

And there it was. "Do you realize how cocky you are?" As soon as she said it, she slapped a hand over her mouth as her eyes flickered to the bulge in his sweats, her face heating. That was definitely the wrong word to use.

He chuckled when she forced herself to look away. "You're like this innocent high school girl."

"Can't you make it, you know, go away?"

"You can help if you want."

Scrunching her nose, Jenna said, "Jeez, could you be any more crude?"

The annoying part was that her fingers itched to help him, and her lady parts were vying for attention, tingling and throbbing at the idea of meeting its counterpart. But her stomach churned at the idea. The conflicting responses played havoc with her mind. How could you want and not want something at the same time? She liked it better when she didn't feel anything. It was much less confusing. Her body felt like it was in a tug-a-war, being pulled in both directions at once.

Shaking her head, Jenna stuffed the diamond in her pocket and stood up. "I'm going to find some food."

"I'll come with you."

Holding her hands up, palms facing him, she said, "Stay. Get rid of that thing first. I'll be back soon."

"I think we've been through this already. I'm coming with you in case that stupid wolf comes back."

Shivering at the idea, she shook her head. "I get that you're concerned, but I need space, Ethan. I won't go far, I promise."

"Bring some food back, and then we'll go to the waterfall together."

"Fine."

She understood why he was worried. The wolf was obviously hungry and had no intention of giving up. It didn't seem to matter how many times she beaned it with a rock the other day. The creature still kept coming at her. She was glad it did in a way, or she wouldn't have found the beautiful gem sitting in her pocket.

Her heart still galloped a million miles a minute when her fingers brushed over it. She was rich, and the thought was mind boggling. Lottery tickets never worked out for her, but now she found something even more awesome. Maybe she'd have some of the diamond turned into a ring or something. She could even pay off the mortgage for her parents, which would help her dad retire.

And it was only fair to split the money with Ethan. Not that he needed it, but she would never have gotten out of the hole without him. She was ecstatic because he loved his boat, and this would help him get a new one. She might even buy one for herself.

Jenna grinned as she imagined hoisting the sails high into the air and riding the wind and the ocean currents. The ocean was her home away from home. She couldn't imagine living in the city full-time again. Being out on the ocean, with no land in sight, felt freeing somehow, like the world went on forever. And she felt safe.

Finding some blackberries, she filled the belly of her shirt, and then began her trek back to the beach. They were lucky that the island had an abundance of fruit. It would keep them alive until someone found them. The place almost felt like a private resort, but without all the fluff. She found it hard to feel freaked out, which was the more logical response to being stranded. But, instead, her body was beginning to relax.

Before she stepped out of the forest onto the beach, she watched Ethan staring out over the ocean, her stomach flip flopping. The man had the physique of a model. He also had strong cheekbones, straight as anything teeth, and a killer smile that was made to melt the heart of any woman. It was no wonder he found himself in hot water with them in the past.

Jeepers, the sun must be melting my brain cells.

As if sensing her presence, he turned that killer smile her way and her heart fluttered.

"What did you find today, sweetheart?"

"Same as yesterday," she replied, swallowing hard as she dropped the berries onto the previously used leaf. Screenwriters were supposed to be nerdy looking and not look like they could grace the front page of Playgirl magazine.

"We should try catching some fish," he said.

"Be my guest. I'd be happy to watch."

"You can do it. I wouldn't mind watching you flounder around in the water."

"In your dreams, sailor."

When he turned towards her, a smirk spread across his face. "My dreams get a little wilder than you catching fish."

"I get that you are love starved here, but I'm not on the menu," she replied, moving a little farther away from him, as if it would protect her somehow from the hormones raging in her body.

People often accused her of being asexual, and she couldn't help but wonder if that was true. Her body had totally shut itself off, going into self-preservation mode. And she'd gotten used to it. Now it decided to wake up, not by choice, and she didn't know what to do with it.

Jenna looked at Ethan out of the corner of her eye and found him staring. "What are you looking at?"

"You."

"Way to be subtle," she said, rolling her eyes.

"I wasn't trying to be. You're different."

"Gee, thanks."

"I don't mean that in a bad way. I've never met anyone like you. You're unique."

Warmth spread through her chest. No one had ever said that to her before, and she was unsure of how to respond. Jenna shrugged her shoulders. "I'm just me."

"That's just it. You're not like other women. You're strong, beautiful, and courageous. And that's just a few off the top of my head."

"Flattery won't work, you know."

"Work with what?"

"Getting in my pants."

Ethan tilted his head toward the sky and laughed. "You're priceless."

His deep, rich laughter vibrated throughout her body. Jenna flopped back on the sand and covered her face with her hands, groaning. This man was going to be the death of her and of all things she considered normal.

"Don't make me move to the other side of the island," she warned.

"I'd follow you."

"Creepy much?"

Ethan rubbed his hands together, cackling like a mad doctor. "Only for you, dearie."

"Oh, my God," Jenna giggled, covering her mouth with her hands. "You didn't really just do that."

Pretending to look offended, Ethan pouted and said, "Hey, I thought I sounded pretty good."

And if her laughter was anything to go by, then his joking around did the trick. Her face lit up when she laughed, which was even more beautiful than the lighting of the Christmas tree in Times Square.

If he never saw another Christmas in the city, seeing her face sparkle would be enough for him. And he was going to do everything in his power to see that she did it more. Break down the walls she had built around herself since the kidnapping. They were slowly coming down, and he loved the glimpse he was getting inside her spirit.

Standing up, he offered her his hand. "Why don't we go and get some water?"

When she took his hand, her soft flesh meeting his, he had to bite his tongue to prevent himself from saying anything that would scare her off. Their connection hit him squarely in the chest, making his heart hammer against his ribcage, threatening to break it. What would it feel like for her dainty hand to touch his body freely? The thought made his cock twitch with delight.

Oh crap. He couldn't get a woody. Not now. Begrudgingly, he released her hand before the twinge could turn into anything more. Hand holding didn't usually do it for him, but his body craved release. Craved her.

"You okay?" she asked.

"Yes, let's go," he said huskily, pushing her towards the forest ahead of him.

"Making the lady go first, huh?" she quipped over her shoulder.

"Only so I can get a clear view of that sweet ass of yours."

She stepped aside, and with an exaggerated flourish of her hand, she said, "Old geezers first."

His lips curled into half a smirk. "Remind me to dunk you in the water."

When he didn't move, she started up the path. "You'll have to catch me first, and with how you're moving on that leg, I don't think you can."

That was a challenge if he'd ever heard one. And he was never one to back down from a dare. When they got to the waterfall, he was going to sweep her up in his arms. She wasn't going to know when or how, but he was going to do it when she least expected it.

Her hips swung from side to side, making his eyes wander to her backside again. For a woman who didn't know her worth, she sure knew how to walk like one. Ethan licked his lips. He couldn't wait to have her in his arms.

She leaned down to move a branch, and he groaned. Walking behind her wasn't helping his situation any, not like he had hoped. Reaching into his pants, he adjusted himself quickly before she turned around. Damn things were a nuisance.

"Keep your eye open, Ethan. That wolf almost got the jump on me last time."

"My eyes are open," he murmured, completely tantalized by her backside. Did they even make them that firm anymore? His hands reached out to test the firmness, but then he pulled them back, not wanting to get knocked on his ass. She stopped suddenly, and he bumped into her, touching her anyway.

Pulling his hands away quickly, he said, "Sorry."

"Shh." She covered his mouth with her hand and tilted her head, listening intently. "I think we're being followed."

Jenna felt his erection pressing against her backside as he stood right behind her, which was distracting her from far more important matters at hand, like the wolf stalking them in the bushes off to their left.

"Aren't you supposed to be as loud as possible," he asked, his breath warm on her neck.

"That's what they say, but this one doesn't seem to care."

"He has an unmet hunger then."

Jenna chuckled nervously, stepping away from him. "Y-you and him both. Come on, let's keep going."

His obvious interest in her unnerved her more than the animal did, especially because her body liked it. No matter how many times she argued with it, it kept responding to him. The sensations travelled through her system like a bolt of sheet lightning, spreading to every corner imaginable.

She continued walking, her mind fighting the electricity between them and the images of Mat's dick in her face. She squeezed her eyes closed. Jenna shivered. She didn't want what happened back then to control her life forever. She didn't want to be afraid anymore.

"Watch out," Ethan said, yanking her backwards.

"What the heck," she cried as she bumped into him, breaking her out of her thoughts.

"You were heading right for a tree."

"Oh."

"I'm surprised you're calm enough to daydream with that sucker out there."

"If he comes after us, he'll catch you first," she said with a straight face as she moved away from him and around the tree. She only had to run faster than the person she was with, or so she read in a Survive the Zombie Apocalypse article.

"Gee, thanks," he said wryly.

Jenna's lips curled upwards as she glanced back over her shoulder at him. "You're welcome."

They walked in silence the rest of the way, and she couldn't help but wonder what he was thinking as he followed her. Was he staring at her butt? She had to fight not to look back and check for herself. Why the heck did she even want to know?

Walking into the open and dying to go for a swim, she relished the sight of the water sparkling in the sunlight. Ethan came to a stop beside her, panting a little in the intense heat with sweat running down his forehead. It didn't take long for him to pull his shirt up over his head, and then he reached for the drawstring on his sweats.

Jenna covered her eyes and turned around. "What are you doing?"

"Going for a dip."

"Don't take your clothes off."

"How else am I supposed to do it then?"

"At least wait till I'm gone."

"I won't get naked, I promise. Come on, pretend you're wearing a bathing suit."

She looked down at her raggedy clothes, drenched in sweat from their hike. The water would feel good. Would it really matter if she stripped down to her bra and panties? He'd already seen her naked anyway. Jenna bit her bottom lip. Uncertain of what to do.

He started wading into the water, wearing his butt hugging underwear, his erection still noticeable. She moaned and groaned all in one go. And, of course, he heard it and chuckled.

"Don't be a chicken. The water is great," he said, backstroking to the centre of the pond, as the water glistened on his skin. "Come on. I won't bite."

"The frogs seem to disagree." She pointed to the previously occupied, but now empty, lily pads.

Ethan shrugged. A smile played loosely on his face as he comfortably floated in the water. "Their loss."

"Hey, what about your leg?" she said, trying to get him to come out of the water and put his clothes back on.

"My leg can handle a little water."

"I'm not sure I can," Jenna muttered to herself. Sitting down on a rock, she tried to tune his suntanned body out of her mind and focused on a loose string on the hem of her shirt. The sun was beating down on her head mercilessly, making her hair cake to her forehead and the back of her neck.

"You're going to bake out there, sweetheart. If I promise to stay on my side, will you come in?"

Jenna looked at the sand, biting her bottom lip. Should she dare? She'd never stripped down to her undies in front of anyone before. She never even wore shorts because it gave them an unadulterated view of her leg. People always stared, and it made her uncomfortable. But the sweat that was rolling down her cheeks had her remove her shirt as she stood up.

Ethan stared at her, amazement rolling across his features.

"Stop staring. You're making me nervous," she said, sticking her tongue out at him. "Turn around."

Spinning in the water, he faced towards the waterfall. "Party pooper."

Slipping off her pants, she dashed into the water and went all the way up to her chin. Jenna shivered in delight as the water acted like an air condition against her warm flesh. "It feels so good."

"Told ya so."

"Shush." Jenna sliced her arm through the water, spraying him.

Ethan ran a hand down his face and removed the water droplets. "Did you really just do that?"

She giggled at the look of surprise written all over his face. Pushing her arm through the water, she splashed him again, forgetting all about the two yellow eyes watching them from the bushes and letting fun reign for a change. Something she didn't allow very often, always being on guard.

When she went to splash him again, she found herself sputtering as a huge wave of water covered her, sailing up her nose causing her to break out coughing.

"You!" she cried, slapping the surface of the pool. Her hair stuck against her head, conforming to the shape of her face, as water dripped down her cheeks.

Ethan burst out laughing. She looked like a drowned rat "Now we're even," he said.

"Are you certain of that?" she asked.

Sweet wickedness flashed in her eyes and the edges of her mouth curled into a mischievous grin. The playful side of Jenna was rearing its sexy head again, and it sent an electric charge through his body, making it hum with sexual energy.

Pulling her hand back, she went to splash water at him again, but he dove under the surface. Ethan swam down to the bottom and looked up at her, her legs moving in a peddling motion as she continued to tread water.

Pulling his lips to one corner, he smirked. He knew exactly what he was going to do next. Raising his arm, he reached for her foot and ran his index finger along the length of it. Immediately, her leg recoiled, but he didn't let that stop him. He wrapped his fingers around her ankle, and then tickled her insole again.

Her laughter cut through the water right into his soul. It was the most beautiful thing he'd ever heard. She wasn't prone to non-stop flirtatious giggling like other women he knew. When she laughed, it was real, and it lit up her eyes so bright that he caught a glimpse of her true spirit.

Running out of air, he floated upwards and ran his fingers against her slippery skin, savouring in the silky feel against his fingertips. Her body trembled beneath his touch, but she didn't swim away from him. When his head breached the surface, they were face to face with his hands resting gently on her waist.

Her eyes searched his. Her pupils were dilated, her breathing rapid and shallow. He wasn't sure if it was from laughing too hard or his touch. Testing his hypothesis, he ran his fingers up her side, brushing the sides of her breasts. Her breath hitched. She gasped slightly, her eyes partially closing as colour bloomed across her cheeks.

"You are so beautiful," he murmured.

There were those words again. Words Jenna wasn't accustomed to hearing, but from his lips they felt authentic. Was she dreaming? Had she hit her head, and none of this was actually real? His touch was like a magic spell taking her under.

"Ethan," she whispered, her voice wavering and resolve caving.

"Touch me," he said hoarsely.

Jenna reached out for him, and then stopped abruptly, her cheeks red. "I don't know how."

They moved towards shallower waters and when their feet touched the sand, he reached for her hand, placing it on his chest. She stared at her hand, unable to lift her eyes to look at him. Light hair spread sparsely across his chest, coarse to her touch as she explored. When her thumb ran over his erect nipple, he drew in a sharp breath.

Thinking it was painful, she drew her hand back. "I'm sorry, did you want me to stop?" she asked, looking up at him.

"Hell, no."

Tilting her head down, she said, "I feel so silly."

Cupping her chin with his palm, he lifted her face to meet his.

"You have nothing to feel silly about, darling. This is the most natural thing in the world."

Easy for him to say, he didn't spend every second of his life fearing the touch of intimacy. Yet, it wasn't fear that accosted her now. It was uncertainty of what she was doing that made her hesitate. These were uncharted waters. She had no idea what she was supposed to do, and whether he would like whatever choice she made.

Leaving his hand where it was, he leaned closer. His lips only a hair's breadth away. "Kiss me, Jenna."

Ethan saw the war of uncertainty rage in her eyes, but he waited for her to make the first move. Jenna needed to make the decision. He knew how important having a choice was to her. Her previous experiences were thrust upon her without her consent. He didn't plan on making the same mistake. No matter how desperately he wanted to taste her lips.

With great anticipation he waited. Seemingly frozen in place for what felt like eternity until she finally touched his lips timidly with her own, gently testing and tasting. And he let her, allowing her to move at her own pace. When her tongue slid across his bottom lip, he fought to hold back a groan. Gripping her waist, he pulled her flush against him, his cock pressing against her belly.

"Look what you do to me," he murmured against her mouth.

She giggled nervously. Her lips tasted like sweet blackberries. He took advantage of her open mouth and swept his tongue inside, mating with hers in a new exotic dance. When she didn't pull away from him or resist, his spirit shouted in ecstasy. This was what he'd been waiting for. Grinding against her, the ache built up inside him. His cock hardened even more.

Whether she was aware or not, he didn't know, but then it happened. Her hand moved. Slowly but surely, it blazed a steaming hot trail down his chest, over his abs, stopping temporarily at the waistband of his underwear. His abdomen tensed as her fingers trailed the elastic around his waist.

Leaning his forehead against hers and his hands loosely on her hips, he moaned, "Jenna." He wanted to let her explore without feeling pressured. But, God, he wanted her. He wanted to run his hands all over her body and slip his fingers into her wet womanhood. A spot that was only inches away.

She ran her hand down the front of his crotch and found the opening in his underwear, brushing the side of his dick. It leapt under her touch and grew harder. He wanted to know if she was as ready as he was but didn't want to scare her.

"You're so soft," Jenna said, filled with wonder.

"I'm not sure what you're touching then," he said, chuckling. "I'm as hard as a rock."

His laughter quickly turned to a moan when she pulled him out of his underwear and wrapped her hand around him. She felt a heady sense of power as she slid her hand down his shaft causing him to tremble under her administrations.

She never expected it to feel like smooth velvet. Mesmerized, she watched her hand move over him through the rippling water, from the base to the tip. Would it hurt to have him inside her?

Jenna snapped her hand back so fast that one would have assumed she burned herself. Horror filled her soul. "Oh, God, what am I doing? I can't do this." Turning, she rushed out of the water, grabbed her clothes, and disappeared into the forest before Ethan even had a chance to respond.

Chapter Thirteen

Jenna picked up a rock and scraped it against another, marking their seventh day stranded. Her hopes and dreams of getting rescued were washing away like the white caps on the ocean waves.

They constantly had their signal fire going, as well as a huge SOS spelled out using large rocks on the beach. But what good would it do if no one flew close enough to see it? They had not seen a boat or a plane pass by the island since they arrived.

She wanted off the island. It was getting increasingly difficult to keep out of arm's reach of Ethan. Now that his leg was healing, he rarely left her alone.

Back when he could barely move, she could go gather berries to give herself some much needed quiet time, but now he insisted on protecting her from the ever-growing wolf menace. It had shown its face a time or two over the last few days and almost took a nip out of her thigh one evening when they were walking back from the waterfall.

"What do you want to do today?" he asked, intruding on her thoughts.

Sitting down across from him, she glanced at the tic-tac-toe designs etched in the sand. "Well, we've had our fair share of x's and o's, so what other game can you think of?"

"I can think of another activity related to x's and o's," he said, smirking.

Jenna pressed her lips together, with one side curling in exasperation as she rolled her eyes. "Only you could twist an innocent game into something more."

"I have an idea."

"Please not another skinny-dipping challenge."

"Can't harm a guy for trying."

She understood his needs. His desires. He was a red-blooded male. But she wasn't about to take a dalliance in that field, despite having almost travelled there a few days back. The moment she thought about doing it, all she could remember was how much it hurt before. Jenna shuddered. She wasn't about to go through that again.

Ethan glanced at her. "Cold?"

Jenna shrugged. She didn't really want to get into it with him. He'd asked enough questions the day she had left him standing in the water with a rather large man-problem. "So, what's your idea?" she asked, hoping he'd stay away from the other topic.

"Why don't we play truth or dare?"

Jenna leaned her head back against the tree and closed her eyes, sighing. "How old did you say you were?"

"Truth or dare has no age limit."

Somehow, his game idea didn't surprise her. He was always trying to find a way to either squeeze new information out of her or make things a little more exciting. She shook her head, declining his suggestion.

"Come on. We've exhausted all the other options already," he begged.

"Why don't we go on a hike instead?" she asked. "Your leg is doing well enough now."

"How about we make a deal? If you'll play truth or dare with me when we get back, I'll go on your hike."

"How about I go on the hike by myself?" she said, standing up.

Ethan had no intention of letting her go by herself, and he wasn't going to let her get off so easily from playing his game. "Are you chicken?"

"Goading me isn't going to work, you know," she said.

He placed his hands under his armpits and flapped his arms up and down as he stood up. "Bwack, bwack, bwack."

"Are you laying an egg or something?"

"Bwack, bwack, bwa—"

She slapped a hand over his mouth. "Okay, okay! I'll play. Just stop sounding like a mutated chicken."

Victory!

Jenna caved earlier than he thought she would. Ethan assumed he would have to badger her all day. A quiet evening every once in a while was okay, but he was itching to do something fun.

"On one condition though," she continued.

"What's that?"

"That we find a way back into that cavern."

"Why do you want to go back down there? It's not like we can do anything with our findings yet."

"It's been killing me. I want to see if there is an easier way down."

He'd seen enough of rocks in his lifetime that it didn't really matter to him either way. However, the sparkle in her eyes brought a smile to his face, and he couldn't help but succumb to it. "Okay, let's go."

Jenna launched herself into his arms. "Thank you. Thank you."

The moment she made contact, he lost his balance and fell over backwards. When they landed, she was on top, one leg trapped between his. Her hair fell like a tent over his face, blocking out everything but her. She went to jump up immediately, but he wrapped his arms around her, holding her in place.

"Can't we just stay like this all day?" he asked.

"You do realize where my leg is, right?" she replied, brushing her leg lightly against his balls.

He flinched but didn't release her. "One kiss and I'll let you go."

"You're a persistent son of a—" she started to say, but Ethan's lips claimed hers, moving over her soft ruby-red lips in a gentle caress, like a lover's massage.

Her breath, her taste—sweet and tangy—mingled with his, waking the lion of desire within him. He slid his hands up her sides, brushing her breasts with his thumbs, revelling in the shiver that rushed through her body.

"We shouldn't do this," she murmured but made no effort to pull away.

"Shhh," he whispered softly. He didn't want her thinking about anything, but what they were doing right now. She deserved to learn how to enjoy the pleasures of the flesh. And he wanted to be the one to teach her. Her innocence was taken from her, and he wanted to give a little of it back by cherishing her body.

He built characters in his story from the ground up, watched them as they grew throughout his work and became the people they were born to be. And he knew they were all on the same journey in life. This glitch, this blip in the ride that left them on this deserted island, was all part of the greater plan.

Ethan let his fingers rest lightly on her neck, as their lips performed a heavenly dance. Her movements tentative and his patient as he waited for her to open to him, letting her take her time. The light touch added kindling to the fire building within him. There was something special about being on this island with her. A glimpse into his own personal paradise.

She was like this exquisite angel sent from heaven. Her kisses were a divine intervention against his steel will to never let another woman into his heart. Gently increasing the pressure on her neck, he pulled her closer and deepened the kiss, encouraging her to open to him. After a moment's hesitation, her lips parted welcoming him inside. When their tongues touched, another shiver rippled through her body. He felt it all the way down to his toes, and his cock leapt at the possibilities.

Her scent intoxicated him and wrapped him in a cocoon. She jumbled his senses. Everything around them ceased to exist, except her. The salty air, mixed with smoke from their fire, didn't exist in that moment. Brushing his thumb along her neck just below her chin, he circled the rapid pulse beating beneath her skin. He loved the fact that she was as affected as he was. Her taut nipples pressed against his chest as she ground her sex into his erection, dry humping him. Something he hadn't done since high school. Normally their clothes would be off by now.

"Jenna," he moaned as she rubbed against him.

She barely heard him, focusing only on the ache causing her sex to swell wonderfully so. Her juices moistened her underwear as she continued moving. Was it supposed to do that? Was she supposed to be so wet?

Who cares.

No concern compared to the pleasurable whirlwind moving through her, taking her body higher and higher to a place above the rainbow. Away from every care in the world.

"I'm going to come," Ethan murmured against her ear.

His warm breath caused another ripple to run through her, stopping right between her legs. Her clitoris pulsated and throbbed. Her body climbed higher and higher towards an unknown peak. Was this what it felt like to have an out of body experience, flying on cloud nine?

Ethan's hands moved between them, slipping into her pants. He needed to feel her excitement on his fingers. She moaned momentarily as his movement put some space between them. Raising her upper body, she braced herself on her hands, digging them into the sand, giving him more room to explore.

When his finger moved between her folds, the intensity magnified a hundred-fold. Her vision blurred, and her hips bucked against him. It was like a lightning bolt passing through her body. All its energy gathering between her legs.

"Oh, God," she cried, her muscles clutching. His finger kept moving deliciously between her folds, pressing against her swollen bud. Tremor after tremor rushed through her, fireworks blinding her temporarily.

She couldn't stop moving and pressed harder against him. Wave after wave of pleasure overcame her senses and her sensibility. His hands suddenly gripped her hips and his eyes squeezed closed as he, too, joined her with his release, moaning her name.

When her vision returned, she looked down at his crotch and couldn't help but giggle. "You look like you peed yourself."

"You don't look that different, missy," he replied as he propped himself up on his elbows, pointing to the spot on her own pants.

Crawling off him, she glanced at herself and then him, her face heating. "I...uh..." she stammered, unsure of what to say.

If the grin spreading across his face was anything to go by, Ethan didn't seem to be too bothered by their predicament. He stood up and offered his hand. "Let's go get cleaned up."

Taking his hand, she allowed him to help her up, her legs wobbling. He waited until she was steady before he released her. He went ahead of her into the forest and for that she was grateful. Her wet underwear was making her walk as though she'd just gotten off a horse. Meanwhile, he was strutting along like he was the king of the jungle.

As he pushed a branch out of the way, the muscles in his tanned back tensed. Jenna wiped her mouth with the back of her hand. *Oh man, he's hot.* She shook her head to clear away the wayward thoughts. *Damn it, Jenna. Stop thinking that way. You don't need the trouble.*

Thwack!

A branch Ethan had pushed out of the way connected with her stomach, making her forget all about admiring him. She rubbed her belly. "Gee, thanks."

He looked over his shoulder. "Just making sure you're awake back there."

"Jerk," she replied, giving him a shove.

How could he be so incredibly sexy one minute and so irritatingly annoying the next? He was a master at leaving her emotions and her body in a heaping mess. One that was too tricky to sort.

"Would you like to walk in front of me instead?" he asked.

"And have your eyes on me the whole way?"

"I wouldn't mind."

"No thanks," she said, pushing him forward.

"You're pushy."

She stuck her tongue out at the back of his head just as another branch flew in her direction, but she managed to stop it. "You're purposely doing that."

"Am I?" he asked, giving her a cheeky grin as they entered into the clearing.

She shoved by him. "You're so infuriating."

He took hold of her arm and tossed her up over his shoulder, lugging her over to the water like a sack of potatoes.

"Don't you dare!" she cried.

"One...two...three."

Splooosh!

Into the water they went, Ethan's arms still wrapped firmly around her as they slipped beneath the surface. She pushed herself out of his arms and scrambled up for air.

When he popped up beside her, she smacked him on the shoulder. "You dolt! I could have drowned."

"Nah, I wouldn't have let that happen."

"My clothes are all wet now," she grumbled.

He shrugged and grinned. "Uh, wasn't that the point of coming here?"

She opened her mouth to refute him, but then snapped it closed. The damn man was always right. Their clothes needed to be washed and as much as she wanted to smack the smirk off his face, they were getting the rinse they needed. Heat rose to her cheeks as she remembered why.

He tapped her on the nose. "You're cute when you blush."

"Shut up," she replied, dunking him under the water. His words created an unaccustomed warm glow in her belly, followed by a growing ache in her nether regions. Why couldn't it disappear into a black hole? Her previous ability to not feel anything was a lot easier than the tornado wreaking havoc on her mind and body right now.

She was about to swim away when his hand wrapped around her ankle, giving it an "I'm pulling you under" warning. Jenna took a deep breath, and then suddenly found herself under water, face to face with the source of her lust and frustration. Floating there with him made her forget about her need to breathe. She was lost in a fantasy world of feelings that shouldn't be.

The sun's rays illuminated his toned body in a strange glow, like a strobe light set on disco, giving him an otherworldly appeal—a Norse god swooping in to capture his woman's heart, taking her captive.

He cupped the back of her neck and drew her in for a kiss, filling her with the breath of passion. His tender caress awakened her suppressed desires that were hidden for almost half a decade. His lips took hers on a journey over the yellow brick road, where the Cowardly Lion found his courage, the Tin Man his heart, and the Scarecrow his brain. Maybe it wasn't too late to find her sexuality and be normal again.

He kicked his feet, and they resurfaced again. He moved them towards the shallow end, not relinquishing her mouth for a second. Jenna loved the smooth feel of his lips against hers, warm and inviting. When his hands slid up her shirt, she shivered. Goosebumps covered her tanned skin.

"Ethan," she whispered huskily, her voice dripping with desire.

Ethan heard the desperate plea to show her the way. And he wasn't about to complain or reject her unspoken proposal. The last time they were here, she ran away. This time, there was no hesitation in her touch, nor in her words. She wanted it as much as he did.

Dipping his head, he kissed her neck. Her pulse vibrated against his lips. Her head rolled back as he sucked, leaving a red mark on her skin. His hands moved over her breasts, squeezing them slightly. She moaned as she leaned into his touch.

He'd almost forgotten what it was like to hold a real woman in his arms and not a money-grabber. The closest he had allowed himself to get to a woman was when he used to watch porn. It had kept his body partially satisfied, but he knew it was staged, so the satisfaction was never quite the same. And touching himself didn't compare to having her hands traveling over his body, leaving trails of lava seeping into his pores, making his blood flood to his groin. How anyone could be satisfied with porn was beyond him.

"Can I take off your shirt?" he begged, grabbing the edge of the material.

Before she even had a chance to finish nodding, he pulled the shirt over her head, tossing it on the beach.

"Boy, you're quick," she murmured, staring down at the water as colour creeped into her cheeks.

"Only when it suits the moment." He stepped back, letting his eyes wander over her newly revealed flesh. "You are absolutely stunning."

She shook her head, her cheeks reddening even more. "No, I'm not."

Lifting his hand, he ran his finger along her cleavage. "I think you should let me be the judge of that."

"I'm not sure you're thinking clearly enough to be a judge."

"My friend thinks you are, too," he said, as he guided her hand below the water. "See."

"That's just sex deprivation."

"And I know just the cure," he replied, undoing the button on her pants. When she didn't slap his hand away, he gave an inward shout of joy. Excitement built within him as he pulled down her zipper.

She gasped when his hand slipped inside her pants and pushed her underwear aside, allowing his fingers to slip between her womanly folds, her silky nectar mixing with the water around them.

"My God, you are so wet."

Jenna held onto his shoulders; afraid she was going to fall. Her legs had taken on a mind of their own, shaking relentlessly. "My pants, take them off," she pleaded. When his hand pulled away to do her bidding, the tsunami of sensations building inside her ebbed. Missing the feeling, she grabbed his hand, pressing it against her. "Wait, no! Don't stop."

He chuckled. "Don't worry. This will just take a sec."

And true to his word, her pants were gone in less than a second, followed by her underwear. The only article of clothing still remaining was her bra. He turned her around in his arms so that her back was to his front, his hard length pressing against her back.

She tried to reach behind herself to touch him, but he grabbed her hands, holding them against her chest with his. "Hey!"

"Time for that later. Just rest your head back and feel."

"But I can't feel what I—" Her words trailed off when his hand slid between her legs again. His fingers made themselves right at home, trailing circles over her clit, making her weak in the knees. "Holy Jeepers. How do you do that?"

He released her hands and wrapped his arm around her waist to help her stay standing. "The best is yet to come," he whispered, giving her a gentle love bite on her shoulder.

"Are you turning into a vampire on me?" she asked, letting out another gasp when his fingers dipped inside her, hitting a spot that came alive at his touch.

"A vampire of pleasure," he said in a hauntingly vampiric voice. "Here to serve."

Jenna's giggle turned into a moan as the speed of his fingers inside her quickened. She wrapped her arm around his neck, her hips moving with the rhythm of his fingers. She had no idea what was happening to her body, but she liked the heat building within her, swirling around like a fiery tornado. The feeling was unlike any other.

Closing her eyes, she allowed herself to take everything he was giving her. How the heck had she missed doing this all these years? It was like her body had previously been a foreign entity and was just now becoming her own again. And she wanted more.

Her hand tightened on the back of his neck, her body racing to the peak. The feel of him against her back, and the way his fingers moved in and out had her seeing fireworks in her mind. Her entire body felt like it was about to be shot out of a cannon, ready to burst into a thousand colours.

Blues...purples...pinks. Oh, God, she could see them all. She rocked against his hand wildly as his fingers took her to new heights.

When her body went over the edge, Jenna cried out loud. Her muscles clenched around him, pushing his fingers out. She wanted to cry out at the loss, but he pressed his hand against her sensitized bud, making her moan with approval. He moved in slow agonizing circles, making her body rock, as wave after wave of sensations rolled through her. Her mind went blank, unable to focus on anything until her body slowly stopped pulsating.

What the heck was that?

She thought the orgasm she had before was intense, but this time it was out of this world. Her mind was still spinning in the aftermath when Ethan pulled away from her, nearly making her fall over. He kept one hand on her back to help steady her.

Her breathing came hard and fast. "Ethan?"

"Don't worry, hun, I'm not going anywhere." He took her hand and turned her to face him. His pants and underwear were both long gone.

"When...h-how?" she asked, staring at his erection bobbing in the water below the surface and then over at his clothes on the beach.

"Does it matter?" he asked, pulling her against him.

She ran her hands up his chest, linking them behind his neck, as she gazed up at him. "Nope."

He slipped his hard length between her legs, moving it back and forth against her wet heat. Her breath caught in her chest as the ache inside her grew.

Cradling her face in his hands, he said, "Jenna, I want to be inside you. If you want me to stop, now would be a good time to tell me."

She rose to her tiptoes and pulled his head down slightly. "I'll knock you on your back if you stop now," she whispered in his ear.

That seemed to be all the encouragement he needed. He had her up in his arms, with her legs wrapped around him in less than a second. Jenna could feel him probing her entrance and for a second, she froze, making him freeze. "You okay?" he asked.

Her mind was trying to form pictures of her past, but she fought the images. They weren't going to wreck this moment. She wasn't going to let them. Ethan hadn't hurt her yet. He wasn't going to hurt her. His gentle movements were a testament to that fact.

Focus on that, Jenna. He rescued you and has been nothing but kind.

He wasn't Mathew. He wasn't Ryan. Her silence must have alarmed him because he loosened his grip on her and slowly lowered her back down.

"Hell no," she said, tightening the grip she had on his waist. She wasn't going to let the memory have power over her anymore. "I want you, Ethan." And she was going to have him, and no past—no memory—was going to get in the way.

"Jenna, if you aren't ready, I understand," he said, pressing his forehead against hers.

Unlocking one hand from behind his neck, she slid it between them and grabbed a hold of him, guiding his length into her before he had a chance to put distance between them. Her body took a second to adjust to him. They both stood there, frozen in this moment of time.

"You're so tight," Ethan moaned, his arms tightening around her again. Her muscles pulsated around him as her body slowly accepted him into hers. She felt like a virgin to him, so fresh and new. He couldn't believe the gift she had given him. Just that fact alone had him on the brink of an orgasm without even moving.

Then she moved. It was subtle. A slight movement of her hips, but it ricocheted through him. "Don't move," he begged, hoping to make it last a little longer, just in case this was the only chance they had.

But she didn't stop. Jenna ground her hips into him like a pro. Her moans mingled with his as he fought to keep control, his breathing rapid and shallow. He held her hips still, but she still found a way to move.

"Jenna," he croaked, his resolve quickly deteriorating.

"Harder, Ethan, please."

All hope of waiting disappeared as she contracted around him, letting him know she was as close as he was. Tightening his grip, his hands splaying across her butt, he thrust into her, harder and faster. His toes dug into the sand as she rode him to greater heights than he's ever been ridden before. His balls tightened painfully against him, fire building within his hardened cock.

He squeezed his eyes closed, as electricity charged through him, aiming right for his gut. His blood pounded in his ears, but all he could focus on was the overwhelming rush to the finish line. She moaned. Her breathing hot and heavy, as her muscles continued to tense around him with her own release.

He couldn't stop himself. He was coming. "Oh, God."

A blinding flash of light overtook him as every single nerve in his body exploded with intensity. His body convulsed as he emptied himself into her. He rocked against her until the last seed was spent. He pressed his forehead against hers and fought to catch his breath, his legs shaking.

"Wow," she whispered.

Unhooking her legs, Ethan let her down gently, not even sure he could respond. He didn't trust his voice not to waver.

He hadn't expected sex with her to be so mind blowing. Hell, he couldn't even remember a time that it ever felt like that with anyone else. Backing away from her, shaken by what they had just experienced, he dunked himself underwater, hoping it would cool his jets. He swam all the way to the waterfall before coming up for air.

Turning, he looked at Jenna, her eyes full of tears. Devastation was written all over her face as she wiped her eyes with the back of her wrists. She shook her head furiously and then waded towards the beach. Grabbing her clothes, she ran into the forest, naked, except for her bra.

Ethan scratched his head. "What the hell?"

Chapter Fourteen

Ethan wasted no time in following her, not allowing her to escape. Much to his surprise, he didn't have to go very far. He saw her behind a tree putting her clothes on, and he took a second to slip his pants on before she saw him.

"Jenna?"

"Leave me alone."

"I don't understand."

"Of course, you don't. Why would you," she snapped, as she yanked her pants up to her hips.

When she was about to run off again, he grabbed her arm, determined to find out what the hell was going through that frustratingly pretty little head of hers. "Please, tell me what's wrong."

"Let me go," she said, ice lacing her voice.

He released her arm and took a step back, brow furrowed in confusion. "I don't know what I did, but I'm sorry."

She sighed and leaned back against the tree, tears flowing down her cheeks. That's when he saw the raw emotion in her eyes, the flash of pain, mixed with hurt. "I know it's not your fault. I just suck at stuff like this."

"At what?"

"Sex."

Ethan bopped his ear with the palm of his hand, certain he'd heard her wrong. "Who told you that?"

"It's okay. I get it," she replied, struggling to pull the shirt over her head. Finally, her head poked through the neckline and as she went to put her arms through, he grabbed the sleeves, tying them up.

"Hang on just a minute," he said, keeping a firm grip on the shirt. Doing so prevented her from flipping him on his back or hitting him. He was going to get a solid answer out of her if it was the last thing he did. "Talk to me."

Jenna tried to back away from him, but the tree got in her way. The last thing she wanted to do was talk about it, especially to him of all people. Why did he want to rub it in her face? "Please, just let me go," she begged.

With great care, he cupped her chin and made her look up at him. "Hun, you definitely didn't suck."

"Yeah, right. That's why you left me standing there like an i-idiot," she replied, her voice breaking.

"Girl, you had my body burning like a flippin' inferno. I needed a few moments to process my own emotions. I haven't let a woman get this close to me in a long time."

Looking into his eyes, she felt like she had just stepped off a cliff and was falling into the endless abyss of her newly awakened feelings of passion. His eyes were dark and full of lustful excitement.

"Really?"

"Do you need proof?" he asked, pulling her against him. "I don't usually get hard again so fast."

His cock pressed against her belly, making her parts begin their dance again, waking up the dormant sexual beast within her. She wasn't exactly sure how to respond. What the heck did she know about a male's anatomy? He could be pulling her leg for all she knew.

"And I'm supposed to believe that?"

"I stopped caring about sex when my name was smeared all over the television."

"Seriously? You all but offered me your bed in our interview," she said, her cheeks reddening at the thought.

He grinned sheepishly. "It was my lousy attempt to scare you off."

"Didn't quite go as you planned then."

"Nope. Thanks to a certain ninja lady, I had my first cold bath of the trip."

"First?" she asked, looking up at him again, wishing against all wishes that she hadn't made eye contact. His were a dark smouldering brown that threatened to devour her silly, knocking her off kilter.

"You've made me take a couple."

"Why?"

"Don't you feel why?" He moved his hips slightly, reminding her of his hard-on.

Her insides twitched, itching to take him inside her again. She'd been tight when he first took her, and it burned a little until her body caved and welcomed him in, but it didn't feel like the way she remembered. It didn't hurt. And the flashbacks she'd been used to getting any time she thought about sex didn't overtake her like before.

The murderous beast caged within her didn't claw its way out. Instead, it stayed away. Could they go two-for-two? Her nipples hardened at the thought and moisture dripped through her already wet panties and down her leg. Jeepers. What was she turning into? A sex fiend?

"Ethan." She cringed at the needy tone that creeped into her voice. Clearing her throat, she tried again. "I think we should start to head back to the beach, before you know who jumps out of the bushes."

He glanced around, head tilted slightly as though he was listening to the sounds of life surrounding them—the birds, the rustling of the leaves in the wind, other critters nattering around them. "I suppose you're right."

Taking a step back, he released her shirt, giving her room to finish getting dressed. She suppressed a moan of displeasure at the distance he'd put between them. The loss of his body heat made her feel like she'd just lost a limb.

How the hell did things turn upside down so fast? She gave him a side glance as she walked past him. The damn man had to be a succubus in disguise. And she was being reeled in like a fish on a line. It was so peculiar, considering these things didn't happen to her in real life. Maybe the island had something to do with it. She could almost believe that there was a love starved ghost hiding somewhere that decided to make them his pet project because he was bored.

He held out his hand. "Ready to go?"

Never! But she took his hand anyway and followed him back to camp, wishing like mad that his sculpted back was covered. Using the back of her hand, she swiped at the drool pooling at the edge of her mouth.

∽

The next night, Jenna was lying on her back beside the fire that Ethan had just finished stoking. Stars filled the night sky, sparkling around a bright full moon. "Do you ever wonder if there is life out there?" she asked.

"It wouldn't surprise me. Our planet is one of thousands out there."

"Do you think they have sick people, too?"

"I doubt we have the universal monopoly on the subject." Ethan shoved the stick back into the fire, embers flying into the air.

"I often dream about waking up on another planet and being normal for once."

"Would you settle for an island?"

Rolling onto her side, she asked, "What do you mean?"

"I think you're more normal than you think."

"Right, that's why I act like the werebeast from hell the minute I wake up."

"I'm not sure if you noticed, but you kissed me this morning as opposed to shoving a stick in my chest. I call that progress."

She caught his gaze. Flames from the fire danced in his eyes, making her cheeks burn. Somehow during the night, she crawled into the makeshift tent next to him unconsciously. When she awoke his arm was around her waist, and it felt like the most natural thing in the world. She had rolled over and kissed him, along with a few other things, too, then he rolled on top of her, and she was out of there like a bat out of hell.

Ethan's face had suddenly changed, becoming Mathew, then Ryan, until she didn't know what was real anymore. His hand became a monster's claw, tearing at her sanity. His lips a black vortex, sucking her into a never-ending nightmare.

"Did you forget that I almost bopped you in the eye?"

"Not intentionally this time, so that's definitely progress." He grinned, his teeth sparkling with the light of campfire. "Shall we try again now that you're more awake?

Her stomach bubbled with excitement as she remembered his lips brushing against her belly, but then a crawling shiver roamed over her body, beginning from the inside out. Squeezing her eyes closed, Jenna pushed the pain away. "I could have hurt you, Ethan."

"I know, but you didn't. You controlled it this time, and you will again."

"You have more faith in me than I do."

"It has to start somewhere, right?" Ethan planned to help her see herself through his eyes. He'd seen the change in her demeanour and attitude ever since she told him her story. It was like a few of her demons were exorcised from her body.

"I suppose."

"Honey, do you realize how far you've come in the time we've been here? I couldn't even touch you before."

And that was not something he was ever going to forget. She gave herself to him—him of all people, even after he told her his story. She could have chosen not to believe him, and that he really did do something to the girl, but she didn't.

Hope was beginning to brighten her disposition, and it was beautiful to watch. It came in spurts, but he would take anything at this point. They could be stuck on the island for a long time, just the two of them, and he'd rather have a companion than an enemy.

"Look, a shooting star!" she said, her words rushed.

By the time he looked, it was already gone. "Did you make a wish?"

"Yep."

"What did you wish for?"

"I never wish and tell?"

"I think that phrase is supposed to be kiss and tell."

"Are you a phrase Nazi?"

"Is that anything like a grammar Nazi?"

Jenna shook her head, but Ethan could see the grin playing on her lips as she threw a blackberry at him. He expertly caught it between his teeth. "Good aim," he said.

"Shut up."

They lapsed into a familiar silence. Something that had become a habit before falling asleep. He loved just listening to the world around them, and to her, as she slipped out of this plane and into the world of dreams. Her sleep was nowhere near as fretful as it once was.

Rolling onto his side, he watched her. Her arms were propped behind her head, and her eyes were closed, lips slightly parted. She was his own personal sleeping beauty but kissing her would likely make him wind up with a stake through the heart. He would have to wait until she was conscious again.

Flopping on his back, he changed the direction of his thoughts. There was no point in letting his mind go where his body couldn't at the moment. However, his mind loved going off on a tangent. It was

Beneath His Hands

the writer's curse. He was always up all hours of the night because his mind would cycle through a story idea, like he was watching a movie, and then he'd have to write it down so he wouldn't forget.

His mom always used to get mad at him. She'd come into his room at midnight and find him awake at his desk with a pen and paper. No one understood his need to write the story down when the ideas were fresh in his mind.

"Mom, I hope you're doing okay."

His dad, Joshua Barrett, had died a few years back. She never really moved on from the loss. Instead, his mom put all her focus on him, and now Ethan was gone, too.

Did she think he was dead? Had she planned the funeral already? He knew that if his crew made it back, they wouldn't have brought any positive news with them. He went overboard, which usually meant a death sentence. And he knew that if it wasn't for the dolphin's help, they would have died.

"Don't give up, Mom. I'm still here," he whispered, praying that the wind would carry his voice to her.

～

Martha, Ethan's mom, walked over to the calendar with a bright red sharpie and marked the 8th red X in a row before slowly lowering her aching body onto the brown flower-patterned couch. Her blood-shot blue eyes focused on the picture of her son on the coffee table. He was sitting on the beach, bucket and shovel in hand. He was only about two years old when it was taken. His chubby baby face, covered with sand, was aglow with smiles.

Picking up the photo, she held it against her chest, hoping to ease the sharp pains that took up residence there. She had been managing okay until she'd heard that the crew was recovered, except for her son and Jenna. Since then, her chest hurt so badly she'd even had a hospital stay while they ran some tests. They had initially suspected a possible heart attack.

It wasn't unusual for her son to go off the grid for days or weeks at a time to finish a screenplay he was working on. She'd grown accustomed to not hearing from him regularly, but this not knowing was killing her slowly. Her heart twisted more and more each day knowing that most of his crew had been found except for them.

She didn't want to think that he was dead, and she didn't want to think she had possibly led Jenna on a trip that would totally destroy what confidence she had built over the years working at Martha's company. That girl was a dream come true. Jenna had helped Martha through her husband's death two years ago.

Her son had been out on the water at the time and all her friends were on cruises. She'd been at the office with Jenna that fateful day when the police arrived. The girl had been her rock, helping her out around the office. Jenna had stayed with her until she could hold herself together long enough to talk to her clients.

She knew that Jenna could help break her son out of his rut. He needed someone as strong-willed as he was. But she didn't know what was going to happen now. They were both missing, and she could only hope they were together.

When the doorbell rang, she carefully put the picture back down on the table and stood up. She opened the door to find Iris standing there, all flustered, cheeks wet with tears.

"What's wrong, dear?" Martha asked.

"Did they call you?"

"Not that I'm aware of, but my phone is on the charger."

"They've called off the rescue."

"Like hell they have!"

Iris paced the room, her hands tugging on her hair. "They said they had already extended the search longer than normal. Something about a seventy-two-hour period, blah, blah, blah."

"Seventy-two hours, my ass."

"They are going based on the reports of the crew, and the fact that they have not found anything else in the area. Apparently, the boat only had one life raft. They don't think they could have survived without one. There is a press conference about it tonight."

"Your husband and his friend are out searching, right? Have you heard from him?"

"Not since the day before yesterday. I'm a little worried though. A storm is moving in again."

A little worried? Martha struggled not to chuckle. The woman didn't know the meaning of the term little. "How many more islands do they have left to check?"

"Not sure, it's moving pretty slowly by the sounds of things. Some of the islands are huge, but they are just skirting around the edge of them, searching for signs of life or debris."

"That sounds smart. If I know my son, he'll make sure they stay in a visible spot."

"Same with Jenna. She's been through something like this already."

Martha nodded her head. She'd heard the story from Jenna's own mouth, including all the trials and tribulations that the girl endured after she was rescued. "I don't know how she managed to keep going. That girl of yours is amazing, Iris."

The woman walked over to the window, resting her shoulder on the frame as she looked outside, appearing to watch the dark clouds swarming above them. "Do you think we'll ever see them again?"

"I'm not going to believe otherwise until the fat lady sings. Have a seat. I'm going to go get ready. We're going to crash that press conference," Martha said.

"Are you sure? I really don't want to go to jail," Iris said hesitantly, ringing her hands together.

"Don't worry. You can hang out at the back while I go and raise hell."

That seemed to appease Jenna's mom because she said, "I'm ready when you are."

Daniel lowered the binoculars and smacked the railing of the boat as they completed their pass around the next island. There were no signs of life. Again. They still had another five islands to check, but there was only one more that was in the vicinity of where the boat went down.

"Hey, don't wreck my boat," Brent said from behind him.

"Sorry," he muttered.

"Don't sweat it. I'd probably be doing the same."

"If I don't bring her home, my marriage is done for. My wife will never forgive me."

"We'll find her." Brent said, clapping Daniel on the back as thunder rumbled overhead.

"Boss, we have a bad storm moving in," Joey, his first mate, yelled from the cockpit.

"Okay, move 'er out into open water."

"Can't we anchor in the cove we saw back there?" Daniel hooked his thumb behind him, where the beach disappeared around a corner. It seemed to be the perfect spot to hide out as they waited for the bad weather to pass.

"It's too dangerous. The cove is on the west side of the island and the storm's moving east. We'd run aground or hit a rock," Brent replied, running a hand through his thick black hair.

"But isn't it more dangerous out there?" Daniel trusted his buddy's expertise, but this man's boat wasn't even half the size of the yacht that Jenna was on and hers went down.

"Nah, we stand a chance riding the waves out here."

"Is there anything I can do?"

"Best for you to stay below deck until the storm passes."

Life jackets were handed out to everyone just in case, but his friend appeared confident that they'd make it out of the storm unscathed. The last thing they needed was to be stranded, too. Iris would find him and kill him for worrying her even more.

Doing up the buckles on the lifejacket, he headed to the cabin below. Life didn't feel real lately. If he were honest with himself, it hadn't felt real since she disappeared the first time. And watching the baby grow in her belly did little to help him forget what happened to her.

How do you watch something like that? He wanted to murder the Mathew for taking advantage of his baby girl. And if the other kid, Derek, wasn't dead already, he would have been more than happy to do it himself. He couldn't imagine what the hell was going through their minds. It still burned him up inside years later.

They'd all gone to counselling to try and muddle their way through the mess, but he couldn't sit there and regurgitate it over and over. He couldn't stomach listening to his daughter suffer and the fleeting glances she'd given him during the sessions.

Yes, he was a weakling. He knew it. But not anymore. His baby girl was going to come home, and he was going to go back to counselling with her. Hopefully, help her see that he wasn't the enemy. They were going to recover together.

"Please, Jenna, be okay."

With the storm coming, their search would be delayed, and the clouds would mess with the satellite. He wouldn't be able to call home and let Iris know the latest news. The weather was as unpredictable as their lives had been.

He stepped into his room and sat down on the chair in the corner, remembering how he used to play checkers with Jenna on the table in the saloon when the weather wasn't very good on their past trips. She loved the game until she grew too old and started thinking it was lame to play checkers. It was then he tried to teach her to fish.

The first fish she caught was a small slimy—her own words—trout. He could never get her to go fishing after that. To eat them was okay, but she'd leave the catching to someone else, namely him or Brent.

Now, his daughter was a regular wilderness go-getter. Her room was full of survival books. He'd seen her gut a fish with the best of them. She didn't do it because she enjoyed it though. She'd become a prepper in case anything ever happened again. She wanted to make sure she was prepared for anything that came her way.

Daniel jerked forward as the boat hit a wave hard, his heart hammering in his chest. The sound of thunder rolled along the wall of his room as wave after wave smashed the hull. He hoped the boat could hold up under the pressure.

If their boat was being knocked around this much, what hope did his daughter have of surviving a storm like this after going overboard? A dark shadow descended upon his spirit, gripping it like a vice, squeezing the life right out of him.

It reminded him of the darkness of his childhood, of the boy who never smiled, nor had a reason to smile. His father was the monster that lurked under every bed, the poltergeist haunting his every waking moment. And when his mother disappeared, he knew that his father was the reason.

His whole family was cursed. What other answer could there be for their run of bad luck? But Daniel was determined to break their losing streak. He wasn't going to allow his life to be turned upside down anymore.

"Bad luck, you're going down!"

As if rebuking him, a huge wave hit the side of the boat, knocking him off the chair. It's like the universe was out to get them, but he wasn't going to let it win. He just wished he could do more to help out during the storm, instead of feeling helpless.

He pulled out his wallet and reached for a picture tucked away inside the bill fold. Unfolding the photo, he smoothed out the creases. Jenna was only 5 years old, and she was sitting on top of his shoulders. They were on a family vacation to Disneyland. She was wearing a princess dress and tiara.

Daniel sighed wistfully. What he wouldn't give to have those happy days back. The days before his adult life and his marriage went to hell. If they were ever together again, he'd take his wife and daughter on a long vacation, focusing only on them for as long as it took to see the excitement and happiness in their eyes again.

When the boat stopped rocking, he put the picture back in his wallet and went to find everyone. Heading out of his room, he found the crew in the cockpit. They were removing their life jackets and checking out the map.

"We'll check out this one next," Brent said, pointing to the island closest to their current location. "We should be there before nightfall."

Daniel slapped his hands on the table. "Sounds good. Let's get the show on the road. It's time to bring my daughter home."

Chapter Fifteen

"Argh, this is so annoying," Jenna complained as she flopped down on the ground, emptying the sand out of her shoe.

They had spent all day searching for another way into the cave, but they couldn't find anything. Ethan did the same and watched the sand pour out of his shoe. How did so much sand wind up in a shoe when it didn't have any holes? Heck, how had his shoes even made it to the beach still on his feet?

"Don't worry. It's not like anyone is going to beat us to it," Ethan said, pulling off his pants, hoping to go for a dip in the water. Their hike took them to the top of a mountain, and he had broken a sweat. "Wanna join me?"

She shook her head. "The water is all yours."

Just the mere question had her blushing, which he loved making her do. Despite their recent dalliances and all she'd been through, she hadn't lost her inner innocence, the inner beauty that shines through, and it was one of the most appealing things about her. She came across as intense and harsh at the beginning, but there was a softness about her.

"Are you sure you aren't just trying to avoid getting wet with me?" he asked, wiggling his eyebrows suggestively.

"As if it were that easy," she mumbled, slipping her shoe back on.

He knew exactly what she meant, and it was for that reason he kneeled down and undid her shoe again, and slowly took it off, letting his fingers caress her instep.

"What are you doing?" she whispered, biting her bottom lip.

"Taking care of our problem."

"Problem?" she echoed.

"It has a very easy solution."

"What if I can't?" A pained expression passed over her face. "What if the last time was a one-off thing?"

"Only one way to know for sure," he replied, removing her other shoe.

"I don't want to hurt you."

Taking her face in his hands, he kissed her softly. "You take the lead, then. Go as far as you feel comfortable."

He knew she needed to feel in control, and as weird as it felt, he chose relinquish control to her. She deserved to make the choices herself.

"I don't want you to get mad."

"I just want whatever we do to be enjoyable for you, Jenna."

Tears sparkled in her eyes as she reached out to him, resting her palm against his cheek. "What are you doing to me, Ethan Barrett?"

"I don't know, but I like it."

"Me, too," she said, her breath hitching quietly.

He covered her hand with his as a flood of warmth moved through him at her words, his heart overflowing with feelings of love for her already. Something he'd never expected to feel again. But if this was how good it felt to be with her, he was more than happy to let the cards fall where they may.

Smiling, he tugged on her shirt. "Come here."

Without hesitation, she moved into his arms, fitting perfectly as though her body was made for his. No one else had ever felt so right in his arms. He couldn't help but wonder if they would have discovered their feelings for each other if they were still on his boat, him distracted by his work and her by her memories.

He was certain they were on this island for a reason. There had to be a master storyteller, carving their lives with his pen. Why else would a dolphin care about helping them? Ethan knew the whole thing couldn't have been a coincidence. Looking down at the woman in his arms, he was absolutely certain someone was stacking the deck in their favour.

Jenna let her fingers roam across his chest, settling his skin ablaze. "I wouldn't expect a writer to be so buff," she commented, circling his nipple with her index finger.

"I work out when I get writer's block. I guess it pays off," he said, giving her a boyish grin.

"Mhmm," she murmured with appreciation. "So, are you going to kiss me or what, sailor?"

"I thought you'd never ask." Taking her face in his hands, he lowered his head and kissed her, loving the warmth of her lips. He could feel his soul reaching out to hers, creating an unbreakable string that would bond them together as soulmates forever. No other woman in his life could ever be what Jenna was becoming in his heart —his woman, his one and only.

Running his tongue along her bottom lip, he coaxed her into opening for him. When their tongues touched, love exploded inside him and aimed right for his heart.

A low purr emanated from her throat as she pressed up against him. He ached to be inside her, but he didn't want to rush her. And he knew she was definitely worth the wait.

Pulling back slightly, he said, "I seem to remember a certain woman who promised to play a game with me."

"So, you'd rather play a game than this?"

"We could make it a sexual game."

"How so?"

"Play never have I ever. If I say something and you've done it, you have to remove an article of clothing."

Her gaze wandered down his half naked body and back up again. "I think you are at a slight disadvantage in that area."

"One second," He stepped away from her, grabbed his pants, and put them on. "How's that?"

"Better, but you're still wearing less than me," she said, the corner of her lips curling upwards.

He knew by the look on her face that she had come up with a solution that wasn't going to be in his favour. "I'd put on my shirt, but it's back at the beach."

Jenna looked down at her crinkled pink shirt and pulled it over her head, offering it to him. "Here you go."

He took it and held it with two fingers as he scrunched up his nose.

Her eyes twinkled with laughter, and she coughed, hoping to cover up the giggle bubbling in her throat. "It isn't going to bite you."

"But it's pink."

She clapped her hands. "Good boy, you know your colours. But, unfortunately, I'm fresh out of stickers for you."

Dropping her shirt on the ground, he grabbed her around the waist and tickled her side.

"Mercy," she cried, laughing as she collapsed to the ground, attempting to protect her sides from his relentless fingers.

"Stop!" Jenna laughed so hard that no sound came out. She tried to crawl away, but he tightened his arm around her waist, digging into her sides again. Whoever invented tickling needed a swift kick in the ass. Finding her way to her knees, she elbowed him in the gut and knocked him down. Without wasting any time, she straddled him.

"That was a dirty play," he grumbled, the annoyance in his tone was betrayed by the twinkle in his eyes as his hands came to rest on her hips.

She winked at him as she ran her fingers lazily across his chest. "Good to know I haven't lost my touch."

"I swear you're packing an army in that body of yours."

Jenna slid her hand between them, touching his bulge. "Feels like you're packing, too,"

Sitting on top of him, she waited for the anxiety to come, like it did that morning, but it didn't; instead, she felt in control, powerful even. There were no feelings of claustrophobia or fear, just anticipation and a strange fluttery feeling in her chest.

"We're ready for action, boss," he said, saluting her.

She rested her forehead on his chest and chuckled. "You are so cheesy."

"I like you like this."

Cocking her head, she looked at him. "Like what?"

"Free as the wind. Island life suits you."

Running her index finger in circles across his chest, she said, "All this feels natural somehow, like it was meant to be this way."

Ethan let his hands wander over her hips and up her sides. "I couldn't agree more."

A full body shiver rippled through her, reaching deep inside her very being. Her spirit was elated that she could finally feel something more than dread. She wanted more of him. Needed more.

His eyes turned dark with need as he watched her, and they filled with an emotion she couldn't place. No one had ever looked at her that way before. No malice or hate existed in his gaze, just heat. Awe struck heat. She felt like her body parts were melting into a rich, elegant, liquidity goodness, getting ready to mould together with him.

"I want to try again," she said, licking her bottom lip.

He grinned. "I'm up for it."

A giggle bubbled inside her. He literally was up, his erection pressing into her crotch. Jenna loved the feel of his hard cock against her. She never thought the day would come when she wanted what everyone else in the world considered normal...sex.

Letting her hand dip between them, she pressed her hand against his swollen length still hidden by his pants. He closed his eyes and moaned softly. Raw energy shot through her, building to a head in her belly, as moisture gathered below.

Reaching for his sweats, she undid the drawstring and tried to pull them down, but they wouldn't budge. "Lift your hips," she ordered.

He smirked but did as he was told. "Bossy little thing, aren't you?"

In one quick motion, she removed both his underwear and his pants, freeing him…maybe even freeing herself a little, too. The monster that haunted her every waking breath was silent. He was still there, lurking in the dark shadows, but lately he was hiding from the light that illuminated her heart.

His light—the man lying beneath her. Somehow, he made the darkness flee, like her own personal saviour. Slowly, she teased him with her hand, running it up and down his shaft. His fingers tightened on her thighs.

"Jenna!" he moaned.

"I wanna watch," she replied, her voice strangely husky.

"Ugh, don't tell me that."

"Why?"

"It's hot hearing you say that," he replied, his breath hitching when her fingers close over him.

She loved having him at her mercy in such a pleasurable way, and he didn't seem to mind in the slightest. "I know I don't have much experience, but isn't that a good thing?"

"Yes…and…no," he said between breaths.

Their talking grew silent and all she could focus on was his body's reaction to her touch. His cock was ramrod straight and hard, yet his skin was soft against her fingers, and she watched as his balls tightened, drawing closer to his body. Ethan's eyes were drifting closed now. His arms were stretched out lazily against the sand.

His tip glistened in the sunlight, a tell-tale sign of his excitement. Leaning down, she ran her tongue over the head of his cock, tasting his sweet saltiness. When her mouth closed around him, taking in his length, his hips bucked off the ground.

"Oh geez, Jenna!" he gasped in surprise, his hands suddenly in her hair, moving with her as she pulled him deeper in her mouth. It reminded her of sucking on a Popsicle, but none tasted as fine as this, nor as exotic. A purring noise formed in the back of her throat, vibrating against him, making him moan out loud.

"You're killing me, woman!"

Jenna glanced up at him. He was propped up on his elbows, watching her administrations with lust boiling in his eyes, panting. She closed her mouth, creating a seal around him, and sucked hard. His eyes rolled into the back of his head as pleasure spread across his face.

"I'm about to come," he warned.

Jenna leaned back on her haunches, all prepared to watch the wonder of him coming unglued at her touch, when suddenly, the wind was knocked out of her lungs as she was hit hard and launched sideways.

Chapter Sixteen

Ethan stared at his blood covered hands, and then over at the mound of unmoving grey fur on the ground. The battle didn't take long, and it was over before he even realized it, leaving him dazed for a moment.

The wolf had caught them unaware. He didn't even have time to put his pants on. Instinctively, he had grabbed the closest decent sized rock and brought it down on the beast's head. He didn't stop until Jenna weakly grabbed his arm and said, 'Enough.'

He took her in his arms, smoothing the hair away from her face. "Are you okay?"

"A little worse for wear, but I think I'll live."

"Come on. Let's get you back to the beach."

"I second that idea." She grimaced as he helped her up. He looked down at her and saw deep puncture wounds on her bloody forearm.

"Shit, he got you good. Let's rinse it off before we go." Helping her over to the pond, they rinsed off her wound, and then Ethan picked up her shirt and wrapped it around her arm. He could only hope it wouldn't get infected. With no antibiotics, they'd be in a whole heap of trouble. As they were walking, he saw the same plants that she had placed on his wound before and grabbed a handful of them.

Jenna smiled, despite the pain running rampant in her eyes. "You've got a good memory."

Ethan helped her to her usual place beside the fire, and she gingerly sat down, cradling her arm. He knew there was no way they could give her stitches, but hopefully the plant-based cure would do the trick, like it did for him.

He shuddered to think what it would have felt like to have his dick chomped on by the animal. It was the thing nightmares were made of. Even having it flailing about as he attacked the animal made him feel sick in his gut, not that he thought about it at the time.

Sitting cross legged in front of her, he placed the plant on his lap and examined her arm. The wolf left a deep bite right around the circumference of her forearm. With all the blood flowing, it was hard to tell whether he nicked an artery, but it wasn't squirting, so that had to be a good sign. Right? "What do I do now?" he asked.

"Roll the leaves in your hand to release the oil."

She guided him through the steps, and soon, her shirt was wrapped tightly around the wound. "I wish you wouldn't have killed him though," she said softly.

"What was I supposed to do? He wouldn't let go of you."

"He was only following his instincts."

Ethan's lips pursed and his jaw line hardened. His eyes dark and intense. "So was I, I wasn't going to let him take you away from me."

"I'm not worth risking your life for, or his life for that matter."

"You are worth it to me."

"That's because I'm the only other person here."

"It's not that and you know it."

Squeezing her eyes closed, she inhaled deeply and breathed in the fresh salty air. She didn't want to contemplate what his words meant. Her newfound feelings still scared her, and she wasn't ready to admit them yet. And she didn't know if she ever would be.

"What's wrong?" Ethan asked.

Opening her eyes, she glanced out over the ocean. "You overwhelm me."

"How so?"

"I don't know if I can even begin to explain it."

"Would it surprise you if I said, I know what you mean?"

"I don't know if you do."

He picked up a piece of seaweed and started picking it apart. "Everything in my life was so simple, and it could be summed up in one word: 'write.' If I could just focus on that, then things would never get out of hand like they did before. And then you came on board, and I forgot all about my rules. I'm falling for you, Jenna, and that scares me too."

Her cheeks burned at his candid admission, and the butterflies in her belly were taking off again. Maybe he did understand, partially, but she wasn't about to tell him that. "It's this place," she said.

"No, it's not. The pull has been there from the beginning."

"I bet you'd be saying that even if another girl was sitting here."

He scooted closer to her and took her cheeks in his hands, studying her eyes. "If you don't feel the same, then tell me now."

Was she ready to say the weird emotions coursing through her out loud, the ones that made her want to hide? She decided for the first time in her life to take a chance. "You know I do," whispered Jenna, her voice barely audible.

He released her cheeks and dropped his hand to squeeze hers, and then pulled back, giving her some much-needed space. Admitting her more vulnerable feelings made fear rush through her blood. She didn't do stuff like that. Her emotions were typically hers and hers alone. Jenna gave him a grateful smile. She loved how he seemed to understand what she needed at any given time. He didn't do that when they first met. It was calming, yet unnerving.

Jenna reached for another blackberry, but her stomach protested the action. She'd eaten enough of them to last a lifetime, but it was the only fruit that was in abundance here. They could set traps to kill the rabbits roaming the area, but she didn't have the heart for it—not when her favourite pet as a kid was a little dwarf rabbit.

Out of the corner of her eye, she watched Ethan lean back on his hands and stare out over the ocean. His normally smooth face was covered in whiskers, giving him an older rugged look, which was quite the contrast to his boyish child-like charm. It took her back to a time when the only challenge she had was making sure that a book was on the right shelf for library patrons and watching over her friend, Cleo, who enjoyed finding a new guy to date every week.

She hoped Cleo was doing okay and not mourning for her. Her friend had a wedding to plan and didn't need to be bogged down with worry or sorrow. Would they be found before her friend walked down the aisle? It pained her to think that her disappearance might mess up this happy time for Cleo.

"Do you think they are still looking for us?" she asked.

"I'm not giving up hope yet."

"My friend is getting married soon, and I promised to be there for her."

"I'm sorry, hun," he replied, his voice solemn.

"If we make it back, would you go with me?"

"Me?"

"Yeah. I'd rather have you there than whatever wacko best man she tries to hook me up with."

Ethan choked back a chuckle. "Would she do that?"

"Apparently everyone thinks I need to get back out there," Jenna said, heat rising in her cheeks as she thought about her more intimate moments with Ethan. In all honesty, she could only see herself locking arms with him, not some strange man she didn't know and didn't want to know.

"If it's any consolation, I think you've done a great job getting back out there."

She looked over at him, and he chose that moment to turn his head, their eyes locking. "You make it easy," she whispered.

"Do I now?"

"You know you do."

Her cheeks were sure to look like tomatoes by now. Embarrassed, Jenna tried to look away, but he took her face gently in his hands and turned her towards him again. "Don't be shy, hun. You can always say what's on your mind with me."

She rested her hands on his forearms and gazed up at him. "How do you do this to me? I feel like an alien in my own body."

"Just don't have an alien burst out of your gut on me, okay."

Jenna giggled. "I'll leave that to Sigourney Weaver."

"Such a cute girly giggle," he said, but as he studied her intently, his eyes grew smoky and dark. "I'm going to kiss you now."

Swallowing hard, she gave him an approving smile. He brushed her cheek with the pad of his thumb, and she couldn't help but lean into his touch.

"Do you know how beautiful you are?" he asked.

His flattery made her heart pitter patter. "Just kiss me, you ole' fool."

"Did we just go back in time?"

Not wanting to chit chat anymore, Jenna took action and jumped on his lap. "Sir, if thou dost wanna kiss me, shut up."

He smirked. "Dost and wanna in the same sentence?"

She jabbed him playfully in the gut. He and his writing brain needed to be shown a thing or two. And she planned to be the one to do it. "You, sir, are driving me mad."

Ethan laughed and wrapped his arms around her, pulling her towards him. "I will give the lady what she wishes."

She rested her hands on the nape of his neck, her fingers playing with his hair. "Sounds good to me."

When their lips touched, their discussion was forgotten. All she could concentrate on was the touch of his lips and the feel of his tongue moving with hers. His fingers trailed up her bare back and down again, leaving a heated pool of nerves in their wake. He deftly undid her bra. She dropped her arms, allowing him to remove the skimpy material.

Focusing on her breasts, he eyed them appreciatively. "Maybe I'll keep you naked, just like this."

He dipped his head and licked her nipple, which puckered immediately. He wasted no time taking it into his mouth.

Jenna rolled her head back, arching towards him. "Ethan," she moaned. How did he do this? Make her body come alive with unkempt desire. A new world never before explored. And no fear existed, just erotic sensations rolling through her body, like waves lapping against the seashore.

While his tongue continued to wonderfully assault her breast, his hand kneaded the other. Moulding and shaping it to his touch, and it went willingly. She did, too. Moisture seeped between her legs, her parts aching for action of their own. She ground her hips into him.

"Take me, please," she begged, her hands diving for the drawstring on his sweats.

He chuckled. The vibration ricocheted through her breast. The newborn sexual beast inside her awoke, and she shoved him to the ground. She made quick work of his sweats and soon he lay gloriously naked under her.

"Impatient, eh," he said, his eyes glowing with a sexual charge of their own. Grinning, she went to remove her own pants, but he stilled her busy hands. "Let me do that. Stand up."

Curious, she stood up, waiting to see what he would do. Ethan kneeled in front of her, his erection curling up to meet her. He undid the button on her pants and slowly pulled her pants and underwear down, letting his fingers brush against her skin along the way.

She stepped out of the pants and kicked them to the side. He grabbed her hips and buried his face against her and breathed in deeply, rubbing his nose against her clitoris. "You smell so good."

Her legs nearly buckled when his tongue replaced his nose, licking her. She bucked her hips. "Holy geez, Ethan."

"So responsive," he murmured huskily. Reaching up, his fingers discovered her waiting arousal, swollen and wet. He slipped his finger inside her, then another. She gasped and found herself pushing down against them.

"Your cock...inside me...now," she pleaded between pants, her words breathy.

He growled his approval and pulled her down onto his lap. Wasting no time, he buried himself inside her, filling her to the brim. Their bodies began moving as one. Their hearts beating frantically in sync to a song only they could hear.

They were oblivious to their surroundings, to the eyes that were watching them from afar. A storm was brewing in the air, but with how distracted they were, lightning could strike the ground beside them, and they wouldn't even hear it outside of their own erotic bubble.

And that was just how the new visitor wanted it. Nothing was better than an unexpected surprise.

∾

The next day, Jenna heard something strange floating in on the evening breeze and lifted her head from where it was resting on Ethan's chest. He was sound asleep, his chest rising and falling softly. She looked out over the water. There was a strange shape closing in on the island. Her heart skipped a beat.

"Ethan, wake up!" she said, shaking him. He only groaned and rolled onto his side, slipping his hand under his cheek. "Wake up, damn it. I see a boat!"

He shot upright, almost knocking her flat on her back. "What? Where?"

"There." She pointed off to the right where rocks jutted out from the island. "A sailboat."

He raised his hand, blocking out the sun. "Hot damn, you're right."

Jenna scrambled to her feet and ran down to the edge of the

water, waving her arms. "Help!" she screamed, but the sound of the waves crashing against the shore drowned out her voice. "Over here!"

Ethan threw a few logs onto the fire, careful not to stifle it. The smoke from their fire barrelled into the sky. If the people on the boat couldn't see it, they were blind. She continued to jump up and down and wave her hands, screaming until her voice cracked.

There didn't appear to be movement on board, but it was too far to see any details clearly. All she could see other than the large masts that towered into the sky was a dark flag that looked too large attached to the top, waving in the strong, but warm, wind.

"Do you think they see us?" she asked, her voice full of uncertainty.

"They don't seem to be moving anywhere, so I'm thinking they're anchored out there. Maybe someone is on the island already."

"Should we look around or stay here?" she asked, letting him make the decision.

"I could always take a quick walk around and see if I see anything. But let me see that arm first."

Turning towards him, she held her arm gingerly, giving him a soft nod of approval. He walked over, untied her shirt, and moved the leaves aside, examining her wound which had started to swell. "Are you in very much pain?"

"It's burning today."

Ethan pressed a hand against her forehead. "You feel a little warm. Are you sure you'll be okay if I leave you?"

"I'm a big girl. I can handle myself," she said with a wave of her hand, swaying slightly when she dropped her arm, eyes blurring. "Oh dear."

He grabbed her elbow, pulling her against him to steady her. "What's wrong?"

"I think I need to sit down."

Helping her to the ground, she rested her head in her hands. *Damn. This wasn't good.* Her wound appeared to be infected. She couldn't say it surprised her. The wolf's mouth was a breeding ground

Beneath His Hands

for bacteria. But, holy crap, if the people on the boat didn't rescue them, it was a for sure death sentence.

"Don't move from this spot. I'm going to take a quick look around," he said.

"I don't think I'm going to go far."

After examining the wound, Ethan wrapped her arm again before giving her a kiss on the cheek and rising to his full height. "I promise I won't be long."

She gave him a vague nod as she stared out at the boat, her vision slowly returning. The last thing she had expected was for it to hit her so fast, especially after they washed her arm. The blood and water should have washed out any bacteria.

Oh, God, what if it had rabies?

Jenna fanned her face, her stomach churning as anxiety welled within her. Was that why it was so aggressive?

Damn wolf.

Damn island.

She was finally becoming her own person, only to have her chance to grow ripped away from her, especially if it had rabies. There was no shot she could take on the island. Of all the things she had survived, she was going to be beaten by a wolf. There was no way she was ready to give up on what she'd built. She had finally stopped hiding in her room. She trained until she could beat her trainer. She found her way back into the workforce, working alongside men, albeit roughly. And now, she finally could touch a guy again and this was her reward?

"Nu uh, no way!" she mumbled.

The guys on the boat just had to find them and get her to a hospital. If she survived, maybe she would get a chance to do something with the diamond they found. Crab-crawling backwards, she stopped when she reached the log and leaned her head back against it. Closing her eyes, Jenna made a wish. A wish that her life could start over again. Fresh and whole.

"Well...well...well," said an unfamiliar voice.

Jenna's eyes shot open just as a hand clamped over her mouth.

∼

Ethan crouched behind a bush and watched as two men descended into the cave that Jenna found the diamond in. And only one word came to mind. *Pirates.* They weren't wearing eye-patches or the typical black style hats that were often associated with them nor did they have wooden legs or parrots resting on their shoulder, but these guys were plunderers. They knew exactly where to go.

He followed them from the beach where he had spotted their rubber dinghy. They were just around the corner from where he and Jenna had set up camp. A second rubber dinghy was already emptied of its occupants, but he had no idea where they went.

"Shit," one of the men yelled. "It's gone."

"The captain isn't going to like this."

"Do you think they found it?"

"If this vine is anything to go by, you can bet on it."

"But how? We hid the opening."

"Beats me. Let's just grab what's left and get out of here. Carter probably has the girl already."

Ethan's eyes widened in horror, and his stomach sunk in a quicksand of emotions. They were talking about Jenna. He bolted back to the beach, as fast as his feet would carry him and skidded to a halt when he saw her sitting on the ground, hands and feet bound.

A tall, burly-looking man stood over her, sneering with a mouth full of missing teeth as though he'd seen one too many fights. He was wearing a white button shirt—half undone—and a pair of ripped jeans covered in sand. "Oh, the captain is gonna have a fun time with you, little lady."

"Let me go before you forget what good times are," Jenna snapped.

How the hell had she let herself get caught? That girl was the embodiment of every warrior that had ever lived. She must have been

Beneath His Hands

worse off than he realized. Studying the guy from the bushes, Ethan wondered if he could take him by surprise. He was about to jump out and tackle him when the man turned sideways, his pistols glinting in the sunlight.

One on one, he would be able to beat him, but the guns put him at a huge disadvantage. Damn it. He should never have left her. But he only had a second before the other guys caught up with them. If he was going to act, now was the time. Ethan picked up a rock. He'd only have one chance to bean the guy and try to disarm him.

Baseball was never his sport, but he hoped like hell it would find its mark. He didn't want to lose her, not when she was finally opening up to him. Testing the weight of the rock and checking his aim, he let it fly.

It hit the guy in the temple, and he crumpled to the ground like a sack of potatoes, clutching his head. Ethan rushed towards Jenna, her eyes widening in surprise. He tossed her up over his shoulder, not wanting to waste time untying her.

"Hey, I can walk," she protested.

"Shush," he said, slapping her on the butt. "Two more guys are on their way."

"I'm too heavy for you to run with. You gotta untie me."

"Later," he said as he hoisted her higher onto his shoulder for a better grip. She was a featherweight. How she managed to pack such a wallop for being a small wisp of a thing he'd never know. He took off down the beach, her butt bouncing close to his face. If they weren't in such dire straits, he could imagine his finger–

"No!" he said, interrupting his train of thought. "Focus, you butthead." There was a time and place for sex, and this wasn't one of them. Just as they disappeared into the bush, he heard a litany of curses stream through the air.

"That was a damn good shot," Jenna said, as she traced his dimples by the waistline of his pants. Her touch sent shots of desire into his loins, his cock twitching.

He ran his hand in a circle over her butt. "I have another good shot if you don't stop trying to turn me on. I have to focus."

"Your butt is in my reach, too, mister dimples." She must really be out of it with how she was behaving. This wasn't like her and that worried him.

He snorted. "Like you can do much with your hands tied. Now be quiet."

Carefully, he manoeuvred his way through the trees. He had no idea where he was going to go, just away from the beach. Away from the guys who wanted to hurt Jenna. The waterfall was too close to the cavern, so he continued to move away from all that was familiar.

"They're looking for their treasure," he said.

"I gathered as much. He said I looked as exquisite as their blue diamond."

"I'm guessing that the other guy knows it's missing now. Where'd you put it?"

"It's in my usual hiding spot, buried in the sand under the log."

"Good."

Ethan wandered around a tree and came across a tiny alcove, surrounded by high bushes with only one tiny entrance. Setting Jenna down, he tilted his head and studied her. He quite liked her tied up. Maybe it would stop her from getting into trouble.

"Stop staring at them and get them off," she demanded with a quick stomp of her tied feet. "I don't like being tied up. Please."

Upon hearing the slight panic lacing her voice, he obliged and removed the ropes. "I'm sorry, I forgot."

She rubbed her wrists as her eyes glazed over with pain. "I wish I could."

"We'll hide in here until they leave."

Her face fell, eyes downcast. "But what about getting off the island?"

"We'll have to find another way."

A flicker of realization passed over her features. "They must have used a dinghy to come to the island. Couldn't we use that to get off the island?"

"We don't stand a chance on the open seas with such a small craft."

"We could stowaway on their boat."

If it were that easy, he would have thought of it himself. "You do realize that they have a whole crew on board, right?"

"We have no choice," she said, her chin trembling as tears filled her eyes. "If we don't go with them, I'm going to die."

The thought made his stomach churn. "No, you're not," he said softly, but even as he looked at her, he knew things weren't going in her favour. Her face was ashen, and her eyes were void of their usual lustre.

"Ethan, my wound is infected, or I could have rabies. Take your pick."

"I'll get more of the plant if we need it."

"We need to get on that—"

Ethan covered her mouth with his hand, shushing her, as he motioned toward the entrance of their hiding spot. "Listen."

Chapter Seventeen

The snapping of a twig made Jenna's heart race, and she grasped Ethan's forearm.

"I thought I heard voices," came an unfamiliar voice from beyond their little alcove.

"I swear I'm going to kill that guy," another groaned.

"So, was she just as sexy up close?" a third voice asked, joining in on the conversation. "I would have loved to have been that guy having sex with her."

"Will you guys shut up! How are we supposed to hear anything?" the first guy snapped.

"Sorry, mate."

She couldn't believe they had watched Ethan and her having sex. The thought of being naked and exposed to more than just his eyes mortified her. That was the last thing she expected the guy to bring up. They totally missed the boat pulling in when their hormones were going crazy.

"We need to find that girl. She'll lead us to the diamond."

If she gave them the diamond, then maybe they'd be nice enough to take them back to the mainland. Leaning towards Ethan, she whispered, "I'm going to barter with them, the diamond for taking us back to the mainland."

He shook his head and leaned towards her. "They're pirates, Jenna."

"At this point, what does it matter?" she said, crawling towards the opening.

Ethan grabbed her foot and dragged her back towards him again. "I'm not going to let you risk your life," he hissed through his teeth.

She kicked at him weakly with her foot and that action alone tuckered her out. Rolling onto her back, she lay there, breathing hard. "I don't see any other choice."

"Stay put and be quiet."

"Let me spell this out for you. My wound is infected. The plant didn't help. It will turn into sepsis, and I will *die!*"

"We'll figure something out. Just not with them, please!"

"How long do you think it's going to take for someone else to get here?"

Ethan turned his head away from her, tips of his ears turning red. She could hear his breath hissing between his teeth. She understood his concern. These men were not honest people. They would turn on them in a heartbeat. That's why she'd have to play it cool.

"Hey boys," she called out.

Ethan clamped a hand over her mouth. "Are you an idiot?" he snarled at her.

She pulled at his hand. "I have an idea. Trust me."

He hid in the corner while she crawled out of their hide-out, a frown etched into his face. She could only hope that she didn't need to fight them. Her strength wouldn't hold out in a battle. Standing up, she found herself surrounded by three men. The one that got beaned in the head with the rock quickly wrapped his filthy paw around her arm, hauling her up against his grubby body.

"That boyfriend of yours had better come out, too, or I won't leave your face as pretty this time," the man threatened.

"I'll tell you where the diamond is," she said, surprising herself by how calm and clear her voice sounded.

"Good girl."

"On one condition."

"The pretty little lady wants to bargain. How about we spare your life in exchange for the diamond?"

"You read my mind."

That seemed to leave them speechless for a second, as though it was too easy. "So where is it?" the man with the scruffy beard asked.

"I'll only tell you after you take me and my *boyfriend* back to the mainland."

"How about I torture your boyfriend piece by piece until you give it to us."

"If you touch one hair on his head or mine, you'll never find the diamond. And I'm pretty certain your boss won't be too happy about that."

The man holding her took out a knife and held it below her chin. "I don't think you have any bargaining power, little lady."

Untying her shirt, she held out her wounded, puss-covered arm to them and watched as they recoiled in disgust. The guy holding her arm released her and stepped away as though she carried a horrible disease he could catch. "I'm already dying, and if I do, you'll never find the diamond."

The three men moved away from her and spoke with each other in a close-knit circle. She couldn't really hear what they were saying, but Jenna knew they'd see things her way. When they broke from their circle, they surrounded her.

"We could always just torture you until you tell us. Have our wicked way with—" Ethan bolted out from his hiding spot and tackled the man talking. "Oomph," the guy groaned as he went down.

"To hell with that idea," Ethan growled, looking much like a crouched werewolf ready to attack, baring his teeth in the sunlight.

The man, who had taken her hostage earlier, pulled his double pistols, aiming right for her newfound love. "Don't even try it," he said, blood still trickling down his cheek from where Ethan had hit him with the rock. "I should put you down right now."

"No, don't," Jenna cried, stepping between them.

"Then we suggest you give us what we want."

"Okay, okay!"

Ethan pulled her down to him. "They're going to kill me anyway. Don't give it to them."

Taking the butt-end of the pistol, the man clocked Ethan on the side of the head, knocking him out. "No," Jenna screamed, knocking the guy flat with a roundhouse kick to the side of his face. As she completed her spin, she dropped to her knees, dizzy and lightheaded.

"It's so not Carter's lucky day," the bearded guy chuckled wryly, shaking his head.

If she weren't seeing double, she could easily take the other two. What a time for her body to screw with her. Couldn't it just give her strength for another five minutes? Fighting to stand back up, she stumbled over Ethan's foot.

"Hell, babe. It's like you've had one too many drinks," the tall gangly man said, grabbing her arm.

"So, if he's Carter, what shall I call you two, other than the bearded lady and the green giant?" she quipped, as she tried to pry his fingers off her arm.

The green giant shoved her in the direction of the beach. "Just take us to the fucking diamond."

His co-abductor picked up Carter and trailed behind them, leaving Ethan in a crumpled heap on the ground. "What about him," Jenna cried.

"We don't need him."

"You do if you want me to take you to the diamond."

"Just move it."

Jenna dropped to the ground, refusing to budge. "You need me to get the diamond, and I won't go anywhere without him."

Reaching down, the man picked her up and tossed her over his shoulder. She screeched at his sudden decision. What the hell was it with men and plopping women over their shoulders? She wasn't a sack of potatoes. When he started walking her face bounced near his armpit and she flung a hand over her nose, suddenly nauseous. "Damn, you need a bath."

"Shut up!"

"I want to talk to your boss."

"Don't worry. You'll meet him."

The feeling of being weak, nauseous, and helpless caught up to her, pulling her back into the dark abyss. The man's fingers were like a hundred crawling spiders as they tightened across her butt. *No. Not backwards. Please, not backwards.* "Please put me down," she begged. "I'll walk."

Her demons clawed their way out of the dark ravine that she'd thrown them into. They swirled around her like a heavy dark fog, robbing her of her breath. "I'm begging you, please. Put me down."

"I like your ass in my face, so no."

"I'll give you the diamond, please."

"Maybe we don't want *just* the diamond."

Her chest tightened and her throat closed. Jenna gasped for air. No. She couldn't go through that again. Reaching down between the man's legs, she grabbed his scrotum and twisted it. He squealed like a pig and dropped to his knees. She rolled away from him, and then kneeled on all fours, trying to catch her breath.

The bearded guy dropped Carter and went to reach for her, but using every ounce of strength she could muster, she kicked her leg out behind her and connected it with his gut. She may be sick, but she refused to become another man's involuntary plaything.

With all the men down, she scrambled to get away, grabbing at branches to help her as she stumbled over her feet. *Focus, Jen, focus!* One foot in front of the other. She had to get away.

She'd rather die than relive her nightmare all over again. Ethan was right. She was an idiot. As she stumbled her way through the forest, twigs snapped behind her, urging her forward. Should she go towards Ethan or lead them away from him?

If either of them deserved a chance, it was him. He had a life. A future in his business. She—what did she have? Her life had no meaning. No real future. Nothing good has ever happened to her, except Ethan. That caused her to pause mid-step. If she gave the men what they want, then maybe she could barter for his freedom? He deserved to live, to get back to his work. And if the only way was to sacrifice herself for him, then she would.

Standing tall, she turned to face her pursuer and slowly raised her hands into the air in surrender. She found herself face to face with the bearded man and the tall guy racing through the bushes behind him. Their pistols pointed straight at her.

Jenna swallowed hard. "Hi."

"Jack, tie her up," the bearded guy said to the other man.

She took a step back, hands in front of her. "No need. I'll go with you willingly on one condition."

"I think we tried that once already."

"I'm serious. You can have me and the diamond. I won't fight you. All I ask is that you promise to get Ethan back to the mainland," she begged. "Safe and sound." The chances of them doing that was slim to none, but she had to try.

"Won't fight us, eh? I think we'll need more proof than just your word," Jack said, circling her. "What do you say, Kal? Should we have some fun?"

"The captain wants the honour of touching her first."

Jack twirled her hair around his finger. "How's he going to know?"

Jenna's chest caved in on itself and the walls of her throat began closing, as the air in her lungs turning stale. She couldn't do this. All she could see now was Mathew's face sneering at her. Covering her face with her hands, she fought to breathe.

No. She didn't come this far to only come this far. *Damn it*. She was going to help Ethan. She had no matter the price. He was worth it more than he knew. And she would make them pay eventually for whatever they do to her. They could bet on that!

For now, she had to do what was needed to save Ethan's life and to get her strength back for the battle ahead.

"I-I'll...o-only...do this, if E-Ethan goes free. I'll st-stay with you guys for as long as you want." She wanted to sound brave, but she sounded like a stuttering chicken instead.

"Let's go back and get Carter. He should be waking up now," Kal said, grabbing her arm. Jack stepped on the other side of her and clasped his spiny, bony fingers around her other arm.

Jack leaned in, brushing his nose against her ear. "I'm looking forward to fucking that ass of yours."

Jenna sucked in a breath and fought to keep control over her twitching arm that wanted to elbow him in the gut. Digging deep in her soul for courage, she said, "How are your balls feeling?"

Jack dug his nails into her arm, cutting off her circulation. "If you do that again, I'll kill your boyfriend myself. Cut him up piece by piece and feed him to the sharks."

"Only if you want to join them," she snapped.

"I'm so going to like having this girl on board. We haven't had anyone we needed to tame in a long time."

"Ease up, Jack," Kal ordered.

They finally made their way back to Carter, who was standing up, rubbing a huge red welt that covered his cheek. When he saw them, fury filled his eyes, and he stormed towards her. Kal stepped in between them. Jenna's eyes widened in surprise.

"She's agreed to come with us."

"Has she now?" Carter sneered. "I hope the captain gives me first dips. Teach the little lady a lesson."

Jenna shuddered. Could she really go through with this? Give herself to these men? That meant stepping into the darkness that claimed her soul before. She knew that if she went there this time, there would be no way out. What she was about to do no sane person would even contemplate.

"Just save Ethan, and I'll do whatever you want."

Beneath His Hands

Ethan sat up and clutched his head, groaning as sharp shooting pains circled his skull. Jenna was going to get a piece of his mind for her cockamamie idea. Didn't she have any idea the lengths these guys would go to get what they want?

He had experienced pirates once before. They had absolutely no honour and no respect for women. With everything she'd been through, you'd think she'd have more street smarts. Her infection must have travelled to her brain.

Holding his breath, he tried to listen for any sounds, aside from the animals, which might tell him which direction the men and Jenna went. Without all the noises of the city, you could hear all around you. It took a few minutes, but he thought he heard a faint cry in the distance.

With blurred vision, he climbed unsteadily to his feet and stumbled his way towards the beach. He had to find her. For the first time since all his crap went down, he felt like he could trust someone. Someone other than his family. Maybe even have a life with her if she'd have him.

Holy hell. Ethan gripped the back of his neck, suddenly feeling like he was struck by a freight train. He'd only just met the girl, and he was already thinking of their future together. Did she want one? Could she find her way out of her own personal hell and accept that he wanted to be a part of her life? Could he?

Shaking his head, he focused on the current task at hand. She was gone, and he had to find her. The future was a moot point if the pirates got their filthy hands on her. She'd revert back to the darkness she lived in before.

And he wasn't about to let her go back into the hellhole she'd lived in before she met him. She deserved so much more than what life was tossing at her, and he found himself wanting to be that more to her and put a smile on her face.

He stepped out onto the beach and glanced up and down the

water's edge, but he didn't see anything. Nausea rolled around in his belly and his mouth went dry. What if he'd lost her already? Running down the beach with his feet sinking into the sand, he yelled, "Jenna!"

Rounding the corner to their camp, he glanced out over the water and saw the two rubber dinghies heading back to the sailboat. "No!" he cried, hitting his thigh with his palm. There was no way he was going to be able to go after her now. "Fuck. Fuck. Fuck!" Picking up a softball sized rock beside him, he tossed it as far as his arm would let him.

"Ethan!" she cried, her voice carrying with the wind. "Help me!"

He linked his hands on the top of his head, pacing back and forth down the beach. There had to be something he could do to help. But what? It wasn't like he could swim out there. He had no gun to shoot. No boat.

Did she give them the diamond? He dropped to his knees beside her favourite log and slipped his hands underneath, pushing some sand to the side. His hand hit something hard. Wrapping his fingers around it, he pulled out the gem.

Ethan glanced out over the water. The dinghy was about halfway to its destination. He couldn't figure out why didn't she give them the diamond. Were they taking her back to the boat to wear the warrior princess down so that she'd tell them where it was?

Oh, God, he hoped not. His fist tightened around the gem. They better not hurt a hair on her head, or so help him God, he'd kill them. With what, he didn't know, but he would. He had to do something to bring them back. There was no way he was going to let them get her onto the boat. He stared at the gem in his hand.

Bingo!

Approaching the edge of the beach where the water lapped the shore, he held the diamond high in the air and waved it around. "Hey assholes, I have something you want."

They didn't even turn around to look at him. "Damn it, look this way!" he yelled.

It was useless. They couldn't hear him. The breeze was pulling his voice into the centre of the island as opposed to out over the water. Leaning back against the log, he really had no choice but to wait for them to come back. If they ever did.

They might just chalk it up to a loss. But he couldn't imagine them leaving behind a multi-million-dollar gem. It wasn't something a thief would pass up. Were they taking Jenna back to the boat to use her as leverage against him or him for her? He wouldn't put it past them.

His stomach twisted in his gut. Ethan sat down on the beach with the diamond on his lap as he rubbed his belly. It was like someone had taken his bowels in their hands and were ringing it like a towel, snapping it against his other organs.

What the hell was he supposed to do now?

∼

"Where's my bloody diamond?" Captain Bartholomew, a heavy-set man, shouted at his men, knocking all the dishes clean off the table. "Didn't I tell you not to come back until you found it?"

"We ran into a little blip in the program," Kal told him in a calm, collected voice, belaying the fear you could see in his eyes.

But Jenna refused to show fear. Fear was what got you killed by almost any animal, including man. No matter what it took, she was going to hold herself together.

"Yes, I can see that," the man sneered as he looked over at Jenna. "How lovely to meet you, my dear."

As kind as his words were, the husky-clip in his tone and the seedy look in his eyes were anything but pleasant. When the man walked over to her, she tugged at the ropes binding her wrists behind her back and took a step back.

"You've got fire in your eyes," he commented, as he reached for her arm. "I like that."

"Don't even think about it." She took another step back and bumped into Jack, who held her firmly against him.

"You can't go anywhere, darling," Jack said in her ear, his breath stinking like beer.

Jenna whipped her head back and cracked him on the nose. After doing so, her legs turned to jelly, and she collapsed to the group, lightheaded.

"You bitch," the man roared, pulling his hand back to slap her.

But Kal knocked his arm out of the way and stepped in between them, helping her back to her feet. "She's sick, boss," he said, glaring at Jack.

Despite everything she'd been through, she looked at the man gratefully. There was something different in his eyes as opposed to the rest of the men on board. Pity, sadness lurked in their depths, almost like he was sorry somehow.

"Get her to the good doctor then," the captain said to Kal and then he faced Jack, a storm cloud passing over his features. The man grabbed Jack by his shirt, pulling him until he was only inches away from his face. "If you lay a hand on that woman, I'll take you to Makena beach and feed you to the sharks. She's mine!"

Jack's eyes narrow and his brow furrows. "But we've always been able to toy with them before?"

"Not this one. I know her."

"Your men haven't been entertained in a while."

"Find your own bloody entertainment. You can stick your shit up each other's asses. She's mine." Captain Bart snapped. "Do you understand?"

Bart had watched the news stories about them, but he never expected to find them on his island. If he could find his gem and keep the girl, he'd hit the jackpot. There was something inside of her, a monster. A flame that sizzled like a forest fire ready to spread. His men were getting a little wayward, and he figured she could knock them down a peg or two. She'd rule the ship with him…one day.

He hadn't met very many women who could knock a man on

their ass. Short of making him beg for sex. Not that he was the begging kind. If he wanted it, he took it. And he was more than happy to keep on taking until he was satisfied.

His men grumbled at his response but nodded their heads. "I want you guys to go back to the island. Corner the guy and threaten him with her life. Once you get the diamond, kill him."

There's no way she'd warm up to him if the other guy was around, and he couldn't bring him to the boat and take him back to the mainland without taking Jenna too. There would be too many questions. Ethan knew she had survived, so he'd sick the police on them, and Bart couldn't have that. The circumstances left him with only one choice. He didn't like to kill unless he had to, but this seemed to be one of those times.

"Actually, maybe I'll take the team to the island." His men's eyes widened. "I gotta do the dirty deeds myself once in a while."

But first he wanted to check on his little lady and see what the doctor had to say. Her eyes had been slightly glazed over, and her skin bore the signs of a fever. Red and flushed.

Moving down the hallway, he skipped down a set of stairs and moved towards the sickbay to find out what was going on with his latest acquisition. When he walked in, he found himself surprised to see that she was cooperating with his doctor. But the minute he walked in the room, her blazing eyes turned in his direction.

"I told your men that I would go with you and give you the diamond as long as my friend was saved."

"I'm sorry for their brutish behaviour. I promise to go back to the island personally and bring your friend back."

She pressed her lips together, and her eyes–full of mistrust–studied him intently. "Really?"

"Of course, my dear. I'm an honourable man, unlike some of my men." He had no intention of bringing him back and would come up with some appeasing excuse, but for now, he was going to play it cool.

The doc raised his eyebrows at him but said nothing to incriminate him. "Her wound is infected like she thought," the doctor said.

"Thankfully, we have some antibiotics that should help. She'll need to be on bed rest for a few days though."

"Did you want her to stay here?" Bart asked.

"Until she's steadier on her feet, I'd like her to stay here so I can keep an eye on her."

"Okay, keep me informed of her health." As he turned to leave the room, one of his deckhands burst into the room.

"Boss, you ain't gonna like this."

"Now what?" Bart snapped.

"We've got company."

Chapter Eighteen

Daniel gripped the railing as he watched their boat near the known pirate ship. He'd seen their kind before. Brent's men were already raiding the gun locker, preparing for a battle they felt sure was coming. They'd given him a pistol in case he got in the middle. He'd never shot a gun before.

What were the odds that they'd come across another ship on their pass around the island? The area had been relatively dead during their search. He was stoked to see a sliver of smoke trailing into the sky on the island, so he knew someone was there. However, the crew's excitement was dashed upon seeing another boat. It was probably that ship's crew that had gone ashore, having a picnic on the beach or something.

But something felt different about this place. Something in his spirit was telling him to pay careful attention, but he didn't want to get his hopes up. They'd been searching for days with no luck. He'd even taken the crew right into the path of danger looking for his daughter.

And now, as he stared at the boat, he couldn't help but think about Jenna and his wife. They deserved so much more in this world, and he intended to give them the moon. He had savings tucked away and wanted to take them on a trip, uninterrupted, so they could bond again. He knew his daughter wanted to travel the world before, so he'd let her pick their destination. No boats or islands though. He'd seen enough to last a lifetime. He couldn't wait to get to know his family and treat them better this time.

When he returned home, he was also going to fire his assistant and go solo for a bit. Iris would probably want to know why, and he'd be honest with her. She deserved that much. It was time to be an honest joe. He was probably the one bringing all the darkness upon his family with his past unrighteous behaviour.

Upon hearing footsteps behind him, Daniel looked over his shoulder and saw Brent approaching him. "So?"

"There is one guy on the beach. No sign of your daughter though," Brent answered.

"Have you guys contacted the other ship?"

Brent nodded. "They are being unusually cordial. They said the guy on shore is one of theirs. He's apparently being punished for misbehaving."

"Do you believe them?" Daniel asked, watching their flag as it blew in the wind. It was too uncanny that there was only one guy there, with a signal fire going to boot. Their own men wouldn't want anyone else encroaching on their territory.

"Well, I'm not about to get into a sparring war with them. They have us outnumbered and outgunned."

That part was true. Their crew was walking non-stop along the outer deck, fully armed to boot, watching Brent's boat carefully. What were they doing here? They hadn't seen any other boat since they started their search. That meant if they ran into trouble against these guys, it would take a while for any rescue boats to come.

Daniel smacked the railing. "What the hell are we supposed to do?"

"Do you have a picture of Ethan?"

"I've seen him online, but that's it. I don't have any of his pictures with me."

Brent ran a hand through his hair. "Damn, and we're offline too. I mean I have a satellite phone, but it's only good for making calls and texting. No surfing."

"We could always take a trip to the island ourselves."

"That might not be a bad idea. We can go around the backside. I seem to remember seeing a small beach as we sailed around the island."

Pushing himself away from the railing, Daniel said, "Let's do it!"

It was the only way to know for sure whether she'd been on the island and whether the man left behind was one of the pirate's men. He couldn't help but think it was a load of hogwash. Didn't they have a brig or something to hold them in? Hell, he wouldn't put it past their captain to kill any man who stepped out of line.

One of the crew walked up behind Brent. "The captain is on the line again. He's giving you an ultimatum."

"Well, I guess the man's lost his cordial bone. Let's go see what he wants," Brent said.

~

Ethan stood on the edge of the beach, his hands on his head as he watched the newer boat turn around and start to leave. "No. No. No!" he grumbled. That wasn't what was supposed to happen. They were supposed to see him on the island and come pick him up. They were supposed to help him rescue Jenna.

He was at a total loss. And it was not a feeling he liked in the slightest. Hell, he should have been able to come up with a solution. He was a writer. Solutions were his middle name. But a blank page was all he could come up with.

"Think, man, think!"

Still nothing.

All he could do was sit there and watch the boat that held the love of his life. And he felt as helpless as a newborn baby. He wanted a chance to be with her. He wanted to see where their relationship could go.

It wasn't fair that as soon as he found a woman he wanted to spend his life with, someone else got their grubby paws on her, and there wasn't a damn thing he could do about it. He had no phone. No radio. No boat. And too many meters to count between him and the sailboat.

The loss he felt was a chasm far wider than any other precipice he found himself on. Not even when he was betrayed had he felt this burning pain in his chest, like his other half had just died. Jenna was perfect, even if she didn't think she was.

Moving back into the shade of the trees, he plunked himself down on the ground, his forearms resting on his bent knees. Ethan glanced at the log beside him. Could he find some branches or some flat pieces of wood that could act as a raft, and then use the vines to tie them together?

"Then what, smartass?" he muttered.

Take on a boat full of pirates, with nothing more than a stick and a rock? Ha. That would end well. He'd either be killed or tossed in their brig and used as blackmail against Jenna. Every muscle in his body tensed. What were they doing to her right now? Were they abusing her? His fists tightened, nails digging into his palm. He wanted to talk with her and find out why she went with them. It didn't even look like she was putting up a fight.

Looking out over the water, he noticed that there appeared to be some activity on the upper deck of the ship. One of their dinghies was being lowered into the water, but he couldn't see how many men were in it.

Did she tell them where the diamond was? He highly doubted it. It was her only leverage against them. Were they coming back for him? Well, standing around and gawking like an idiot as they neared the island wasn't going to give him any answers. He needed to decide what to do and fast.

After burying the diamond in Jenna's secret location, he moved into the tree line, out of sight from the boat coming in. It was obvious they were coming straight towards camp, unlike earlier when they went around to the other side.

Ducking behind a bush, he watched as they waded ashore and pulled their boat onto the sand. One man didn't get out until his boots could touch dry ground, his men giving him room to disembark. He had to be the captain. He had that certain air about him.

"I know you're here," the man called out. "We just want to talk.'

Yeah, sure. No one who ever said that meant it. He wasn't going to be the stupid one at this party. Sitting silently, he waited. The men moved about the camp, upturning every rock and looking under every bush, moving closer and closer to where he was hiding. Quietly, he moved deeper into the forest. It was times like this he wished he knew kung fu. He knew he would land flat on his ass if he tried anything.

"If you don't come out, I'll contact my men to hurt your girl."

The dark, evil tone in the man's voice made him cringe. There was no doubt in Ethan's mind that he'd do exactly what he said he would. But did he have a means to contact his men? There hadn't been a single radio squawk since they arrived.

"I just want the diamond. You have one minute to decide."

Ethan wanted to shout out his frustration at being trapped like an animal. Was this what she felt like when she was kidnapped before, struggling with the inability to do anything about the situation? If so, then he really felt her pain.

"Come out!" the guy said. "Come out, wherever you are."

If he gave them the diamond, they'd have no reason to keep him alive. Yet, if he didn't give it to them, she might die. And he would certainly die if he revealed himself. Neither scenario ended good for him.

"Bring her back to the island, and I'll give you the diamond," he said, taking a chance as he attempted to project his voice, like he'd seen in the movies.

"So, the screenwriter speaks."

"Do we have a deal?" Ethan asked, cutting to the chase.

"I think I quite like having her on my boat. She's feisty that one."

"If you hurt her, I'll kill you," Ethan growled. That's when a gun clicked beside him, making him freeze. "Shit!"

The captain distracted him long enough for his man to get the jump on him. "For being a writer, you sure aren't quick on the uptake," a voice said.

Slowly, Ethan stood up and turned to face his captor. It was the tall burly guy from earlier. Carter was the name if he remembered correctly. "You!"

"Move." Carter shoved the gun into his back, pushing Ethan out onto the beach. Now what was he supposed to do? They surrounded him in a semicircle, only Carter remaining behind him.

"Ethan Barrett, the infamous screenwriter. I've seen your movies," the captain said, folding his arms across his chest. "Quite the impressive portfolio." He did have appreciation in his eyes, but they quickly clouded over with greed. "Give me my diamond."

"I couldn't care less about your diamond, and I'll give it to you gladly, but please bring Jenna back."

"If I bring her back here, she'll die in days."

"Then do the honorable thing for once and drop us off on the mainland."

The captain dismissed him with a wave of the hand. "You only have one choice here. Give us the diamond or she dies."

Ethan rubbed the top of his head. His stomach twisting in fear. He'd heard it said that fear wasn't real, but God dammit, it sure felt real. The ground beneath him was like quicksand, and he couldn't seem to find any way out. "If you kill her, you won't ever find the diamond."

Unhooking the large flashlight off his belt, the captain gave four quick flashes back to the boat. "If I give another two flashes, they'll toss her over the side with her hands and feet tied. And she will be given a live burial at sea."

No," Ethan begged, holding his hands out. "Stop. I'll give you what you want."

Kneeling in front of the log, Ethan brushed the sand aside, revealing the diamond. He didn't really care about it one way or another. He only cared about getting Jenna back, but he had a feeling that wouldn't happen either.

But if giving it to him meant she stayed alive, then that was better than nothing. Eventually, she'd have her strength back and fight her own way off the ship—a female Steven Seagal. His own life didn't matter to him as long as he could save hers.

"You know what's ironic about this," the man said. "She came with us willingly, thinking we'd save you."

"And let me guess, you have no intention of keeping your word."

"We can't very well take you back to the mainland and not her, and we can't leave you here. You'd squeal if someone found you, and I don't really want the coastguard on my tail."

That somehow didn't surprise Ethan. He knew that the moment they came back, his goose was cooked. Defeated, with his shoulders slumped, he wandered over to the log and kneeled down, knowing full well that the barrel of the gun was pointing directly at his head. "Sorry, mom," he whispered, his eyes burning with unshed tears of a life he would never get to live.

He'd never bless her with grandchildren. He'd never get to see the smile spread across her face as he accepted another award for his writing. And would never get to see her grow older beyond her years and be able to care for her as a son should. All he could offer her now was pain and loss.

The thought of begging had occurred to him, but there was no dignity in begging for his life. They'd just laugh at him and tell him to take it like a man, not that they were men themselves. Would his mom close up shop, unable to deal with the sadness? He hoped not.

He picked up the diamond and held it in his hands. The sun made the surface of the gem sparkle, making him think of an engagement ring—one that he would never have a chance to give.

Carter reached down and snatched it out of his hand, holding the gun up to Ethan's head. "Shall I boss?"

Instead of cowering, Ethan pulled his shoulders back and looked straight ahead, refusing to close his eyes. He was going to go out with dignity and honour, as much as one could while on their knees. His one consolation in all this was the fact that he knew Jenna would bring the crew to their own knees once she recovered. And he would watch over her from above with a smile on his face.

The captain waved his hand at Carter, giving him the go ahead. Ethan held his breath, waiting for the shot that would send him into the great unknown. A gunshot reverberated through the air. He waited for the searing pain that was sure to follow, surprised that he'd even have time to hear the sound. After another rapid succession of bangs filled the air, he opened his eyes and watched the men around him duck for cover. He patted himself across the chest and sighed in relief when he found no blood on his hands.

Glancing behind him, he saw Carter on the ground. His eyes were wide open, and blood was seeping out of a hole in the middle of his forehead, pooling in the sand beneath him. Ethan grabbed the diamond out of Carter's hand and scrambled behind the log, surveying his surroundings. Two men lay dead. The rest had taken cover and were shooting at their attackers.

Taking advantage of the distraction, Ethan took off into the bush and worked his way to the ones who saved his life. It had to be the people from the other boat. They must have known something wasn't quite right.

"Find him," the captain yelled to his last man standing. Only four of them had come to the island and with two of them dead, the odds were a lot more even. They couldn't have too many more bullets in their guns either. Keeping low to the ground, he followed the sound of the other men.

Ethan ducked as a bullet whizzed by his head, hitting the tree in front of him. Looking back, he saw Jack hot on his tail. He slid down an embankment and ducked behind a large tree, breathing hard. If he made it out of this, he'd definitely make a screenplay of their adventure. No one could make this stuff up.

As soon as the man rounded the side of the tree, Ethan struck out his arm and clocked him across the bridge of the nose. Jack's gun went flying. The man grunted and staggered around as he held his nose. "Damn it, I think you broke my nose," he growled, sounding an awful lot like a chipmunk. Ethan chuckled.

Jack took a swing at him while his other hand still covered his nose. Ethan ducked and landed a good shot to the man's stomach, making him double over. "That's for touching my girl." He reached down and picked up the man's gun.

Jack held up his hands in surrender. "You'll never get her off the boat, you know."

"That's where you're wrong." He grabbed the guy by the collar and hauled him up. "Let's go," he said, shoving him in the same direction he'd been going.

The gunshots had finally subsided, which meant the show had to be over. Ethan guided the man back out onto the beach. The captain was on the ground, holding his side, and three men were approaching him. They all stopped and turned to look at Ethan and Jack.

"Ethan?" asked a man with black hair, still keeping his distance, gun ready. Next to him was a man with a head of sparse dirty blond hair, bearing a remarkable resemblance to Jenna.

"Yes." Ethan nodded his head towards him, as he shoved Jack next to the captain. "You Jenna's father?"

The man's eyes lit up, full of hope, as he looked around. "Yes. I'm Daniel. This is my friend, Brent. Is Jenna here?"

"They took her to the boat."

"Shit," Daniel's hands balled into fists. "But she's alive?"

"Yes. She's sick, though. She caught an infection from a bite."

The man's face paled and the hopeful look in his eyes faded. "Brent?"

Brent placed a hand on Daniel's shoulder. "Don't worry. We'll get her back. Let's get back to the boat and radio our location to the coastguard."

"What about them?" Ethan pointed towards the pirates on the ground. He just wanted to finish them off and make them pay for taking Jenna.

"We'll use them as our insurance policy. What's that in your hand?" Brent asked.

Opening his hand, Ethan showed them the diamond. "This was what they were looking for, and they found her instead."

"Wow, even better," Brent gasped. "I think that might be the one that was reported missing last year. There's like a five-million-dollar reward for whoever finds it."

Ethan must have been hiding under a rock when that was announced. He hadn't heard anything about it. They might not be able to get the full price for the diamond, but what they could get would help Jenna follow after her dreams and build a new life for herself.

"Come on, guys," Daniel pleaded. "Let's go get my daughter. I have a lot to make up for."

Brent hauled the captain up by his shirt. Easy for him to do since he was almost twice the man's size. "Let's go, big boy."

"I'm going to lose my boat and the girl," the man grumped, clutching his side. "Just let me die already."

"That ain't going to happen," Brent said. "You are going to jail for a long, long time."

Things were finally looking up. Ethan couldn't wait until Jenna was in his arms. He'd never let her out of his sight again. Climbing into the small, motorized boat, the men made their way back to the other sailboat.

"How long were you guys searching for us?"

"Ever since we heard that your boat went down," Daniel replied, glaring at the two pirates. "The coastguard stopped searching a few days ago, but I'm glad we didn't."

"Me, too. Did any of my men make it back?"

"Last I heard, three of them were found."

Ethan sighed with relief. He'd been worried that he'd led his entire crew to their death. He'd tried hard not to think about it while he was with Jenna, but the guilt almost ate him alive. They all came on his trips willingly, but that didn't stop him from feeling the punch in his gut.

"So, my daughter, did she handle everything okay? Did you take care of her?" Daniel asked, his hands rubbing his legs nervously as worry wrinkled his brow.

Ethan chuckled. "I think you already know that your daughter can take care of herself."

"You found that out, did you?" the man replied wryly.

"Kinda hard to miss when she flips you on your back a few times."

Daniel raised one eyebrow at him. "Did she now?"

"I learned very quickly not to piss her off."

The small motorboat pulled alongside the sailboat, and Brent anchored it to the back dock. Ethan followed the men onto the ship. He was eager to see his warrior princess again. He only hoped she wouldn't push him away after their dream-like bubble popped and reality set in.

"Let's go call it in," Brent said.

~

"What's your name?" Jenna asked the doctor, as she watched him move about the room. He wasn't as tall as Ethan, but the man's shoulders were broad, and he walked with an air of grace about him. Almost like he didn't belong on board.

"Lars."

"Well, Lars, how did you come to be on this ship?"

"Much like you actually."

That intrigued her. She felt that there was a little animosity between the two men but didn't know what was behind it all.

"He captured you?"

"In a manner of speaking," was all the man said.

He seemed reluctant to spill the beans, so Jenna let it go for the time being. She imagined she had plenty of time to fish the news out of him. Maybe he could even help her get out off the boat.

"You should start to feel better in a few days, but I'll keep you out of his clutches for as long as I can."

"How long have you been on the boat now?" she asked him.

"About five years I think."

What would make him stay that long? They no doubt docked once in a while, which would give him a chance to escape. Questions bubbled inside her, but she didn't want to rock the boat and push him too far.

"Have you eaten anything?" he asked.

"Not recently."

"If you promise to stay here, I'll run to the galley and grab you something."

He was going to leave her alone. She tried to control her excitement at possibly being able to escape. Giving him a nod, she pressed her lips into a thin line, trying to prevent a smile from breaking free.

Lars folded his arms across his chest as he stood in front of the door. "I know that look in your eye. I've seen it before, hun."

"Can't you just say I knocked you out or something?"

"Please don't mess this up for me. People's lives are staked on my behaviour here," he said, pleading with her.

Her heart softened and she found herself agreeing to stay. Enough lives have been affected by her actions, and she didn't have the heart to add more. She'd have to find another way. Hopefully the captain would keep his word and bring Ethan, and then she'd have a comrade in arms.

He turned to leave the room, but then turned and walked over to a cabinet, grabbing out a pair of handcuffs. "Do I need to use these?" he asked, studying her.

Jenna let out a soft gasp and shook her head. She didn't want to be tied up. She hated being constricted, trapped. "I promise. I'll still be here."

It's not like she had the strength to fight her way off the boat right now anyway and with her vision going wonky, she'd just get caught again and be worse off than she was right now. They'd probably tie her up in a room somewhere. At least in the sickbay, she had someone watching over her that seemed to care about her wellbeing.

The man nodded his head and disappeared out the door. Sliding off the bed, Jenna wandered over to a tall cabinet in the corner of the room. It had three shelves along the top and one pull out drawer. There had to be something she could use to escape later. A scalpel. Anything.

Lars had everything medical at his disposal. Pulling open the drawer, she saw a scalpel encased in plastic. Grabbing her shirt off the bed, she pulled it on and then hid the scalpel in the waistband of her pants before sitting back on the bed.

It didn't take long for the man to return to the small room with a muffin and butter in hand. "I'm afraid this was all that they had for now. Dinner will be ready in a bit."

"I'm grateful for anything, thank you."

"And thank you for staying put, although I wouldn't have blamed you if you did try to run."

"Do you mind if I ask what keeps you here?"

The man sighed and sat down on the bed beside her. "Bart is my brother."

"Holy fuck!"

"My words exactly. When my daughter got sick, she needed all sorts of expensive medical treatments that her mother and I couldn't afford. Bart helped us out and then threatened to cut us off if I didn't come to work on the ship."

"But you're a doctor. Wouldn't you make enough on land to afford medical care?"

"He messed up my practice."

"I'm sorry," she said, resting her hand on his forearm. Lars didn't deserve to be put through this just because of health care costs.

Patting it gently, he said, "Thank you. You're too sweet to get mixed up in all this. I'll try to talk to my brother."

"I appreciate that, thank you. I think I'm going to try and get some rest."

"Yes. Sure. Sorry." Lars helped her lift her legs onto the bed and covered her up with the sheets. "I'll come back in a bit and see how you're doing."

As he went to walk out the door, she asked, "Do you really think he'll bring Ethan back?"

"Do you want my honest opinion?"

The tone of his voice didn't hold much promise. "Forget I asked."

"Get some sleep."

"I'll try."

"I'll be right across the hall if you need me." Lars dimmed the lights, and then left the room, leaving the door ajar.

As soon as he left the room, she threw back the sheets. Walking over to the counter where he'd placed her pills, she stuffed them into her pocket. If Bart wasn't going to rescue Ethan, then she was going to go back and rescue him herself.

Jenna stuck her head out the door, looking left and right. Once she was sure the coast was clear, she took her first tentative step out of the room and then bolted down the hall. Where she was going, she had no clue, but she was going to get off the boat and save her first love from the captain's clutches.

As she raced down the hall, a man came around the corner and she skidded to a halt, landing flat on her ass. "Damn." She rolled onto all fours and was about to run back the other way, but Lars stepped out of his room.

"Crud."

So much for that idea.

Chapter Nineteen

In the silence and darkness of the night, Ethan helped Daniel lower the paddle boat into the water while Brent slept. They climbed into it and started the journey towards the other boat. No activity could be seen on the upper deck of the ship, which allowed them to approach unawares.

They didn't speak. Both were far too focused on getting to the ship, and too deep in thought as to what would happen when they found her. Would she push them both away or welcome them into her arms? Hopefully, no one had hurt her yet. Ethan would kill anyone who put their hands on her.

He didn't want this to change what had started between them, but he was scared that it would prove to be too much for her. And, of course, he wouldn't blame her in the slightest. But he was going to do everything in his power to help her get her life back, even if she might not let him into it.

Pulling up alongside the ladder, they tied the boat to a hook and quietly scrambled up to the deck of the ship, ducking behind the closest barrel. "Where do you think they have her?" Ethan asked.

"I'm guessing down in one of the cabins below." Daniel replied.

Ethan's fingers tightened on the handle of the gun, and he flicked the safety off. It was a good thing he had to research guns for one of his stories. At least he knew how they worked. Whether he was a good shot or not was another matter. He'd probably shoot himself in the foot.

Daniel waved for him to take the portside while he took starboard. Cautiously and quietly, they roamed the deck of the ship. Ethan was surprised that no one was around. They must be in a meeting or sleeping, but one would think they'd have a lookout, considering their situation.

As they neared the cabin, he stood on one side of the door and Daniel stood on the other. They listened for any signs of life, but things were quiet. Maybe they went to the island looking for their captain. Slipping inside the saloon, they wandered over to the stairs and quietly went down to the next deck. They entered a long hallway, with rooms branching off on both sides.

As they stood with their backs against the wall, voices could be heard ahead of them. It sounded like they were all together. Slowly and quietly, they side-stepped their way down the hall. That's when they heard her cry out in the distance. As much as he wanted to bolt down the hallway, he knew it would alert whoever was on their floor, and they wouldn't get anywhere.

Ethan's heart raced in his chest, sweat beading on his forehead. It was hard to hold back and take his time when he didn't know what was going on. But if he got killed before he reached her, what good would that do them? Step by step, they neared another staircase. About five feet away, they found a door that was ajar, and the voices made them pause.

"They should have been back by now," a guy said, his voice high-pitched with worry.

"We might have to accept that they're all dead and ain't coming back," another deeper voice said, weighing in on the conversation.

"That would put me in charge." The last voice sounded oddly friendly and out of place, despite his attempt at being authoritative.

"Just because you're his brother? Hell no. I've been on this ship longer than you," the deep husky voice argued.

Since they all appeared to be in the room that left the ship open for Daniel and Ethan to explore. Slipping past the door, they continued their track to the next set of stairs. The only trouble Ethan could foresee was trying to make their way back up if they had to retrace their steps and go by this door again.

The next floor down was designed much the same way as the one they were just on. They made their way down the hall, checking each room as they went. Ethan approached a door that was ajar and heard a familiar voice mumbling a complaint from inside. He motioned towards the door with a grin, his heart jumping for joy. Daniel's eyes filled with excitement, and he nodded his head.

Ethan couldn't believe they actually made it to this level of the ship without being detected. Something didn't feel right. It felt a lot like a setup. But he knew most of them were in that room arguing, so his brain was probably overthinking again.

Holding up his hand, Daniel counted.

1...2...

～

Jenna couldn't believe they had finally left her alone, and there was nothing she could do to break free from the handcuffs. She was cuffed to the metal railing on the bed and couldn't reach anything that she could shove into the keyhole.

"Damn it all to hell," she grumbled, smacking the bed with her free hand. If she ever got her hands on the men who took her, she'd kick them up the wazoo. They wouldn't be able to sit down for the rest of their lives.

A sound in the hallway made Jenna's head snap towards the door. "Who's there?" she called, unnerved by her inability to hide. She couldn't blame Lars for handcuffing her, but she still wanted to kick his ass for not letting her go. He could have knocked out the guy who brought her back to the sickbay instead of handcuffing her, and then they could have helped him. But she should have guessed that he wouldn't risk his daughter's safety to help her.

When door creaked and slowly opened, her head whipped in its direction. "I'm going to ki–" She stopped when a set of familiar brown eyes peeked inside, his gun entering the room before the rest of him. After a moment, they pushed the door open completely. Ethan rushed to the bed, yanking at the handcuffs.

She yelped in pain. "Careful!"

"Where's the key?" he asked.

"Lars must have it."

Ethan's eyes clouded over in anger. He reached for her, turning her head to the left and then to the right, examining her. "Did they hurt you?"

She tried to shake her head, but his hands prevented her from doing so. "No," she replied, as a heaviness filled her from the inside out, her chest constricting. "What are you doing here? They want to kill you. You have to go."

Another person cleared his throat, and she moved Ethan aside to see who it was. "What the fuck!" she cried, and then slapped a hand over her mouth and mumbled sorry for swearing and for being so loud. "Daddy...how?"

Tears welled up in her eyes. She never thought she would see him again. And she was pretty certain he wouldn't want to see her either. She'd been horrible to him and didn't realize just how much until after she'd opened herself up to Ethan.

Daniel poked his head out the door before turning to look at her. "I've been looking for you non-stop since you disappeared."

"Why?"

"I think your questions need to wait until we're out of here," Ethan said, as he glanced around the room. "Daniel, we need to get that key or find something to break the cuffs."

The men turned the room upside down, trying to find either bolt cutters, or something they could use to cut through the metal cuffs. They came across a saw and looked at each other. It wouldn't get the cuff off her wrist, but she knew they could use it to cut the chain.

She watched the two men in her life work on setting her free. Her heart swelled with love for them, and also fear that they wouldn't make it off the boat alive. They shouldn't be risking their lives for her.

When the saw failed, so did her hope. "Please, guys, just save yourselves. I came here hoping to save you, Ethan. Don't let that be in vain."

"Hell, no. I'm not going anywhere until you can," he growled.

"Damn you, Ethan!"

"Damn me all you want," he said, his voice husky and low. "Daniel, stay with her. I'm going to go hunt the bastard down who has the key."

As he walked to the door, she said, "Wait. Please."

He turned to look at her, impatience written all over his face. She didn't want him rushing into the situation without knowledge first.

"The doctor will have the key, but don't hurt him. He's only here because the captain is blackmailing him. If you get him alone, I'm sure you could get him to help you. He's wearing a white dress shirt, black pants, and has jet black hair and grey eyes."

"Did he handcuff you?"

"Yes, but—"

Ethan scowled. "Then it makes no difference to me."

"He has a sick kid. Bart is making him do his bidding by threatening to cut the kid off from medical funds. Please, Ethan. He needs our help."

"You're a regular humanitarian, aren't you," he grumbled, but reluctantly agreed to try to help the man. Ethan wasn't exactly sure how he was going to do that though.

"Take Daddy with you."

"One of us has to stay here to protect you," Ethan said.

"You're a writer. Don't you know how bad splitting up usually turns out in horror movies?"

Trust her to point out the obvious, but he wasn't about to leave her here by herself.

As if reading his mind, she said, "They aren't going to hurt me. They were told to leave me alone. The captain wants me for himself."

"We have the captain, so all bets will be off when they find out."

Footsteps at the end of the hallway made them freeze.

"Hide," Jenna whispered.

They both ducked beside Jenna's bed, it was the only solid surface that was away from the wall. He hated the idea of being behind Jenna. What if the person coming down the hall decided to shoot first and ask questions later? They might hit her.

And he didn't come on this rescue mission to bring a corpse back. Standing up, he rushed to hide behind the door—ready to pounce on whoever walked in. He could only hope that Jenna's eyes wouldn't let the visitor know others were in the room with them.

As the person walked by the crack in the door, Ethan held his index finger against his lips, reminding Jenna to not give their presence away. But it caused her to glance his way, making the new visitor turn around as well.

"Damn," Ethan grumbled and dove at the man. They crashed to the ground in a heap of limbs and groans.

~

Daniel leaped up from behind the bed and trained his gun on the two men rolling around on the floor.

Jenna pushed the gun away. "Daddy, Ethan, that's Lars. It's okay."

Ethan stared at the man he had in a headlock, his legs wrapped around his middle. The man did seem to fit the description that Jenna had given him. "He still handcuffed you," Ethan complained, as he untangled himself from the man.

Lars, much to his surprise, didn't hit him, yell, or call for help; instead, he stood up and shut the door. "How'd you guys get on board?"

"No one was watching the deck," Daniel commented.

"The captain went after you," Lars pointed to Ethan. "Is he dead?"

"No. We have him and are willing to exchange him for Jenna."

A battle raged in the man's eyes, and he looked over at her. "This puts me in a tough spot now."

"I don't think it does," she said softly.

"We have the captain and the diamond. Right, Ethan?" she asked. Ethan nodded his head, and Jenna turned to look at Lars again, saying, "A diamond which would more than pay for your daughter's medical bills. You can take your family and run."

Lars' jaw dropped in surprise. "You'd be willing to give me the diamond?"

"You need it more than I do, but I can't help you if you don't let me go." She held her cuffed hand out to him.

"How do I know you have the captain and that he's alive?" Lars' eyes narrowed, his lips pressing together tightly, as if unsure of what he should do and whether they were telling the truth.

"You captured my girl, and you're still alive, that should say something. Look, the coast guard is on their way, and you'll be arrested with the rest of them," Ethan told him, trying to find some way to reason with the man. "Unless you help us."

That seemed to do the trick. Lars pulled the key out of his pocket and moved around to the other side of the bed to uncuff her.

Jenna placed her hand on the doctor's cheek, causing Daniel's eyebrows to raise. "I'm going to do everything I can to help your daughter," she said.

Lars touched her hand with his and gave her a weary smile. "I'm going to hold you to that. Come on, let's get you guys out of here."

Daniel poked his head out the door, and then turned to look at them. "Our boat has probably been detected by now."

The moment he spoke, it was like his words had jinxed them. A flood of footsteps sounded above them, along with some loud shouts along the way.

"Shoot. They'll be down here any second." Lars swore under his breath.

They were going to have to fight their way out after all. Ethan handed Jenna the extra pistol that was tucked into his waistband. "Do you have a gun, Lars?" he asked.

Lars nodded and pulled a rifle out from under the bed. That made Ethan a little more comfortable about the situation. Sort of. An enemy—turned possible friend—was wielding it. The man could turn on them in a second though, but Jenna was hell bent on helping him.

Each enemy footstep reverberated inside him, and Ethan's worry grew, knowing that any one of his allies could be closer to their death. His nerves made his eyelid twitch. He swiped at it, as well as the sweat gathering on his forehead. He wasn't an army person. He sat behind a desk. He didn't duke it out with the warriors.

That wasn't the same for Jenna though. Her eyes were ready to blaze a trail of gunfire ahead of them. They'd already be shooting bullets if they were capable of it. It was kind of strange that she hadn't joined the army. She'd wipe the floor with any militant out there. He was definitely going to create a character based on her. Very discreetly, of course, or she'd wipe the floor with him personally.

Daniel pressed his back against the wall on the left side of the door. "How many people are on board, Lars?"

"There are usually 20 of us, but ten are off visiting family. So, given that you took out 4, that means there are 5, not counting me. This was a side trip for us while we waited for the others to get back."

"How many exits off this deck?"

"One at either end of the hallway."

Ethan knew they'd have to disarm every man on the ship before they escaped. There was no way they would get away otherwise. *God.* This had the makings of a Hollywood movie. Hostages, pirates, boats, water, islands, diamonds. He was going to make sure it had its chance to shine with Jenna's permission. Things like this don't normally happen in real life. Not that you ever read about anyway.

Upon hearing footsteps on the stairs, Daniel stuck his head out the door. He took aim and shot the gun before the men had a chance to know what was happening. By the loud cry and multiple thumps as the men fell in tandem down the stairs, Ethan knew a bullet found its mark.

A litany of curses filled the air as the men scrambled back up the stairs, leaving one wounded man down at the bottom. "Well," Ethan said from behind the door, not wanting to stick his head out too far. If he did, he ran the risk of his face becoming bullet fodder.

"One guy is on the ground, clutching his stomach. The others took off, probably to regroup."

"Do we wait, or do we make a run for it?" Jenna asked, hopping off the bed. "Wowzers." She reached for the wall as her body swayed.

Both Ethan and Daniel rushed to her side. Ethan beat him there, putting an arm around her waist, holding her up. "Easy, hun."

"I think you should wait here until we clear the ship," Daniel suggested. "You aren't in any condition to run."

Lars fidgeted where he was standing. "Do we have to kill everyone? These guys have families that depend on them."

"What do you suggest then, genius? These men won't hesitate to kill us." Ethan folded his arms across his chest.

"Guys, please, let's just get out of here. Find the dinghy and get off the ship," Jenna pleaded. She didn't want anyone else hurt because of her. Her dad, Ethan—whatever she was meant to call him now—wouldn't even be on this ship if it wasn't for her.

"Okay, Lars, you know the way around this boat, so you'll guide us. Daniel, watch our backs and I'll help cover Lars. Since they came from over there." He pointed down the hall. "We'll go the opposite way."

The injured man wasn't moving anymore, and so they cautiously moved out of the room, with Jenna in the middle. Her legs were shaking as they moved in tandem. And she hoped to God she wouldn't have to try and fight. She was too weak.

Would she ever stop having bad experiences? It was like, out of everyone, in the world, Mother Nature or God—whoever was in control—wanted to pick on her family for whatever reason.

And it was her known bad luck in this moment that scared her. She didn't want anyone to be killed or permanently scarred for being involved with her. And with her being sick and weak, she had to rely on someone else, and that didn't sit well with her psyche or her fears.

Following behind Lars, Jenna stumbled into Ethan who slipped his arm around her. Warmth flooded her, and she snuggled in closer as they moved towards the stairs. She knew he needed two hands, but she was grateful for the extra support, otherwise she'd be on her knees.

The infection was sending her for a loop. One minute she felt somewhat fine and the next, her legs were like wobbly jello. She couldn't trust her body to behave from one minute to the next.

A flurry of footsteps on the stairs at the other end of the hallway had them scrambling into one of the side rooms, not wanting to be out in the open to get shot at. Jenna looked around. There was a worn pool table in the middle of the room and on the wall behind it was a dart board, full of darts, which she watched Ethan make a beeline for.

"We don't have time for a game of darts," she commented, glancing towards the door.

"And we don't have enough bullets for an all-out gun war, so I'm improvising," Ethan said, collecting the darts. He'd been a good dart player back in his day, winning a pub championship. Not anything to brag home about, but it was fun. It was the one thing, other than story writing, that he was good at. Barely poking his head out the door, he let a dart fly as fast as he could throw it. A yelp told him that it found its mark.

"Okay, there is only one way to do this. We need to hop between rooms, each taking turns providing cover," Daniel said. "I'll go first. On the count of three, run to the next room. One—"

Jenna bit her lip, her forehead creasing. "Wait. What if it's locked?"

"We can't just stay here."

Someone was going to get hurt because of her. She couldn't stand the thought of Ethan or her dad losing their life over trying to save her, but they were stuck, and nothing could be done except to fight their way out.

"One...two...three," Daniel yelled and rushed out the door, shooting in their attackers' direction. He covered them while they ran into the next room. Jenna fell to her knees in the room, fighting for air. She felt like she'd run a marathon.

"Jenna!" Ethan dropped beside her. "You okay?"

"I can't do this."

"Her activity is probably making the infection spread faster," Lars commented. "We have to get her out of here."

"No duh, doc," Ethan snapped.

Daniel poked his head out the door and then pulled it in quickly as bullets whizzed past his head. If only they could get them to run out of bullets, then maybe they'd have a chance to escape.

"Let's fake them out," she murmured.

"What was that?" Lars asked, as he leaned in to listen. "I didn't catch what you said."

"Let's fake them out," she said again, forcing herself to speak more clearly.

"What do you have in mind?"

"Get them to use their bullets."

"It will take forever to wait out their bullets. Their pistols have like 15 rounds, and they probably have another magazine in their pocket. We have to come up with something else." Lars tapped his chin, looking up at the roof as he deliberated on what to do.

"Let's dangle a carrot," Ethan suggested.

"Surrender," yelled a deep voice. "You have nowhere to go."

"We have the diamond, the captain, and the girl," Ethan yelled back. "And the coastguard is on their way right now. If you want any chance of getting away, you need to let us go now."

"Do it, guys," Lars pushed them to accept the terms. "You have families counting on you. Joel, your wife is about to have a baby.

Chris, your daughter has her graduation ceremony coming up in September. This ship isn't worth the pain that it will cost your kids if you die."

Jenna placed a hand on Lars' shoulder, "Thank you," she whispered, giving him a kiss on the cheek.

"Okay, who are you and what have you done with my daughter?" Daniel said jokingly.

It felt oddly satisfying to Jenna to be able to touch people again, without feeling super weirded out and all panicky about it.

"Get on your knees and crawl out of the room. Once you do that, slide your guns towards us and put your hands on your heads," Ethan commanded, "No funny business and maybe you'll get out of this in one piece."

One by one, the three men came out of the room and did as instructed.

"Stay like that for 10 minutes until we get off this boat and then you guys are free to take off before the coastguard gets here," Daniel said, holding his gun at them just in case any of them decided to do something different.

"Be careful." Lars warned as they started their trek to the upper deck to the dinghy. "There's still one more guy."

Jenna's heart lightened as they neared the boat. They were actually going to make it off the boat and get back to the city again.

She glanced over at Ethan and wondered what the future would hold for them. Would he want her? Would she want him? The island surrounded them in a mystery, their own little bubble, and it was easy to step aside and let him in when it was just the two of them.

Something about him just invited her in, and she couldn't quite figure out what it was. She stumbled as she walked in the dark and reached out for him. He wrapped his arm around her, pulling her close to his side, and they took the last few steps towards the boat.

No one heard the person approaching them from behind, his feet strangely silent on the deck. The man raised his gun and pulled the trigger.

Chapter Twenty

Daniel slumped against Jenna, knocking them both to the ground. The gunshot echoed around them. Jenna screamed and tried to twist around to face her dad, but she was pinned beneath his unmoving body. She knew that things were going too good to be true.

Ethan turned and immediately got a shot off, hitting the guy square in the chest. The man took a moment and looked down as a giant red mark spread across his shirt before collapsing to the ground.

They loaded Daniel quickly into the boat and raced across the water as Lars put pressure on her father's sucking chest wound. "Hurry, I need to seal the wound," Lars ordered, as Daniel gasped for air.

"No. No. No," Jenna cried, holding his hand and burying her face in his shoulder. She should have listened to her mom. Wherever she went bad luck followed. "Daddy, I'm sorry."

Ethan pulled up alongside their ship and tied the dinghy to the boat. He helped unload Daniel and took him to the sickbay. "What the hell happened?" Brent yelled, stumbling into the madhouse. "I told you guys not to go over there."

Brent watched Lars move around the sickbay. "Who the hell is he, and what's he doing on my boat."

Jenna turned on him, eyes blazing. "He's trying to save my father, asshole."

Ethan put a hand on her shoulder. "Easy, hun. He didn't know that we went over to save you."

"Don't hun me." Tears streamed down her face as she turned and pushed him, hitting his chest with her fists. "Why'd you come? Why'd the hell did you come? I was fine. Now my father is going to die because of me."

He wrapped his arms around her and pulled her close. She struggled against him, but in her weakened state, she couldn't break free. Her knees buckled under her exhaustion, and Ethan scooped her up in his arms.

She buried her face in his chest and cried as Lars worked on her dad. Life wasn't fair. Why the hell did her family have to suffer so much? She needed to go. Get away from everything. And everyone. Her family deserved better than the life she was giving them. Ethan deserved better, too. There was no way she was going to bring her curse of bad luck into his life.

"Shh, hun. He'll make it through this," Ethan said as he rubbed her back, pressing a light kiss to her forehead.

His gentleness unglued her even more, and she bawled her eyes out. Her life wasn't going to be the same without Ethan, but there was no way she could stay with him and bring the same curse upon his life as well. He'd already lost his friend, Chris, and his boat, and his newest story because of her. Now her dad was dying because of her. Again.

"Please, put me down," Jenna pleaded, her voice breaking something fierce. Her stomach felt like it had burst wide open, emptying all its contents into the deepest sea. Her spirit quickly plummeted along with it.

"Are you the captain?" Lars asked Brent.

Pale-faced Brent nodded his head as he stared at the blood

Beneath His Hands

leaking around Lars's hand.

"Get this boat back to the mainland as fast as you can," Lars instructed. "Ethan, I need your hands."

Placing Jenna on her feet, he crossed over to the doctor, glancing back at her; clearly torn on who he should be helping. She nodded her head, giving him permission to help the doctor.

Collapsing into the chair in the corner, she wrapped her arms around herself, her body shaking, as goosebumps covered her skin.

"Please, Daddy," she whispered, "don't die."

∽

Jenna wrapped her hand around her dad's as she sat beside his bedside. A heavy weight balled in her stomach, growing by the minute. They had finally arrived at the hospital and her dad had been rushed right into surgery. Now he was in his room. Still unconscious.

Various news medias were waiting in the lobby to interview them and find out what happened during their time away. Police were situated outside their door to prevent any media from sneaking in.

The hospital had placed them in two separate rooms, which were right across from each other. Her white blood cell count was off the charts from her infection, and they were keeping her in for monitoring until they felt the infection was under control. She hadn't spent this much time with her dad in years.

Tracing the lines on her dad's palm with her finger, she couldn't help but lean forward and kiss his forehead, breathing in his familiar scent. How had she gone so long without touching him? How could she have even thought she had anything to fear from him?

She wanted to rest her head on his chest, but too many tubes and wires were in the way. She wanted to hear and feel his real heartbeat, as the lines on the machine were not as convincing as hearing it herself. He looked pale like a ghost.

"Oh, Daddy," she cried softly. "I've put you and mom through so much. Why would you even come after me after what I've done to you?"

"Because he loves you," said a voice from behind her, making her jump.

With a hand on her chest, she cursed, "Holy shit, Ethan, you scared me."

Looking abashed, he replied, "Sorry. I didn't realize you were so deep in thought."

Returning her attention back to her father, she gently placed his hand on the bed so as to not disturb the IV. "Why would he even love me after the person I've been?"

"A father's love never dies, Jenna. Just like your love for him has always been there, even when your fear was masking it."

"I'm scared."

Taking her hand, he pulled her to the large recliner chair in the corner, setting her down on his lap. He wrapped his arms around her and sat back in the seat. "The doctor has given him a good prognosis. He should make a full recovery."

She allowed him to hold her close, snuggling right up against him. He smelled different than her father. He smelled minty, like he'd just had a shower and brushed his teeth. Her father's smell had been comforting, but Ethan's brought vivid images from back on the beach. Images of heat, spicy and everything sexually nice.

But as much as she wanted to stay in his embrace, she had to break it off. The last thing she wanted was for him to wind up trapped in the wild generational curse that had its grip on her family. She sighed and started to extricate herself from his grip, but he tightened his hold.

"No," he said, his voice stern as though he knew what she was thinking. "Please, don't."

"Don't what?"

"Run away."

"I'm not good for you, Ethan."

"That's for me to decide, not you."

Beneath His Hands

"You don't even know everything about me yet."

"Then tell me."

Just then, her mom walked in the room and Jenna's hands flew up to her mouth, a small cry breaking free. She scrambled off Ethan's lap and Iris gave Ethan a peculiar look. In her mother's arms was the box she thought she had lost.

Taking it from her mom, she cradled it in her arms, tears streaming down her cheeks. She thought she'd never see it again. A knot formed in her throat as she held it against her chest. "How?" she asked. "How'd you find it?"

"The crew saw it floating and picked it up."

Ethan took her arm and pulled her back onto his lap, and she went willingly, earning him another raised eyebrow from her mom. "What's inside?" he asked.

She was torn between telling him the truth and running away, keeping the sad hard truth to herself. Not too many people knew this part of her story, except her parents.

"Is this the part I don't know yet?"

"Yes," she whispered, barely able to speak. Jenna ran her hand over the pink embroidered name patch on top that said 'Savannah.'

Ethan remained silent as she opened the box and pulled out a necklace with an angel on the end. She held it up to her chest as tears cascaded down her cheeks. It didn't make any sense that she could feel this type of pain from a loss that should never have existed in the first place, but the intensity was still as strong as on that fateful day.

"Remember how I told you that I got pregnant, right?"

"By that bastard, ya."

Opening her hand, she ran the pad of her thumb over the angel. "This is my daughter, Savannah. I didn't have the heart to get an abortion, but I didn't feel like I had the strength to have her either." Jenna took a deep troubled breath. "After I found out I was pregnant, I tried to kill myself. I figured if we both died, I'd never have to make that choice. People always said that those who get an abortion regret it later, and I had enough regrets in my life."

Ethan ran a hand soothingly up and down her back, kissing her neck lightly, and she sighed at his loving touch. How could he even still touch her after everything she's said?

"When the first attempt didn't succeed, I tried again. But I guess it wasn't my time to go yet. Eventually, I found the strength to continue with life and my pregnancy. Sadly, there were some ramifications of my attempts," she said, suppressing the bitter taste that always filled her throat when talking about what happened. "She was born with a brain defect and died within a few weeks."

"Oh, honey, I'm so s-sorry," he said, his voice catching. "You've been through so much that I couldn't even begin to imagine how you must feel."

"In the end, I turned out to be no better than him with all the people I hurt by my actions."

Taking her cheeks in his palms, he turned her to face him. "Don't. You are nothing like him."

Jenna pulled away and buried her face in her hands, crying. "My baby died because of me, and now my dad might die, too."

All the pain she had suppressed over the years poured out of her. Pain for the baby she'd never see again. Pain for the innocence she could never get back. Pain for her family that kept building over the years with one painful experience after another. Pain for a marriage that her parents never got to have because of her.

Suddenly, the weight once again became too much to bear, and the well of hell opened inside her like a super volcano. Unable to be touched, she pushed away from Ethan. She couldn't bring the same disaster upon his life.

But he wouldn't let her go and held her firmly.

"Let me go before you get my curse, too," she cried. Her family was fine before she was born. She was a jinx, a bad luck charm. 'I need to go. I gotta get away."

"Stop," a voice croaked from the bed.

All their heads swivelled to Daniel. His glistening eyes were open, and a world of pain filled their depths. "You are not a curse.

You are my daughter who deserves to be happy for once in her life. Bad things are going to happen. It's inevitable. The only way to get through them is by holding onto all that is good. And Ethan, he's good for you."

She looked over at her mom, Iris, who was now standing beside her husband, nodding in agreement.

"I want us all to go away together on a trip," Daniel continued, as he grunted in pain. "Ethan included."

"I couldn't impose," Ethan replied, shaking his head.

"Non-nonsense," Daniel said, struggling to get the word out.

"Dad, please. Save your energy," Jenna pleaded, not wanting to cause him any more pain. Her father looked over at Iris, begging her to continue the discussion.

Iris took her husband's hand in hers and then looked at Jenna. "Your father is right, honey. It's time to stop running. You've pushed everyone away until now. There has to be a reason for that."

There was, but what if it didn't work out between them? What if her life got upended all over again, and she had to go through even more pain than what she had already? Ethan brought her a little piece of heaven that she didn't deserve. Turning she looked at him, searching his eyes. For what she didn't know.

"I want to spend my life with you Jenna, in the good and in the bad. Whatever we face, I want to face together with you."

"Why? Why me?"

"Because there is no one else in my life that gets me like you do. Hell, we made it through being stranded together, and we didn't kill each other. How many other couples get to say that?"

Jenna gave a chuckle, mixed with a sob. That was true. They did work well together. But what if something happened and she lost him? She didn't think she could handle another loss. Or what if he left her somewhere down the line? "I'm afraid."

"Then we'll be afraid together because I'm just as scared. Just say you'll give us a chance. That's all I want is a chance to show you that I'm here to stay. I want to marry you, Jenna."

Jenna looked at her parents who were smiling as they held hands, encouraging her. Maybe if they could survive the mess they called their lives, then so could she.

She turned her attention back to the man whose lap she was sitting on. No matter what she told Ethan, he never turned away in disgust. He never made her feel less of a human. Could this be her happily ever after?

He made her feel things she didn't even know existed in real life, and she wanted to explore that more than anything, despite being afraid. "I don't want to let you down," she said quietly.

"Honey, the only way you could let me down is by never giving us a chance to explore our feelings in the normal world."

She sighed. He just didn't seem to understand. "That's the thing. All the stuff that has happened is my normal world."

"Then it's time to let you see a different kind of normal," he said, not missing a beat.

She couldn't help but smile and feel all gooey inside. He really was adorable when he was trying to be encouraging. "Okay."

He tilted his head, studying her. "Okay?"

"I'll give us a shot."

He leaned in and brushed his lips against hers. "That's all I ask."

After a minute of him ravishing her lips, Daniel cleared his throat. "Okay, get out of here, love birds. Iris and I have things to talk about."

Jenna glanced between the two of them. There was a genuine smile on her dad's face. In his eyes, his own love for her mother shone through. And for the first time since her tragic kidnapping, she felt at peace. The monsters lurking in the dark were fading away. It would seem that Ethan's love and her newfound strength were scaring them away.

Ethan set her on her feet and stood up. After walking a few steps ahead of her, he turned and held out his hand. "Ready?"

"Just a second." Jenna wandered over to the other side of the bed, opposite her mom, and leaned down, giving her dad the biggest hug in the world. "I love you."

Her dad took a second to respond, tears forming in his eyes. "Oh, sweetheart, I love you so much," he whispered as his arms wrapped around her, enveloping her in the warmth of his embrace. "Thank you, baby girl. I needed that."

Giving her dad a quick peck on the cheek, she stood up and faced the newest man in her life, taking his outstretched hand with a smile on her face as she wiped tears from her eyes.

"Now I'm ready."

Epilogue

Three weeks later...

Jenna stared at the diamond in her hand, revelling in how it sparkled in the overhead light of the museum. They were waiting in the curator's office while he went and got the reward cheque signed by his managers.

She would love to keep the reward all for themselves, but she knew that she had to honour her promise to Lars. He took her to meet his daughter the other day, and she was just the sweetest little thing ever. Jenna knew that she wanted to do everything in her power to give the little girl the life she deserved with her daddy.

"Here you go, Ms. McCay," Mr. Stevens said, as he handed her a cheque with seven huge digits—five million dollars.

After wiping her shaky hands on her pants, she reached for it. She'd never had that much money in her hands before, and it felt a little daunting.

"It's just money, honey," Ethan said, patting her on the leg.

She gave him a light tap on the shoulder. "I know, but I'm so excited. I can't wait to see the look on Lars' face when we tell him that his daughter can finally get the wheelchair she's always wanted."

"You really are an amazing person, Jenna McCay," Ethan said, squeezing her hand.

She blushed.

"No really. I mean it. Not too many people would give away 2.5 million dollars, half of their reward."

"He needs it more than I do."

"And I need you, Jenna, forever and always. Will you marry me?"

If he would have asked her when they first met, she would have run the other way. She didn't want to get involved with anyone, much less a man who could easily turn her world upside down. But she found her solace and healing in the palm of his hands and that's where she wanted to stay for the rest of her life.

"On one condition," she said, unable to resist antagonizing him a little.

"What's that?"

The curator slipped out of the room silently, giving them a moment alone. Jenna wandered over to the door before looking over her shoulder at him with a womanly smile on her face. "That you show me exactly how much you love me."

"What...here?" he asked, swallowing hard.

"The door does have a lock." She turned the lock until it clicked into place.

"You've become insatiable, woman!"

"I plan to be insatiable for the rest of my life. Think you can keep up?"

"I'll match you play for play."

Running her hands up his arms and over his biceps, she linked her hands behind his neck and looked up at him from under her lashes. "Prove it."

"It would be my pleasure." With that, he pushed her up against the wall, held her hands above her head, and kissed her like the world was ending.

And for her, the old horrible part of her world did end. As she opened her mouth to thank him again, his tongue swept inside, and all of her thoughts and words were forgotten as their bodies molded together.

And little did they know, it was in those few moments a new life came into existence, which would fill their life with a happiness they both deserved...and maybe even a few challenges that keep every new parent on their toes.

But Jenna wouldn't have it any other way.

THE END

INTERNATIONAL AWARD-WINNING AUTHOR

Patricia Elliott

...Patricia offers a nuanced exploration of human relationships filled with engaging and multi-faceted characters that will keep readers captivated until the last page.

Literary Titan

For a complete list of titles, please visit:
https://patriciaelliottromance.com/books

Newsletter

Join Patricia Elliott's "Where love meets suspense" newsletter. She'll be sharing tidbits about her current books, updates about upcoming releases, exclusive content and more. You'll also have the opportunity to contact her and ask whatever questions your heart desires.

Head to her website to join now:

https://patriciaelliottromance.com/newsletter